to

with much affection,

Roman

CONVERSATIONS
with a
CLOWN

▼
▲

CONVERSATIONS
with a
CLOWN
▼

Michael Welzenbach

THE ATLANTIC MONTHLY PRESS
NEW YORK
•

Lyrics from "When I Paint My Masterpiece" by Bob Dylan
© 1971, 1972 by Big Sky Music. All rights reserved.
International copyright secured. Reprinted by permission.

Printed in the United States of America
FIRST EDITION

Library of Congress Cataloging-in-Publication Data

Welzenbach, Michael.
    Conversations with a clown / Michael Welzenbach.
    IBSN 0-87113-395-4
    I. Title.
    PS3573.E4974C66   1991   813'.54—dc20   90-869

The Atlantic Monthly Press
19 Union Square West
New York, NY 10003

FIRST PRINTING

FOR GARY HALE
fiat lux

ACKNOWLEDGMENTS

▼
▲

THERE ISN'T ROOM IN THIS ENTIRE BOOK TO THANK
personally all those whose support and encouragement have made it
possible for me to write at all. But first and foremost, thanks to my
parents, Don and Lanora, for their continued—even stubborn—faith
despite all the hell I've put them through over the years.

Warmest love and gratitude also to my dear departed grand-
mother, Velma Wilkin Miller, whose orneriness, restless intellect,
and sheer love of life would be an inspiration to any young writer.
I dearly hope she knew what she meant to me.

Thanks, too, to Steve, Kathy, and Brian Young, Hank and
Carol Goldberg, Tony Buzzanca, Benny and Hanna Levy, Kenny and
Sandy Kittel, John Sheringham, Robert Gillmor, Eric Ennion, Roger
Piantadosi, Jeff Stein, Curt Suplee, Calvin LeCompte, Charles
Freund, Paul Richard, Ramon Osuna, Bill Gildea, Ben and Gabrielle
Forgey, Henry Mitchell, Gael Jacques, Jane Loftus Nickel, and Bill
and Ann Newman, without all of whom none of this would have been
possible. Love to you all.

To my hardworking and attentive agent—but mostly friend—
Gail Ross, hugs and kisses, 'cause no one could have a better. And
to the very best goddamned editor in the whole world, Ann Godoff,
for being a hardass, a sweetheart, and a more perceptive intellect than
any author rightly deserves, my deepest respect and admiration.
(Don't you even think about leaving again!)

Lastly, by no means, thanks to Suzanne, just for being herself,
and to Kerry Margaret Nickel, just for being my darling daughter—
and living proof of the power of magic.

"Got to hurry on back to my hotel room,
Where I've got me a date with Botticelli's niece.
She promised that she'd be right there with me
When I paint my masterpiece."
—Bob Dylan
"When I Paint My Masterpiece"

PREFACE

▼
▲

WHEN I WAS A SMALL BOY LIVING IN THE TROPICAL wonderland of Okinawa, scrambling after butterflies and lizards, getting wounded in dirt-clod fights in the boondocks, and copying faithfully, page by page, the notebooks of Leonardo da Vinci, I believed that artists were magicians who could transport the mind and soul of any human being to places of mystery and profound sentience.

Now, after years of writing and editing, painting and sculpting, lecturing and listening, I know it.

This book is addressed to everyone who has ever seen a picture—be it a poster in a boardwalk stall or a painting in the Tate Gallery—that they just had to have; that they took home and thumbtacked to the wall because it spoke to them. Because it struck a chord somewhere in them that they simply could not keep from resonating. What art *is* neither I nor anyone else I know of is qualified to assert. What the unique power of good art is we are all qualified to assert, even if we are not all equipped to describe it adequately. And, of course, none of us is.

The role of art in society has always been a topic of considerable discourse and acrimony, and in the past few years has become a topic of national concern in the United States. Whether or not such interest and debate results in censorship or acceptance, it is a tribute to the power of the crafted image that it can arouse such spirited discourse and energetic contemplation. This book was designed to challenge conventional perceptions of what art is and what its function is in contemporary society. I obviously have my own views on the subject—else I wouldn't have gone to the trouble to write the

▼

damned thing—but what is more important is that you form yours. Given the baffling flux and flow of the world today, it's vital that we all consider the role art plays in our lives. Remember: there's precious little magic left.

M. Welzenbach

1

▼
▲

IT CAN BE DAMNED HARD TO ACCOUNT FOR SOME
things. And sometimes, I guess, you're better off not trying.

Of course he's gone now—well, not *gone* exactly, although I
have no idea where he is just at the moment. Chances are that
somewhere—even as we speak—on some shady boulevard in Paris,
perhaps, or in the woody-brown womb of a *Stube* in Cologne, some
creative soul is experiencing the distinctive if confounding pleasure of
his company: a tall, pale character, avuncular but young, athletic but
frail, sybaritic to the point of laziness, yet mentally as agile as any
acrobat. Perhaps, like myself, the unwary object of his attentions will
not at first recognize this odd and honored personage; only a vague
intuition, a reluctant wish, will in time ripen into conviction and,
ultimately, gratitude. Beyond a point, I suppose, no introductions
are necessary. The livid face and black skullcap like an overlarge
yarmulke; the expressive dark eyes and inkspot nostrils—you have
only to bundle down with a volume of Flaubert, Gautier, or Baudelaire, or dawdle through an exhibit of Picasso to make his acquaintance. His gracefully clumsy presence informs almost five hundred
years of painting, literature, theater, and poetry. No circus would be
complete without him; no opera entirely true to its staged grandeur.
Yet for all that, he works his magic in small and intimate ways.

As I say, he's difficult to account for. I hear rumors of him now
and then from London and Madrid, Frankfurt and Rome—even
Moscow. Here in New York though, things have been ominously
quiet. He's gone—just up and left. And along the once fashionable
promenades of Greene and Prince streets in SoHo, on the crowded

sidewalks of shoppish Madison Avenue in the shadow of the Whitney, and throughout the formerly bohemian communities of TriBeCa and the East Village, the clamor of artists has all but stopped. He's skipped town, boys, headed for greener pastures—or redder, or bluer, or the comparative adjectives of colors yet unnamed. Where he'll wind up at last is anybody's guess. But if we make it to Mars, it's even odds he'll get there, too. Might even stay awhile—after all, somebody's got to civilize the place. I mean, what would a space colony be without love, hate, jealousy, avarice, and all the other foibles and all the grandiose, improbable aspirations that brand us human?

Well, we'll all see what develops, I'm sure. But just for the record, here's how I first met the guy, back when he was much, much older:

▼
▲

Probably most people have some sort of obsession, and mine, remarkably unblunted by years on the reviewer's beat, has always been painting. So whenever business allows me the luxury of spending a week or two at home in Washington, I'm in the habit of sneaking off by myself on Sunday afternoons to enjoy a few solitary hours in the National Gallery of Art. During the winter months especially, the high-ceilinged, skylighted rooms of the old building and the vast quiet spaces of I. M. Pei's east wing provide a restorative haven for the world-weary. And when the place isn't teeming with tourists one has a chance to sit and consider at leisure many favorite paintings, sometimes for hours on end. At such times the gallery is one of the best places I know for avoiding people—a sentiment that thankfully appears to be shared by the few other lone wolves I occasionally encounter there. Myself, I generally start with the Vermeers and Rembrandts in the west wing, with the ageless riveting faces that gaze wistfully from the oaken-paneled walls, and I end up in the newer building with a visit to the Giacomettis and, as a parting treat—always—Picasso's haunting *Les Saltimbanques*.

One particular December day—the day after Christmas, in

fact—I'd lingered longer than usual with my silent old friends. Stretched comfortably on the soft couch in the middle of the room, I was contemplating for what must have been the hundredth time the melancholy magic of Rembrandt's *Windmill* and trying to relax. I allowed my mind to splash along the edge of the evening river; tried to divine the thoughts of the few people gathered at the shore under the shadow of the towering stone wall that to this day keeps a beetling vigil over the passing boats.

It had been an especially hectic week, what with having just returned from a prolonged stay in Europe to a house teeming with noisy and nosy relatives, who out of the blue had taken it upon themselves to drop in on me for the holidays—en masse. It had been some time since I'd seen any of them, for they rarely ventured beyond their hometowns in Illinois and Ohio, and I had lived on the East Coast for many years. Besides, being a journalist I was almost always on the road—a circumstance that made familial visitations mercifully tough to accommodate. I'd always been too restless and curious to tolerate the idea of being landlocked in the Midwest, and had therefore come to be regarded as the peripatetic black sheep of my sedentary and gregarious clan.

Perceptions founded on estrangement often have a funny way of becoming self-fulfilling prophecies, and I'd grown somewhat misanthropic over the years and tended to avoid relatives wherever possible. It hadn't helped things, either, that my marriage to Fran, whom everyone in the family adored, had failed so precipitously. We'd been divorced for over ten years now, but family members had an irritating way of reminding me of her—sometimes intentionally. All things considered, being related by letter was by far the most comfortable situation for me, so having had to entertain hordes of relatives I barely recognized—coupled with the fact that I normally dread the Christmas season anyway—had made this year's holiday enough to make me forswear family and religion all in one fell swoop.

But now, with no sound intruding on my mind but the ghostly voices of the pictures whispering through the vacant halls and the occasional distant echoing footfall, I breathed a sigh of relief: alone at last. Just one more night in a house that offered no sanctuary so long as I had to tiptoe about after dark (so as not to wake up the visiting rug-rats), then off again to New York first thing Monday morning to see the new season's opening exhibits and start writing the end-of-the-decade wrap-up I'd promised my editor several months ago. End-of-the-year summaries were tough enough to write, and I wasn't exactly dying to dig into this one—in fact I'd been doing my best to put it out of my mind. But, work aside, I always enjoyed my trips to Manhattan because I could get lost there for a time. It would be good to be anonymous again; to dine in thronged solitude.

New York sometimes has a curious way of imposing solitude on a person—seemingly just by virtue of its human hugeness; its vast artificiality. Though I never liked to stay too long in the city—I sometimes felt downright frantic after a week or so—there were occasions when, shoving and being shoved along the crowded sidewalks of Sixth Avenue at rush hour, I'd been surprised to suddenly feel remarkably detached from it all: a sort of welcome, secure loneliness such as I'd otherwise only experienced far from cities and cars and babbling crowds. It was a sensation I'd only just recently relished during a brief getaway excursion to the Normandy coast a few weeks before. Setting out one morning from the little bed-and-breakfast place I'd found in a tiny village that wasn't even on my road map, I had walked down to the sea. I'd had Fran on my mind again. It was an overcast but brilliant day; the sun's rays so scattered and bounced by the mists that everything in the rocky landscape appeared to be slightly magnified, evenly lighted, and shadowless. Working my way down from the high cliffs to a narrow strip of dark shingle beach, I stood for maybe an hour by the thundering green water, exhilarated by the feeling of puniness it caused, and thrilled by the shaking, shimmering salty air. Watching the waves dash and suck about the mountainous jagged black rocks for so long, I became dizzy. To regain my balance, I fixed my gaze for a moment on the litter of sea-sculpted pebbles at my feet. Amid these, by the toe of my shoe, I spotted an egg-sized, rounded, and flattish jewel of a stone.

My first thought had been what a perfect skipping stone it would make, and I picked it up to heft it in my palm. It was then that I noticed what an incredibly lovely object it was; all smooth and gleaming and moist, its surface a marvel of puzzling reticulations in agate reds, rich greens, and streaks of ebony. On its underside was what looked like a fossil of some sort—that, or an unusually symmetrical natural decoration. Two tapering rows of bone-white oval spots formed a fernlike pattern across its length, almost as if someone had painted it with a view to selling it as a paperweight. I was absorbed with my find for quite a while before the growling of my stomach reminded me that I hadn't eaten breakfast yet. And so, wedging the lovely stone snugly between my thumb and forefinger, I waited until the emerald water retreated to feed an incoming wave, then flung it hard and low across the surface. I had been right. It skipped seven times before finally sinking into the massive swell.

I remember I felt immensely proud of myself for having accomplished such a feat—despite there having been no one there to witness it—and I walked back to the little inn as happy as I'd been in months. As if with the stone I'd thrown away all my distressing memories.

But now, as I sat quietly pondering such small but precious things in the empty gallery before Rembrandt's enduring vision, another, more disquieting, thought disturbed my ruminations: in five days it would be New Year's Eve. Not just any New Year's, either. It suddenly occurred to me that only certain generations of people live to witness a complete change in the calendar—like the one coming up. And the ramifications of that were daunting: in five short days, I reminded myself, all my old checks would be useless because they all bore a date beginning "19" in the upper right-hand corner, and I knew from experience that it would take me the better part of a year to get used to writing 2000. Hell, it had always been hard enough just to remember to change the last digit. And somehow the very number seemed ominous; the sound of it unpleasant and awkward on the tongue. Perhaps because it made the tumultuous, promising sixties of my youth seem so dreadfully far away. I remembered going to see the premiere of Kubrick's *2001* so many years ago, and how the date of the title was then simply too remote to visualize. Anything might have been possible by the turn of the century. Yet here we were, and after all the dramatic global political changes of the last several decades, things in general seemed considerably worse rather than better. It wasn't just the environment or overpopulation. It was the state of art that had me worried, and that made the prospect of writing what would be an end-of-the-millennium wrap-up almost more than I could tolerate. I had precious little good to say about the art of the last twenty years.

Contemplating all this in the presence of the windmill made me feel ornery enough to want to get up and joust with it. I was entertaining myself with visions of how the self-important museum guards might react to someone tilting at an Old Master, when the waning light reminded me that I'd already stayed dangerously close to closing time, and if I was going to get in my customary visit with Picasso's itinerant clowns I'd best get a move on over to the new wing.

As I hurried through the fountain square on the way over I ran into Carter, an elderly guard who'd been at the museum as long as I could remember going there.

"Have a nice Christmas, Mr. Peters?" he asked cheerfully as he strode by on some errand.

"Bloody marvelous," I said, none too enthusiastically.

The old fart grinned and touched his cap. "New Year's just 'round the corner!" he said, and passed into the building behind me.

He was all right, was Carter—although he sometimes gave me a hard time about "hogging the pictures" if I had to do a review when the galleries were crowded.

The other building, too, was nearly deserted but for the yawning uniformed guards, no doubt anxious to get back home to their wives and leftover Christmas turkeys, yet I hurried upstairs without pausing to look in on Giacometti's scored and slender figures. Arriving slightly out of breath in the spacious, well-lighted room that harbored my favorite painting in the world, I was unpleasantly surprised to find standing before it an old, old man, obviously very much absorbed.

Tall and painfully thin, he wore a long cream-colored coat buttoned tightly up to his throat. It had obviously been an expensive item once, but was now threadbare and shiny at the elbows, faded and stained in spots. His trousers and shoes were white and, with white-

▲

gloved hands clasped firmly behind his back, he stooped to inspect the picture closely, paying especial attention to the seated figure of a woman on the right side of the composition; the lovely, lonely looking lady in the ill-fitting flowered hat, reaching to her tresses with one slender hand.

I was rather annoyed to find the strange-looking old fellow there. Though I had no right to feel any monopoly over the painting, on winter weekend evenings I was accustomed to having it all to myself. And anyway, he was blocking my view. There was no one else in the gallery, so for a time I just loitered about the room in what I hoped looked like a disinterested fashion, glancing impatiently at the other pictures and waiting for him to leave. But he was so singular looking I couldn't take my eyes off of him—and when after some five minutes he still showed no signs of moving on, I worked my way around the room toward him, thinking by this to remind him that *other* people might want to see the painting, too. Presently I became aware that he was muttering audibly—having what sounded like a fairly involved debate with himself or some invisible companion. Or perhaps with *Les Saltimbanques*. Great, I thought, now some senile old geezer's going to hog the whole damned thing till closing. What a fitting end to a miserable holiday week. With my luck he'd probably turn out to be a relation of some sort (there being any number of whom I wouldn't have known by sight). I resolved to edge up and get a good look at him. But the moment I started to sidle in his direction he turned a most merry face to me and announced loudly: "I am in your way."

"Oh, no . . ." I began disingenuously, shrugging and forcing a smile. He had taken me by surprise, and there wasn't a hint of shakiness or uncertainty in his firm, foreign-sounding voice. His slightly amused and candid expression left me no doubt that he was quite in control of his faculties.

He must have sensed my embarrassment for he gave a little laugh and said with hearty friendliness, *"Je vous prie me pardon*—I am so sorry. It is a painting that I love and I am sometimes too greedy with it."

Again I shrugged as if it were nothing at all to me.

"You, too. *Non?*" he inquired, head tilted to one side like a schoolteacher who *knows* you've been smoking round the back of the gym during recess.

Now I am normally quite capable of maintaining a poker face—something that comes with long years reviewing exhibits of awful paintings under the anxious gaze of greedy art dealers—but the old man had such a disarming air about him that I found myself breaking into an involuntary grin. His accent, I noticed, didn't seem to be French, but it wasn't anything else I could handily place, either. And on closer scrutiny I found that he did look familiar, though at the time I had no idea where I might have known him from. At any rate I was relieved to find that he didn't look at all like a relative; rather, he had a distinctly Mediterranean appearance. Despite a complex map of wrinkles about his eyes and forehead, there was something sweetly young about his nose and mouth, as if the marks of age were but a disguise; a ruse applied by a master makeup artist. His hair, combed flatly back from his forehead to leave a pronounced widow's peak, was obviously naturally bright white and thinning so that the pink of his scalp glowed through. His large eyes were heavy-lidded and of a brown so deep as to appear black. But his mouth was his most startling feature: set above an unusually long, pointed chin, the lips were unnaturally red, as if he wore some sort of lipstick—rather like the Joker of Batman comics fame, come to think of it.

It was, in short, a face seemingly designed to keep one off balance, so I felt even sillier when, with light-footed grace I'd scarcely have credited someone of his years, he fairly danced over and took me by the elbow. I was so surprised at this move that I let him guide me gently back to the painting. "Come, my friend," he said, "let's share it together. Perhaps I can atone for my rudeness by telling you some things about it that only I am in a position to know."

When we stood before the picture he tapped me on the shoulder and, with a ducal sweep of his hand, presented the image to me as if it were the stage on which a performance was about to begin. Every one of the curious old gent's movements appeared to be calculated; scripted. And I watched him the way one might stop to admire the precision of one of those guys who mimic windup mannequins in department store windows—indeed, the analogy struck me at the time as being uncannily accurate. In a mechanical fashion, he brought his forefinger to his lips as an exaggerated gesture of silence and whispered, "Listen. Do you hear?"

At this I began to reassess my reassessment of his sanity, and I watched him guardedly as he cocked an ear in the direction of the big canvas. Part of me simply wanted to walk away from him; leave the gallery and come back another day when I could visit with the painting in peace. But equally, part of me was intrigued.

"Hear what?" I asked at length.

"Why, the sound of memory, of course," he said, as if it were the most obvious thing on earth. "All paintings have memories—if they are good enough. Pablo's best works have wonderful memories. And now that I am here, I have my own to add to them."

His mildly patronizing tone grated. After all, didn't I know this painting by heart? Hadn't I pondered each of its six figures for years? And wouldn't I have known the original from any copy, no matter how faithful, by the tiny inch-long stroke of white-edged grey under the red-and-black-clad harlequin's left heel? But I stared at the familiar image through narrowed eyes nonetheless, kept my mouth shut, and listened. Sure enough, my eccentric companion began to mutter again—this time, though, to me.

"I can't deny there's something in the face that's caught me," he began. "In the set of the brows, perhaps. The eyes. Yes, the eyes are quite good. But I never had such a chin. Why, it's flattering, but it's quite all wrong, for goodness sakes. *Mon Dieu!* Did you ever see such a weak little chin? Look at this chin, would you?" At this he grabbed my elbow once more and tugged it vigorously. Startled, I jerked away and stepped back to look at him, rapidly becoming convinced I was in the presence of a madman.

"Why," he continued, oblivious to what must have been a really priceless expression on my face, "why even in whiteface it sticks out like a fist. Observe." So saying, he held his hand under his chin palm up, as if serving it to me on a platter.

▼

The guy appeared to be suggesting that it was he Picasso had portrayed in the picture. But the painting, as I well knew, had been made almost a hundred years ago. Still, just to humor him—and to give me the opportunity of backing off even farther—I dutifully examined his proffered chin, then scanned the picture.

And then it hit me like a slap. The resemblance was uncanny: the tall harlequin standing with his back to us, one hand crooked behind him, was the crazy gentleman next to me. At least if it wasn't him it was someone who might very well have been him when he was much younger. Same eyes, same forehead, same nose—even the way he held his arm bent behind his back, the way the old man was doing even now. The only real difference was the age—and, of course, the size of the chin, which to be truthful is somewhat obscured by the attitude of the harlequin's shoulder as he thoughtfully stares across at the lovely woman on the other side of the composition. Following his line of sight I too looked at her. She gazed back out at me with a knowing, introspective expression. I had to catch myself when I fancied I saw her eyes dart briefly toward the old man.

Wide-eyed, I turned back to him, whereupon he broke into a broad grin, reinforcing the Joker impression I mentioned earlier.

"You see?" he exclaimed gleefully. "Do you not agree that the chin is too small?"

I watched him dumbly.

"Don't you see," he prattled on, "that that is why Callot used to caricature me so cruelly? It is why Pablo has me with my shoulder up at such an odd angle. It hides my chin and makes it not so obvious that it is I, and not Arlequin, posing for the portrait. He might, of course, have done it out of kindness, but that was not in his nature. At any rate, there was not much else to be done with it, because Arlequin—the silly snob—had refused to pose and so it fell to me to do it. And I did, of course. I always do. I don't know that Arlequin would have approved of the costume. It is not, strictly speaking, what he was accustomed to wearing for Funambulesque, but then that would be his own fault, wouldn't it? Besides, Pablo always did have his own way of doing things, and I guess we're all the better for that, *n'est-ce pas?*"

▲

I nodded vaguely, aware that I was entranced in spite of my-self. This extraordinary character seemed to have some hypnotic power that kept me rapt—or maybe it was just that he was without question the oddest human being I'd ever run into, and those sorts of people tended to get my attention in a big way. At any rate he was now obviously encouraged at the thought that he might be getting through to me, however dimly.

"He was certainly a genius," the old man concluded with a wink, "but frankly not even the great Picasso did me as faithfully as ever-dear Antoine did."

"Antoine?" I asked as mildly as I could manage and, forcing myself from his spell, glanced at my watch. I knew that soon we would be asked by the guard to leave. Lounging by the entranceway he had evidently been following our exchange with some interest. As I looked toward his post he promptly pretended to be deeply con-cerned with one of his fingernails.

"Antoine," sighed the old man, "dear young Antoine. Forever young now, I expect. But what a painter! Do you not agree?"

"I'm afraid I don't know your friend," I said—rather shortly, I admit—and started to explain that as it was getting late I should probably be moving along. But before I'd said three more words he interjected:

"But of course you know Antoine!" He sounded terribly ur-gent all of a sudden; a note almost of desperation quavering in his voice and a look on his face as if this were an issue of global impor-tance. "Everyone knows him now. And I myself have seen you staring at his work for years and years. Do you deny it?"

The question was practically an accusation. "Look," I began, "Mister . . . ?"

"Pedrolino," he said, straightening his back and affecting a slight, elegant bow of the head. "Gilles Pedrolino, at your service. My friends call me Pierrot—a nickname, you understand, but you may call me that if you wish."

"All right then, Pierrot," I began, at first unconscious of the silliness of what I had just said. "Look, I don't know what on earth you are talking about or, for that matter, what you've been talking about all this time. But it's getting very late and it's been lovely chatting with you but I really must be getting along now. Good-bye!" I finished up all in a rush, afraid I wouldn't have another chance to get a word in edgewise.

But I stopped my heel in mid-turn.

Pierrot? This guy had just introduced himself as Pierrot—the white clown. The mime. And all of a sudden I knew whom he meant by "Antoine." Watteau, of course. No one had devoted more energy to painting the minstrels and clowns, or had done more portraits of the Pierrot, than he had. In fact, I'd visited with his "Gilles" earlier that very afternoon. But the notion that the old man could have known the great Flemish painter was obviously even more absurd than the idea that Picasso might have painted him. Watteau had died in 1721.

Monsieur "Pedrolino" evidently read my mind. "It is, I admit, somewhat unconventional to live so long," he said apologetically, again with that idiotic Joker grin.

You may be wondering why at this point I didn't just up and leave.

Me, too. But I couldn't. It wasn't only that I had always been fascinated with the subject of the white clown figuring in the work of so many painters, but, as crazy as this sounds, the weird old guy somehow struck me as genuine—which is to say I could think of no way to account for him. And even if he were pathologically self-deluded—as he patently was—I found myself perversely wanting to hear him out. I looked once again at the figure in Picasso's painting. Still unable to get over the resemblance, I decided to humor him a little longer.

"Pierrot, huh?"

"I did not expect that you would believe me so soon," he said with a wry smile, and lowered his heavy eyelids. "But I know how much you love the art, so I saw no harm in introducing myself."

"You've seen me here before?" I tried to recall having ever noticed him in the gallery, but I was pretty confident I hadn't.

"Why of course, monsieur! I see everyone who loves the paint-ings. You cannot expect to be always looking so intently at me without expecting that I will not look back at you. That is hardly logical, now is it?"

I shook my head, first up and down, then sideways. It was, you understand, a rather difficult sort of question to answer. As I was about to open my mouth to reply, he again began talking about *Les Saltimbanques*.

"Of course," he said, "we never dressed this way for the Funambules shows. I wore a black skullcap and a lovely long white gown with beautiful, big fluffy buttons on it. And obviously I was always *enfariné*—in whiteface, you see. So it never really mattered who was playing me on stage—Deburau, Legrand, Najac . . . whomever. You would not have known it wasn't me when it wasn't. Of course," he said, turning reflective for a moment, "by the time young Picasso arrived in Paris, we weren't really—how shall I say?—fashionable. Yes, to be extra kind, that's the word. Our best days, those glorious days when the audiences stamped and clapped and hooted at the fun, were well behind us. We were reduced to playing to the rabble; the critics no longer took an interest. The great writers had turned to other things, and poor Pierrot was all but forgotten."

He looked at me with a theatrically sad expression, then resumed: "But Pablo, he loved the circus. Of course, back in those early days when he was poor and working at the Bateau-Lavoir, it was all he could afford. He and his lady friends, and sometimes Braque, would come down to catch the shows. They were not much, compared to the days of the great acts at Funambules, the Follies-Bérgères, the Moulin Rouge. But Pablo loved the acrobats and the clowns. To be candid, though, I believe he was more attached to Arlequin than to me." Monsieur Pedrolino lowered his voice almost to a whisper, as if the canvas might hear. "Closer to his own personality, if you take my meaning.

"But one day he demanded that we all come to the studio to pose. I remember the occasion well, because his old friend—and one of my best clowns, if I do say so myself—El Tio Pepe Don José—was in town. He's the big fat fellow there; the one with the grim face."

I glanced at the stocky, patriarchal character with the granite-like visage. He cemented the lovely composition like a well-placed rock in a Japanese flower bed.

"A fine, fat clown," the old man said wistfully, and went on. "Well, of course we were all delighted to go—all except Arlequin, naturally. The ass! So self-centered, so uncaring for anything but trying to bed every woman in sight. I tell you that man's libido is quite out of proportion to his ability on stage, and that's a fact. Would you believe he even tried to lock Colombina in the theater to keep her from going? Of course I managed to free her. She desperately wanted to pose for Pablo—not, you understand, because of the painting, but because she wanted to sleep with him." Pedrolino shook his head sadly. "It is the great injustice of my life that while I am always trying to inspire artists, my darling Colombina is always trying to fuck them. And she made it so painfully obvious. And that horribly jealous girlfriend of his, Fernande, I think, was hovering around like a protective mongrel bitch . . ."

Abruptly the old man left off, covered his mouth with one gloved hand, and stared at me round-eyed. *"Oh, je suis désolé!* I am so sorry," he said, and half closed his eyes in mock anguish. "I didn't mean to assault you with such rank vulgarity. But I am so very good at it, you see. Please forgive me."

His expression again caused me to grin in spite of myself, and I shook my head.

"Well then," he continued, with an air of immense relief, "Colombina, whom I have loved dearly for centuries . . . I mean, of course, for many years now . . . she was determined to . . ."

Just at that moment the guard, who I'm sure had allowed us to remain in the gallery well past the posted hour, strode deliberately in our direction. When he detected this, the old man suddenly snapped his mouth shut, motioned to me, and walked away. With a second's hesitation, I followed him out of the gallery.

▼
▲

▲

Outside it was nearly dark. The argon streetlamps had come on, washing everything with a pinkish-blue light. A sharp wind kicked up leaves and litter along Pennsylvania Avenue. The old man walked on ahead of me past the still fountain and out to the street, where he stopped at the sidewalk and looked back. The wind fluttered his collar against his pale cheek.

Now, should I have wanted to, I could simply have walked away; averted my eyes and pretended I'd never seen him before. I had, after all, visited the museum with the express aim of avoiding company, not seeking it. For a moment I stood undecided. Should I make a beeline for the metro and go home? He watched me closely, probably guessing my thoughts.

Curiosity is a powerful thing. It may well be that it's stronger in journalists, who are after all conditioned to investigate anything out of the ordinary. But that's mere conjecture, and maybe sidestepping the issue anyhow. I'm not sure why I followed M. Pedrolino. I had, in fact, begun to suspect the old fellow's motives. He might have been selling drugs for all I knew. But as an acquaintance of mine was so fond of saying, "Once in a while you just gotta jump and not know where you're gonna land." Anyway, I'd always had an uncanny knack for getting myself into some of the most ridiculous situations, purely on account of some bizarre—and perhaps injudicious—taste for adventure. Besides, I'd always found myself curiously attracted to oddballs, maybe because they always made me feel a bit less peculiar myself. And who could tell?—maybe there was a story here. If anyone would even believe it so far. The old gentleman was definitely the oddest ball I'd ever run into. I reminded myself that I'd been the one who, while in São Paulo, Brazil, for the Biennal some years ago, had gone traipsing off in pursuit of a woman who several people claimed had the ability to turn herself into a giant bat at will. Evidently she was suspected as being responsible for the disappearance of a number of small children from a remote area of the jungle. Excited at the prospect of maybe discovering something concerning the origins of the belief in vampires and other ghoulish things, I hired a driver and set out on a miserable daylong journey in unbelievably humid weather to a ramshackle little village in the middle of nowhere. Here I found a crazy old lady squatted on a straw bed in a filthy hut, babbling away to herself in some obscure local Indian tongue. But, members of the village (according to my driver) having solemnly sworn that if I watched her long enough she would indeed turn into a huge bat, I hung around through the night and most of the next day—attended by swarms of vicious mosquitoes. Of course she didn't turn into a bat. As a matter of fact she died the following afternoon. She jabbered to herself for hours incessantly while a number of people whom I presumed to be family members sat and gawked at her. And finally, with a loud, highly un-batlike wail, she fell back and rattled her last. The old crone may indeed have felt like a bat on occasion—I feel small and blind myself once in a while—but she had obviously been suffering some disease-induced delirium which the villagers had interpreted as voodoo or some such thing. To this day I don't know why they insisted I sit up another night by her hastily dug grave. They seemed earnest enough, but perhaps they had a better sense of humor than I gave them credit for at the time, and saw an opportunity to pull one over on an old gringo. Whatever the case, I looked back on the excursion fondly. And anyway, how could I have resisted?

And so, without being conscious of having taken a single step in his direction, I found myself standing by the strange old man, hunching my shoulders against the cold and waiting to see what would happen next.

"A beer, I think," he announced, again appearing to have read my mind. "Is there a pub nearby you are accustomed to frequenting?"

"Not really," I answered truthfully. I wasn't much of a barfly, and though I enjoyed visiting the Cedar Tavern near Union Square when in New York, when home I generally stayed home. Coming from a family of Irish-stock tipplers with a prodigious capacity for beer, I'd become—out of sheer contrariness, I suppose—a very moderate drinker. But I had no objection to a martini or two on special occasions, and it looked like this was shaping up to be one.

"Then," said the old man, "if you would be so kind as to join me, may I suggest a favorite spot of mine? The Childe Harold is not so far from here—at Dupont Circle. And it is a fine, dark bar with many pretty women and amicable young people."

Marking my hesitancy, he laid a cautious, slender hand on my shoulder. "It is only that I would appreciate the company," he said, suddenly looking very old indeed, and very lonely. "That is all. I thought perhaps you might enjoy talking of the art some more. But of course, if you have other plans . . ." He turned away and shrugged.

Again I stopped to consider: I had to catch a train in the morning, so I had to pack. Also, I should probably be wise to go over my itinerary and make a few phone calls. But then I thought of the residual relatives potentially still lurking about the house. Almost certainly my divorced aunt Christa and her three screaming brats—which is to say children, or cousins, or whatever. Christa would insist on making me dinner, talking about when I was very young and, no doubt, advising me on how I should pack my suitcase.

Oh, what the hell.

I will be eternally grateful to her for having expedited my decision to throw caution to the wind and make a new acquaintance. "No," I told the old man. "No plans."

"*Bon!* Excellent," he exclaimed delightedly. "Let's hail a taxi, then."

Quite a few heads turned when we entered the long dark bar. The old man's appearance wasn't calculated to make him blend into a crowd of designer-tailored Washington yuppies. It had been more than a year since I'd last been in the place, but I recognized the burly, mustachioed bartender, and was surprised to find that he obviously knew my companion well.

"Mister Pierrot!" he boomed in hearty greeting as we elbowed our way to the bar—he pronounced it "Parrot," more or less—and without waiting for an order produced a bottle of Bass ale and a glass and set them before the old man. *"Bonsoir, mon ami,"* Mr. Pedrolino said and, disdaining the glass, grabbed the bottle and tilted fully half the contents down his skinny throat in one gulp. Then he motioned to me and led the way to a seat at the end of the bar where it was relatively quiet. I ordered a martini from the bartender, who introduced himself as Big Ron, and took a stool beside him.

"There, that's better," my strange companion said, smacking his lips appreciatively. Then he drained the remainder of the bottle and ordered another.

"Always a genuinely thirsty man, this one," Big Ron said with a wink.

"Now, my friend," said the old man when he'd gulped down about half of the second bottle, "I perceive that you do not know what to make of me, *n'est-ce pas?*"

That being the understatement of the decade, I sipped my drink and considered how best to reply. I'd followed the guy this far, so I might as well humor him all the way. In any event it was reassuring to see that he was known to the bartender, as it gave him, and the moniker he claimed, an element of legitimacy. It was also good to see the affection with which he had been greeted, as that indicated that he had to have some good points—all delusions or mental imbalances aside, of course.

"I'm curious," I replied, trying hard not to sound too curious.

"Ça va sans dire," he said with a grin. "That goes without saying. And I am curious also. Would it be improprietous of me to ask what sort of things you paint, Monsieur . . . ?"

"Peters. Corry Peters. And I'm not a painter."

The old man paused with the bottle halfway to his lips and looked suddenly anxious.

"Not a painter?" It was as if someone had just pointed out to him that the world was actually round.

"I'm a writer."

"A writer," he repeated, deadpan. Then, "What sort of a writer, Mr. Peters?"

"An art critic."

In spite of the general hubbub in the crowded bar, I felt as if this response had prompted so profound a silence that everyone could hear us. Judging by the expression on the old man's face, I gathered I'd taken him totally unawares. For a moment he sat stock-still, staring at his beer bottle.

"Oh dear!" he muttered finally, obviously chapfallen. "That is most unfortunate. Very bad indeed!" With a throwaway gesture he drained his beer and waved the bottle pointedly at Big Ron. I watched him closely. "What I mean to say is," he went on after a time, weighing his words carefully, "I don't mean to imply that it is bad you are a writer, you understand. Only that I was under the misapprehension that you were an artist. Please forgive the mistake."

"I wasn't aware you'd made one."

"Yes, yes of course. I understand that. Quite. But . . . but I have never particularly liked critics, you see."

"Lots of people don't like critics," I said, and ordered another drink for myself. "I'm sorry if I disappointed you. But as I recall, it was you who asked me to join you for a drink."

"Of course, yes," he replied, adopting a faintly pained expression. "Please forgive my manners. I was only somewhat disappointed." The arrival of a fresh beer seemed to pick up his spirits somewhat. "You see, Mr. Peters," he continued, wiping his mouth on his sleeve (so *that's* where those stains came from), "you see, it is artists who are my special concern. And after having seen you study the paintings for so many years, it did not occur to me that you might be a critic." He stopped and looked at me searchingly. "You do love the paintings, do you not?"

"Why the hell else do you think I'd spend so much time with them?" I said with some asperity, unable at the moment to keep down the knee-jerk reaction I sometimes get when I sense someone is implying that a critic could not possibly *like* art. I was beginning to feel that, rather than shedding any light on this mystery, our conversation was making things substantially muddier by the minute. Both my tone of voice and the rhetorical nature of my question were evidently lost on the old man, for he only looked at me with an expression that announced plain as day that as far as he was concerned a critic could only be in a museum for one reason: to find something nasty to say about the works.

"Oh dear," he said again, and finished off his beer. Not surprisingly, he was by this time beginning to look a bit tipsy, and I wondered how much more he could drink before falling off his stool. I didn't have to wait long to find out. Signaling the bartender for yet another beer, he tottered to his feet, said, "Please s'cuse me for one moment," and turned to make his way toward the men's room. Within a pace he tripped hard on some unseen obstacle in the middle of the floor and pitched forward. He struck his head with an audible thump, did an ear spin Buster Keaton would have envied, and came crashing down with his feet landing in the middle of a table full of food and wine. The animated chatter in the room stopped, and there was a collective intake of breath as heads craned to see the old man lying spread-eagled on the floor, looking, frankly, quite dead. It took me a second to recover my wits enough to get up and run to his assistance. But a young woman beat me to it. Kneeling down beside him, she reached out a cautious hand to his face and asked anxiously, "Mister? Are you okay?"

He startled her—and all the rest of us—when, with a sudden jackknife action of his legs, he vaulted nimbly to his feet, smoothed his coat sleeves, and announced with a merry smile, "But of course, my dear. How very kind of you to ask."

Needless to say, he no longer looked even the least bit inebriated.

Big Ron the bartender, who was evidently familiar with the old man's antics, broke the tension in the room by booming, "What a clown!" At that, people turned back to their conversations with general nervous laughter. A busboy appeared with a broom and mop and began to clean up the mess. With a deep bow, Mr. Pedrolino apologized to the food- and wine-soaked couple whose table he had demolished, told the angry-looking waitress that he would pay for their meal, and walked back to the restrooms, waving to the crowd with the air of a performer leaving a stage.

And that should have been the last I ever saw of him. Enough was enough. I was tired and had two martinis under my belt. The old man was obviously a complete put-on, and I no longer felt up to playing straight man to his act—which, after this last little stunt, looked as if it might get downright dangerous any time now. So I laid the money for my drinks on the bar, buttoned my coat, and slipped out the door. Sure I felt a little underhanded sneaking off like that. But not much.

2

▼
▲

BEING THE FIRST DAY OF ANOTHER WORK WEEK, I HAD
by Monday morning all but forgotten about the crazy old man. Aunt
Christa and her brats were still asleep when I left them in possession
of the house at 6 A.M. and caught a taxi to Union Station to make the
6:20 Metroliner.

It felt good to get back on the road. Not that I don't look
forward to getting home now and then, but as often as not, I no
sooner get there than I'm looking forward to leaving again. I bought
a morning paper and a pack of cigarettes at the newsstand, a giant cup
of coffee from the stall near the gate, and boarded the train. Finding
that I had practically the entire smoking car to myself, I stashed my
bags in the overhead rack and set about the business of making myself
as comfortable as possible. After spreading a few notes on the seat
beside me to make me feel as if I were already working—or at any rate
to make myself look that way to anyone who happened by—I opened
the paper and settled down to read and sip away the first hundred
miles or so. The train gently lurched into motion, and for a moment
I watched as the grey and rusty railyard with its sprawling clutter of
old engines and abandoned cars and the sooty backs of decrepit brick
buildings with their faded advertising rolled away, until it all vanished
behind a misty thicket of bare trees.

I love train rides. There is to my mind no more relaxing
sensation than rocking along the rails, one's seat tilted back, the
scenery rippling by outside the window. The ride to New York always
calmed me no matter how hectic the schedule ahead, and I smiled to

▼

myself in anticipation of the soothing three-hour journey before me.

But some things were never meant to be.

No sooner had I unfolded the newspaper and pried the top from my coffee than I became aware of someone standing by my seat. Assuming it was the conductor, I fished in my pocket for my ticket and held it out to him without looking up.

"Thank you ever so much, *mon ami,*" said a voice I recognized immediately, "but I already have one of my own."

Was it really possible? I was almost afraid to look up and verify what my ears had already made perfectly clear. But sure enough, there stood the crazy old man, beaming down at me like a grandfather about to present his grandson with a particularly chewy piece of caramel. I shot him the coldest basilisk stare I could muster—to no effect whatever.

"What a pleasant surprise!" Mr. Pedrolino said, as if I had just laughed aloud for the joy of meeting him. "I was sorely afraid I wouldn't see you again. I'm so sorry I missed you yesterday evening. But then, you must have had some very pressing business to attend to, *non?*"

I said nothing.

"Ah," he continued, "but all's well that ends well, as they say. May I join you?"

That was it. My beautiful, relaxing journey was irrevocably ruined. It had begun to look as if I would never shake the old man, and I caught myself wondering if he weren't some ghost of Christmas sent to punish me for my less-than-enthusiastic celebration of the Lord's birthday. Perhaps the best thing would be to ignore him; concentrate on my paper and pretend he wasn't there.

"Certainly," I said stupidly, and gathered up my notes.

That done, I determinedly focused on the headlines as he settled himself beside me. Not that there was anything riveting to read: stock market down again. So what? It had been down for the last fifteen years. Murder rate on the rise nationally. Big deal. When was the last time you saw an American newspaper reporting a falling murder rate? Let's see; a gubernatorial race in Tennessee. Boy, I'll bet *that's* an exciting piece of reporting. The newly elected president of the Soviet Union delivered his acceptance speech—calling for the right of citizens to bear arms—and an early Prendergast painting had been auctioned to Japan for $500 million—bloody bargain at half the price.

The news was all pretty much predictable these days, and by the time I'd finished reading the front page twice I was yawning. But I dared not even lift my eyes to look out the window. Presently the conductor came by to collect our tickets, wish us both a pleasant ride, and inform us that the club car was now open for breakfast.

"Well," said the old man when he had moved on, "I think I shall get myself something to eat. Would you care to join me?"

I stubbornly pretended I hadn't heard him and attended to the front page. But I couldn't concentrate. He sat quite still beside me for almost a full minute, his question unanswered. Then he said sharply: "Oh my goodness, look!"

I turned quickly to see him pull a long, wicked-looking knife from his pocket and, holding his left hand flat against the back of the seat in front of him, drive the blade into it with a sickening *thunk!* It all happened too fast to prevent.

My jaw dropped as blood spurted over his white sleeve and spattered onto my opened paper.

"My God!" I gasped when I found my voice. "You're fucking insane!"

"Yes, yes, perhaps," he replied with a dry chuckle. "But not *that* insane." So saying he withdrew the knife and I saw that it was a stage prop; a gag knife with a retractable blade. His eyes twinkled with amusement as he folded it up, then took a handkerchief from his breast pocket and carefully wiped the "blood" from his hands and lap.

"You do make wonderful faces," he observed. Then, "May I speak with you now? I'm sorry to have startled you, but you were being very difficult. And you have to admit it got your attention." He giggled and covered his mouth girlishly. "It always does."

"Mr. Pedrolino," I said, exasperated, "I only want to travel in peace, that's all. Why the hell are you following me?"

"You are being most unjust, Mr. Peters," he said sternly. "I am not following you. Indeed, I had no idea you would be on this train. I am only going home. But when I saw you boarding, I thought I might take the opportunity to renew our acquaintance, that is all." He paused to bat me a hurt and accusatory glance. "And besides," he went on, "we never did have that discussion about art." He shoved the knife back into his pocket, folded his arms, and pouted at the seat ahead of him.

My fate was sealed. There was simply no way out. From one minute to the next this infernal old man had successfully bugged the hell out of me, scared me half to death, and then made me feel like the world's biggest cad. I folded up my paper in defeat.

"Okay," I said. "Let's get some breakfast."

▼
▲

Train food being one of the few drawbacks to that mode of travel, I had little appetite, so for twenty minutes I sat and watched with distaste as Pierrot wolfed down two full plates of rubbery eggs and cold sausage, smacking his lips loudly between bites. It seemed that with all things alimentary his only object was to get the stuff to his stomach by the shortest possible route. Finally he finished and we headed back to our seats. It was then I noticed that the fake blood that had soaked his white sleeve had completely disappeared. "Magic," was all he said when I mentioned it.

By that point I had no inclination whatever to pursue the subject further. But on noticing my intentionally vacant expression I suppose he just couldn't resist the chance to expound on his practical joke. Someday I'll learn to keep my mouth shut.

"You see my friend," he began reflectively, "it is impulsive with me, I'm afraid. There was a time, before the writers pulled my teeth and tried to make me into a pathetic, witless blow-about, when I was the master of the stage. I was not at the mercy of any situation; rather, it was I who determined the plot of every sketch. There was a time when, in my role, I was perfectly capable of committing murder if it

▲

were necessary to win the favor of my darling Colombina. And I did so, often. Back when Théophile Gautier was writing for me, I could—and did—determine my own path to gratification; which is to say Colombina. But by the time that task was taken over by the likes of Carné and his film *Les Enfants du Paradis,* I was merely a melancholy shadow character; the epitome of pathos, soft as goat's-milk cheese. So every now and then, because I am no longer tied to the stage, to the whims of writers and the gluttony of audiences, I feel a need to assert my capricious, heedless, and to you, no doubt, obnoxious self. Can you understand that?"

I nodded vaguely. To be perfectly honest I didn't have the foggiest notion what he was getting at; nor had I been prepared for such a river of reminiscence. But I couldn't quarrel with his self-description.

Pedrolino flashed his Joker grin. "It will come clear to you in time, my friend," he said. "You must understand why I was, and am, always so intent on winning Colombina. You see . . ." he paused for a moment to gather his words carefully, "you see, Colombina is, for want of a better way of putting it, the soul of my art; its ultimate metaphor—Erato, if you prefer. She is what every artist strives for: The Ideal. And she is, of course, entirely unattainable. Am I being clear?"

"Clear as mud."

The old man chuckled appreciatively. "As a critic, my friend, you know that discussions of art often are. But then, that is why I am trying to make it clear to you. You asked what happened to the red dye on my sleeve? I tell you again that it disappeared by magic— perhaps not the most precise choice of words, but the only one that suffices. Our Indo-European languages are sometimes sadly ill-equipped to define such things."

How true, I thought, and considered suggesting that he conduct the rest of the explication in Pali. But I decided against it on the off-chance that he would be tempted to do just that.

"Let me try to be plainer," he went on. "Any successful work of art, be it a play, a poem, a piece of music, or a painting is in effect a gestalt, a magical blend of calculated intent and inspired caprice, forming a whole system that is completed with the participation of the audience. Truly fundamental differences in methodology exist only between music and poetry on the one hand, and the visual and stage arts on the other. This is because, while the eye can be fooled—the way I fooled you just now—the ear cannot. Meter, rhythm, and pitch are such integral parts of our everyday speech that we are already, by virtue of being speaking animals, born critics of art forms that appeal to the ear. Do you follow me so far?"

This was all beginning to sound alarmingly like a Socratic lecture—which I needed first thing in the morning like I needed a case of smallpox. But being determined to err on the side of politeness so as not to incur any more sulky behavior, I nodded and did my best to look attentive.

"Bon," he said, and rubbed his hands, warming to his work. "So, this fact sets the visual arts—and above all, painting—apart from the rest. A painting, as you are aware, is not merely an image; it is not a photograph. Nothing is concealed. And that which cannot be expressed purely in terms of the image can be intimated by other, purely plastic means—the texture of the paint, for example; the gestures employed to describe the subject, or lack of one. A truly good painting reaches straight from the heart of the artist to the eye of the viewer. It is an immensely intricate process, creating, as it does, an intellectual expression from an emotional root. And in art, emotion is the font, the origin of all communication. It is indeed rather like humor—which is where I come in."

"Right," I muttered. "Like humor." But the old man was undeterred by my facetious tone, and proceeded with his dissertation like a guest on a TV talk show.

"I will explain: I'm sure you would agree that it is impossible to note-by-note dissect the magic conveyed by a figure of music—Beethoven's Ninth Symphony, let's say." The old man closed his eyes and, conducting with an imaginary baton, began to hum the melody to the chorale finale. "You see?" he said gleefully, "it is simply a sequence of fifteen notes which roughly travel up, then down a scale, then up, then down again partway. Arpeggios; that is all. And yet, who would deny the effect it has on the soul?"

I shrugged in agreement.

"*Bien sûr.* No one. So, we may deduce that its heartfelt impact is, though obviously constructed within the rather rigid bounds of an accepted musical structure, nevertheless purely magical in nature. So it is with painting. But it goes further, because painting employs many more devices. This is because painting can never be the perfect abstraction that music is. A painting, in terms of the many moments in which it can be beheld and contemplated, is not a fleeting thing. It is, for better or for worse, a dual entity: an image on the one hand, and an object on the other. 'Art' occurs when a dialectic is provoked between what an object *is,* and what it *signifies.* Do we agree on this?"

I'd never heard it put quite that way before, but it actually seemed a rather succinct description of what constituted an art object, and I said so.

"So it does," he said, obviously pleased that I'd agreed with him on something. "But what is not so easily defined is how the gestalt of a painting—its magic—works. There are, of course, many components that can be isolated and analyzed with some degree of accuracy: various symbols, for example, which are remarkably universal in some instances, crossing and encompassing many cultures. There is the inherent emotional dynamic the painter can evoke by composing on the vertical or the horizontal; a horizontal, naturally enough, evokes a rather placid, calming, or bucolic feeling, simply because it implies landscape; a horizon—a common enough phenomenon to almost anyone but the poor soul who has never left the inner city of, say, Manhattan. The vertical inspires just the opposite response, because it implies enclosure and visual restriction. Such devices are analogous to the way a composer employs sweet, high-pitched violins or deep, sonorous basses to establish moods within the context of a musical work.

"Such devices are fairly obvious. But many others are not. And, curiously, such components of painting are shared by abstract, nonobjective, and realist works alike—or at least the *implications* of them are. You wonder how all of this is related to my profession; to humor. It is like this: Something may strike people as funny because it is a play on words—generally and most successfully of a scatological nature; it may be slapstick derived from commonplace events gone haywire. It might be a satirical reference to a specific occurrence or character within a specific context—contemporary politics, for example. Or, to illustrate the fine line so often drawn between the sublime and the ridiculous, it may simply be complete and utter nonsense, such as the unforgivably crass stunt I pulled on you with the knife just now. And, while you may not have found the prank particularly funny, I can assure you by dint of long experience that many onlookers would have. But however we dissect the actions or events that elicit a humorous response, we can never fully explain *why* they cause someone to laugh. And yet someone trained like myself to make people laugh can do so ninety percent of the time—at will. How can that be, if such a phenomenon cannot even be adequately explained? If we invoke the definition of magic I applied to art, then the analogy holds. Do you follow me so far?"

I lighted a cigarette and watched him closely. My recent experience of the crazy old fellow had not prepared me for such a complex argument, and frankly he had begun to lose me again. "If I understand you correctly," I said, "you seem to be saying that a good painter is essentially a wizard, and his paintbrush a magic wand. It all sounds a tad abstruse to me. I'm afraid I personally place a bit more faith in formal training; in knowing how to make a picture according to well-established rules of composition and mastery of technique. Besides, when you blithely draw an analogy between art and humor, you seem to forget that lots of things people consider funny are unintentionally so—that there is, in fact, a pretty morbid, if not downright cruel, side to humor. Take accidents, for example. We tend to laugh at other people's misfortunes just as readily as at their intentional jokes. And to be honest, I don't for a moment believe that great painters make great paintings by accident."

He listened attentively, nodded, then paused for a moment to blow his nose loudly into his handkerchief—which I noticed was also quite free of red stains—and proceeded. "I didn't say that painters made great paintings by accident," he continued at length. "Nor did I claim that humor is always intentional. But whether the laughter was provoked intentionally or unintentionally has no bearing on my argument. We can no more easily explain why an unintentional action is funny than an intended one. The thing is that beyond a point we can only agree that something was funny. By the same token, if we agree that making a painting is often a process of making decisions—which is to say making decisions to leave certain elements, whether they were intentional or not—then the artist, too, recognizes that there are certain things beyond his control. If he inadvertently slips with his brush and causes a particularly pleasing line, then it is up to him to leave it or delete it as he sees fit. So he has made a conscious decision, yes. But he first had to have the expertise to recognize that something was worth saving; to recognize that it was aesthetically significant. But I hold that that significance is essentially inexplicable, and I invoke the word *magic* to describe such inexplicable things. You wouldn't, I'm sure, argue that just because someone studies painting for ten years at an academy, and learns to master the techniques you mentioned, he will automatically emerge as an artist capable of producing great works!"

"Of course not!"

"Quite right. Of course not. And yet, of all people, I would be the last to disparage the value of good training in any art. But that is not my point. My point has to do with impulse and, to a degree, innate ability. I contend that the very impulse that causes certain individuals—regardless of training—to want to create images or a piece of music is itself magical. How else do we explain it? Certainly there are those people who are gifted almost from birth with an ability to, say, draw instinctively a recognizable representation of what they see in front of them. And there are others who possess an uncanny ability to make beautiful sounds on almost any instrument—a Mozart, for example—although genius of that magnitude is admittedly rare. But beyond raw talent, which I suppose would be explained these days in terms of hand-to-eye coordination, or by the number of synapses present in the brain—in other words, in purely somatic or morphological terms—beyond that, there is an impulse which is much harder, if not impossible, to define. It is the impulse that compels someone to refine such an ability to the degree that he or she can express almost any emotion, any thought or feeling, through an artificial—meaning an essentially *human*—medium. It is this impulse that concerns me.

"Why do you suppose it is that throughout history there have been artists and musicians willing to sacrifice their very lives—to endure poverty, addiction, even scorn—to pursue such an impulse? We say cavalierly, 'So-and-so had to follow his *muse.'* That's what we say. But who, or what, is that muse?"

I watched him attentively.

"Ah," he said, "for me that muse is Colombina. The unattainable. I have killed her many times in my career—not out of hate but from jealousy and infatuation." The old man paused to cover his mouth with his hand and giggle girlishly. "You know, I once even tickled her to death, if you can believe it. Yet she is not dead. The great paradox is that she can never truly die, because if she did, there would be no drama; no story. No Pierrot. She is the source, you see; the reason for my existence, and Arlequin's, and Leandre's. All together we make the magic. And the magic has no true name but art."

The train slowed to rumble loudly through the darkness of the Thirtieth Street station in Philadelphia, then picked up speed again as we raced on toward New York. The old man fell silent for a time, moodily watching the dreary landscape spinning by beyond the window. Intent on what he had been saying, I said nothing and waited. Presently, he began talking again, more reflectively now.

"In the Tate Gallery in London is a huge painting by that wonderful German painter Anselm Kiefer. You know his work, of course?"

"Oh," I replied with as much sarcasm as I could muster, "I might have heard the name somewhere."

The old man smiled indulgently. "Yes, of course, forgive me. This painting's title is not important because, like all great paintings,

▲

its imagery is profound. It is a picture of an empty attic; an old, high-ceilinged wooden one, dark and whispering with the memory of treasured things once left there to be forgotten. In the center of the picture, buried solidly in one of the raw wooden rafters, is an arrow. Do you know the piece?"

Come to think of it, I hadn't seen that particular image. But I'd seen other Kiefers of that nature—works he'd executed, for the most part, in the late seventies. "I'm familiar with the style," I said. "He made quite a few paintings along those lines some years ago."

"Good," he said. "Well, that's it—the whole picture. Yet it is a remarkable one. The arrow is of the sort a Plains Indian might once have slung at the shaggy neck of a bison. It is painted red and white and festooned with a tassel of feathers. Given its angle of penetration into the beam, it would have to have been shot from somewhere up near the corner of the steeply louvered roof—an absurd notion, of course, but the only possible explanation. The attic itself, to judge by its structure and general appearance, obviously belongs to a very old European—probably German—house. In other words, just about the last place you'd expect to find somebody shooting Sioux arrows about, *non?*

"The arrow's very presence (and it is the only prominently featured subject of the painting) is a complete incongruity. Yet it gives the entire composition a haunting, dreamlike quality that persists long after the picture has been passed by or left thousands of miles behind. There is nothing fancy about the way the image is rendered. No flashy technique or hidden, unexpected twists to the composition. Just plain, straightforward depiction. In fact, the style verges on the childish: the grain of the wooden beams, for example, is drawn in the way a youngster might do it; a stylized pattern of concentric ovals and parallel lines forming a universal visual signature that announces quite plainly, 'This is wood.' Yet still the painting conveys an aura of magic; an intensity and significance that is undeniable—one that goes beyond the mere physical fact of the object itself. Why?"

"Go on."

▼

"It is the picture's gestalt, of course. In other words, more contributes to this painting's power than just the startling incongruity of its subject. Which, of course, is not to say that it isn't precisely this unconventional juxtaposition of elements that sets us to pondering its meaning. But think about it: a simple incongruity in nature—or on a city street—does not necessarily move us to contemplate magic. Who of us, for instance, has not at some time seen an otherwise sartorially subdued individual on the subway who just happens to be wearing one odd or outrageous article of clothing or jewelry? Or, how often have you seen in the depths of an otherwise seemingly virgin wood the wreck of an automobile or some other man-made contraption of plastic or brightly painted metal? No, it is not enough to focus solely on the arrow in Kiefer's attic, though the arrow is indeed the focus of the painting; a device; a symbol. It is a question of how that symbol relates to its surroundings. It is a matter of context, and that context has been determined and defined by the painter's imagination.

"Of course, whether or not the artist consciously intended it, it isn't hard to see the arrow as a symbol of barbarism—tribal, totemic, boorish, even threatening. And it takes little imagination to decipher the attic's significance as a warehouse of long-standing cultural tradition; like the mind of Western man, a place to store the intellectual and ethical accoutrements of centuries of civilization. These things the viewer can bring to the picture of his own accord; indeed, it is vital that he do so, lest it remain only at the level of a curious pattern on the wall. But what is more remarkable about this painting is the fact that a combination of devices used to seduce the eye is so deftly incorporated and orchestrated as to pass virtually undetected on first encounter. The devices are there, but they are unobtrusive. It is an example of accomplished, almost effortless, legerdemain, and the longer one studies it, the more the virtuosity of the artist becomes apparent.

"You see, what Kiefer has done here is employ an overarching device that's as old as the hills—or at least as old as Renaissance and Late Gothic German painting; a device so obvious that few artists

these days—being, as they are, the inheritors of the Modernist tradition—even consider using it, or recognize it when they see it. And
yet it is this single age-old compositional element that gives the work
its power and makes the blatant incongruity of the arrow work. That
device, my friend, is the same one I use: the stage."

So far I had followed the old man carefully. But I confess that
this last pronouncement escaped me. "How do you mean, 'the
stage'?"

"Why the entire picture is a stage! A simple one, but a stage
nevertheless. Just look at it," he exclaimed, as if it were right there
in front of us. "By the use of dramatic perspective, sheer size, and
powerful diagonals that draw the eye unerringly to the central subject,
Kiefer has visually set up a conventional stage, with a performing area,
backdrop, wings—everything but curtains and an usher. It's a dynamic area he gives us to contemplate. Put it this way: if you walked
into a dark theater and saw, there upon the spotlighted stage, a single
arrow quivering in the boards, what would you think?"

I thought carefully before I answered, but I was beginning to
get his drift. "I would think," I said, "that it was probably a prelude
to some drama about to take place there. Or perhaps an omen signify-
ing violence of some sort."

"Of course. And you would be right to assume this. A stage,
after all, is a place where one expects something to happen. And this
is precisely the expectation Kiefer anticipates with his picture, you
see? A painting, obviously, cannot perform action for us or vocalize
a dialogue. But it can set up its audience, then let our imaginations
take over to provide the drama. And the artist has simplified—or at
least facilitated—this process for us. He has given us the arrow. And
this mundane object becomes the focus not only of the composition,
but of our imagination."

"It sounds plausible enough," I said. "But what about the
arrow itself. Surely there is more to it than just a token of barbarism,
or an item of weaponry. I mean, why an arrow as opposed to maybe
a garden spade, or a pickax, or a drill bit?"

"Ah," said the old man, "very good. But in fact Kiefer has

▼

done other pictures of a similar nature where the object is a dagger. But the arrow has a special significance all its own. What is an arrow? Does it only kill things? No, of course not. In the vernacular of almost any Western tongue, the arrow *points* to things. It is a symbol of direction. In this case, I might suggest that Kiefer's is 'the arrow of time,' if I may borrow a phrase from Stephen Hawking's essay on entropy. It symbolizes the persistent direction of time and the tendency to disorder; to decay. It is irresistible and mono-directional. It points, in other words, in the same direction as chaos—perhaps the greatest enemy recognized by civilization. What time has decided, no power on earth can alter. We stand before Kiefer's painting and, as in daily life, we are transfixed by time's arrow. For a moment, it's true, we may be unaware of the one great enemy we all share to one degree or another . . ." Here, the old man stopped and gave me a curious look. "But," he continued shortly, "by the use of this one universal symbol driven into the calm and complacent dark of an old and venerable attic, Kiefer reminds us that time recognizes no civilization; no creed, no philosophy—much less any aesthetic, sentiment, or other human attribute. It is the ultimate paradox of the nature of art: a refined human artifice informing us of the innate futility of itself. Structured artifice employed for the purpose of showing us the depth of its own artificiality in the face of uncontrollable nature. Kiefer's arrow, you see, is not lodged, immovable. Its forward motion has not been entirely stopped; only its tangible presence has. Its direction and impetus go on before it. It digs into the ancient wood of the attic as surely as grooves of laughter and sorrow will score all of our faces. And it is in the pursuit of this impetus—that intangible but very real element that leaves marks of its passage on everything—it is for this that the artist gives so much. The artist must pursue his Colombina as assiduously as I. He has no choice. And if sometimes he appears to kill his muse, it is merely an illusion. Like my knife trick, it's an act, performed upon a stage of his own devising."

His torrent of words dried up suddenly, and again the old man threw me a quizzical look, as if he suspected I thought he'd been talking gibberish. I lighted another cigarette and glanced out the window. New Jersey enveloped us in a smudge of early morning light, and neon twinkled on the horizon. I wasn't sure I could reconcile the impulse that motivated the great and wonderful paintings I had loved so long with the cheapness of a parlor trick such as the one M. Pedrolino had pulled on me. I thought of some of the ridiculous characters who figured in the world's great literature—Quasimodo, for example, and Hamlet and Cyrano de Bergerac. But these dramatis personae had all been pitted against overwhelming odds—odds only aggravated by their own physical deficiencies and private demons—and all had either come out heroes or failures of shattering magnitude. Frans Hals may indeed have been a drunkard and a philanderer, but the marks of his genius were there for the world to see, and I had to believe that he triumphed in spite of his faults, not because of them.

"So," I asked at length, "you really believe that art is fundamentally such an insubstantial thing—an illusion, and a contradictory one at that?"

"I did not say so, my friend. And if I implied it, then I have failed you. No, I meant to express that the impulse to make it, to uncover the nature of the world through it, is timeless. But that the process by which that knowledge is conveyed is often a matter of devices—parlor tricks, if you like."

I looked at him sharply. He smiled archly and fluttered his heavy lids.

"Let me posit something to you," he went on after a moment's silence. "You are no doubt familiar with the famous cave paintings of Lascaux and Altamira?"

"Certainly."

"Do you then go along with the notion so popular with many scholars that these were merely records, or ritual figures, or impromptu depictions of hunts dashed off by some inspired Cro-Magnon of a wintry evening when there was nothing else to do—to illustrate what animals of the hunt looked like for a youngster?"

"I don't think I've ever thought much about it."

"Precisely. Then let me put this to you for your consideration:

that these beautiful paintings have so captured our imaginations because they represent the culmination of months of study and work on
the part of the artists who made them. That somewhere, if we only
knew where to look for it, there is a leaf of studies; sketches by one
of these artists rendered, perhaps, on a sheet of bark or scraped hide.
Studies not only of how the animals looked fresh in his memory, but
of ways to formalize their shapes; capture with a line or two their
vitality and the nature of their movements. There must be, because
all of this is certainly present in the finished products as we see them
today, however faintly. These are no mere ritualistic spatterings of
blown ochre and smeared iron dust. These are masterpieces of their
time, drafted and composed with all the care and attention Rivera
brought to one of his murals. And wouldn't it be marvelous to find
such a relic? To see how a draftsman of seventeen or twenty thousand
years ago worked out his images; perfected his line and volumes?"

It had in fact never occurred to me that works of such antiquity might be products of as refined an artistic impulse as that which
prompted Michelangelo, say, to design the Sistine Chapel ceiling.
And, frankly, I doubted it. But the old man appeared to be driving
at something that had so far eluded me.

"What exactly is the point to all this?" I asked after some
consideration.

"My point is only this: that the urge to make art is as old as
mankind; and that it will continue, no matter what the current state
of affairs politically or economically. You see," he continued pen-
sively, "there has been so much talk recently of the 'death of art,' the
'death of history,' and so forth. It seems that every time I pick up an
art magazine or listen in on an artist's conversation, all I hear is this
pessimistic pondering about the state of the arts in the so-called
'Postmodern' period. Why, even you have entertained such perturba-
tions, have you not?"

"Me and everybody else with any sense," I admitted. Whether
he'd intended to or not, the old man had struck a chord; hit on an
issue that was very close to my heart and had nagged my thoughts for
quite a few years. "I've thought for some time now," I said, "that

certain values have gotten lost; the belief in art for its own sake, for example. It's almost as if, since the last efforts of pure abstraction—Minimalism—in the seventies, there's been a purely cynical, purely political approach to making art. And I'm not sure I can honestly say why this has happened, but I can say that I don't particularly like it, and that I don't see much of a future for painting. It's all being eaten up by degrees, by media saturation, by advertising and sloganism; by 'deconstruction' theory and so on. It's so damned popular these days to talk about how very far off base artists I admired, like Rothko, were. So popular to talk about how artists are merely mirrors of Baudrillard's 'simulacrum' society: that great and trendy idée fixe that presumably no artist and no critic can be taken seriously without paying lip service to. And, of course, it's popular to rant on about how pernicious Modernist tenets are, or how connoisseurship is some kind of capitalist plot. But all anybody seems able to offer to replace the things they rail against is sophomoric bullshit. Doesn't that bother you, too?"

"Non," he said with a smile. "I see a degree of uncertainty, of course. Perhaps even a temporary stasis and lack of imagination in the plastic arts. But then I have seen many such periods." He looked at me and winked. "You may not yet believe it, but I am who I say I am. And for the sake of argument, let's accept that I have seen a number of centuries roll past my windows. I submit that such periods of seeming disarray and lack of direction are indicative of perfectly natural periodic political and economic unrest. And that these periods of unrest predictably occur at fins de siécle—at the turns of the century. It's partly to do with social psychology, and partly to do with the natural cycle of things. It takes, I believe, a certain number of generations for economic or political systems to prove themselves or work themselves to a close. And with the close of the twentieth century—which I remind you has witnessed more change in human life more rapidly than any previous era in history—we are approaching something even more portentous: the turn of a millennium. Even I have not lived through such a time.

"But I contend, *mon ami*, that times such as these are transitory. Don't you see that that is why I brought up Kiefer's arrow? The artistic impulse is not dictated by anything so flimsy and artificial as a change in the date on a calendar! Goodness, my friend. How many such changes has art already seen come and go? Can you honestly believe that the muse is so unfaithful a lover?"

"Go on."

"I understand your concern with what you perceive as a breakdown in values, in aesthetic concerns. Of course I sympathize entirely. But these are perfectly predictable manifestations of unrest; reflections of the unease of contemporary society. We live at present—in this country, at least—in a society of unparalleled greed. A society whose overriding impulse is the acquisition of material things, to the neglect of the spiritual and intellectual. And all this has affected art profoundly. How could it not? Artists are, after all, among the most sensitive and perspicacious of humans. That is why they are artists. But we must not allow ourselves to be so easily swayed by cynics spouting Baudrillard—or more especially, Hegel. It is of no use to anyone to dig up the dubious reasonings of long-dead philosophers to explain the problematic realities of the present. It can only be counterproductive. We need new philosophers; new ideas. Ideas that deal with those realities and not pet theories, however intriguing."

Despite my reservations about him, the old man appeared to be making sense, and again I found myself reassessing my opinion of him. Whatever else he was, he was an accomplished interlocutor. In any event, he had certainly made the journey speed by. I was surprised when the conductor's voice came over the loudspeaker, announcing, "Ladies and gentlemen, in about three minutes we will be arriving at Pennsylvania Station, New York City. Please be sure to check around your seats for your belongings . . ." Looking out the window I saw that we were already crossing the stagnant, polluted marshes of the Jersey shore, with the flashing, glassy spires of Manhattan rising swiftly in the near distance. Pedrolino watched them too, a strained expression on his face. Tentatively, he reached out and laid his bony hand on my arm.

"My friend," he said, "I do apologize for having monopolized

▲

your time so—and of course for my little prank earlier. But I would be delighted if you would give me the opportunity to show you something that would, I am sure, be of considerable interest to you."

"And what could that be?"

"Quite the rarest and most complete collection of master paintings you will ever see."

Misunderstanding him, I replied, "I've been to the Metropolitan many times, Mr. Pedrolino. It's my job. But I'm not sure I'd call it the rarest or most complete."

He laughed. "Nor would I, my friend. And I was not speaking of the Met."

"What collection did you have in mind then?" I asked, trying to recall the names of all the private New York collectors I'd ever heard of.

"Why mine, of course. And I assure you, it is the only one of its kind in the world."

3

▼
▲

DON'T ASK. I HAVE ABSOLUTELY NO IDEA WHAT IDI-
otic impulse made me, after all I'd been through with M. Pedrolino,
agree to go and see his "collection." Maybe I was still feeling guilty
about having walked off and left him the night before. I don't know.

I don't mean to give the impression that I went along with his
proposal right off the bat. We rumbled into Penn Station more or less
just as he made the suggestion, so I was able to avoid making a
decision while I got my bags together and exited the train. All the
old man had with him was a dirty white canvas carrying case, and he
offered to carry one of my suitcases for me when we'd taken the
escalator up into the crowded building.

"Thanks, I can manage," I said. "I'm just going right out to
Thirty-fourth Street to catch a cab uptown."

He walked me out to the curb. As I was about to step into a
taxi he took my arm. "Monsieur Peters," he said, "a moment, please."
He withdrew a dog-eared calling card from his coat pocket and thrust
it into my hand. "This is my address," he said. "I have no telephone,
I'm afraid. They are such irritating contraptions. But should you have
a chance in your busy schedule, please feel free to drop in on me any
time. I am leaving shortly for Europe and have to set my affairs in
order, so you will find me home almost anytime this week. I would
be interested to hear your opinion of my collection."

"What sort of a collection is it?" I asked—a shade facetiously,
I admit. By the looks of him the old man couldn't have had money
enough to rent a decent apartment, much less purchase art.

"Ah, *mon ami*. That you will see when you come. I can only assure you that it will be well worth your while." He stepped back and gave a deep bow. *"Adieu,"* he said, and strode off in the direction of 7th Avenue.

I glanced at the card in my hand. PIERROT, it said, and under that, A REAL CLOWN. The address was Avenue B in the East Village. Beside this, in parentheses, it said, BY APPOINTMENT ONLY. How did one make an appointment if he didn't have a telephone?

"Monsieur Pedrolino!" I called after him. He turned around and stood looking at me expectantly.

"I'll stop by in a day or two," I said. "Promise."

"Très bien," he called back with a broad Joker smile. "Any time, my friend. Any time." Then he waved and walked away.

I checked in at the hotel, unpacked my bags, and called room service for a nine o'clock wake-up call the next morning. Then I went back out and flagged a cab down to SoHo. It was quite chilly outside and few people were about on West Broadway or Greene Street. After ambling about the galleries for a bit, seeing only two shows I thought worth a damn—some recent Robert Therrien sculpture at Castelli, and a retrospective of Jim Nutt's funky cartoons at Phylis Kind—I stopped into The Cupping Room Cafe for some lunch. The normally quiet little restaurant was unusually crowded, and it took me almost fifteen minutes to get a seat. I'd no sooner sat down than I spotted Robert Moskowitz walking in. An artist I liked and admired, I invited him to join me.

I'd first met Moskowitz some ten years before, when his retrospective opened at the Hirshhorn Museum in Washington, although I'd been familiar with his refreshingly original and untrendy work for many years before that. Slightly built and self-effacing, Moskowitz painted powerful pictures that made high art out of all-American icons. A rarity in the contemporary art world, he was one of those who preserved and displayed a respect for the painting as object; slyly humorous and critical as they were, his large canvases and pastel drawings such as the justly famous *Eddystone Light, Red Windmill,* and the *Empire State Building* were more than mere aping of pop imagery to satisfy the whims of pop culture; they were studies in subtlety, in intention more akin to Monet's Rouen Cathedral pictures or Ad Reinhardt's black paintings than anything else. To a degree his works were reverent abstractions, in homage, perhaps, to the work of one of his teachers, Adolph Gottlieb. In other words, the man had a way with paint.

He looked tired.

"Just working hard," he said. "What are you up to?"

"Recovering from the holidays."

"I know just what you mean."

We ordered lunch and bantered about this and that over coffee while we waited. And then a thought occurred to me.

"Bob," I said tentatively, "do you know a guy named Gilles Pedrolino? European guy, lives in the East Village?"

Moskowitz adjusted his round wire-rimmed glasses and rubbed his grizzled chin thoughtfully. He regarded me with a wary expression, as if debating whether he should answer the question. Finally he said, "Yeah, sure I know him. Usually goes by the name of Pierrot, though—you know, like the clown."

I felt relieved. So far only Big Ron the bartender had provided any verification of the old man's identity.

"What exactly does he do, Bob?"

Moskowitz put his hands in his pockets, rocked back in his chair, and contemplated this question.

"Where do you know him from, Corry?" he asked at length—almost suspiciously, I felt.

"Met him at the National Gallery yesterday. Rode up on the train with him this morning. I just don't know what to make of him. I mean, he seems pretty knowledgeable about art, but . . . Well, you know, he claims to be about five hundred years old or something. Do you know what I mean? I mean, I just don't know what to make of him. And now he wants me to visit his 'collection.' "

"It's a good collection," said Moskowitz with a laugh. "Like nothing *you* ever saw before."

"You mean you've seen it?"

"Sure I've seen it. Lots of artists have seen it." Bob suddenly rocked forward again and took a sip of coffee. "But not too many critics have, I don't think," he added thoughtfully. "He doesn't like critics much."

You can imagine how this news struck me. Here was a major artist blithely corroborating the old man's extraordinary story, like it was nothing at all out of the ordinary. I watched Moskowitz dumbly as our food arrived and he started eating hungrily.

"You're not putting me on or anything, are you, Bob?"

He laughed. "No, man. I'm not putting you on. He's for real. But," he said, lowering his voice, "I wouldn't go blabbing it all over town that you've run into him. He likes to keep it kind of quiet, you know."

"Sure, sure," I said. Like I was really out to make everybody in the whole damned city think I was loony-toons! I took a bite of my sandwich but discovered I had little appetite. "Bob," I said, "what's this collection like? I mean, what is it a collection of?"

Moskowitz grinned around a mouthful of food. "Well," he said, "long as you were invited, I guess you'd better go see for yourself."

▼
▲

That night I slept fitfully. The crazy old man haunted my dreams. I couldn't shake his odd Joker grin, his uncouth manners, or his remarkably learned conversation. The next morning I woke early, got dressed, and breakfasted in my room. Then I went downstairs and hailed a cab for the East Village.

As we turned onto Avenue A and East Tenth, my head was filled with memories of a decade and a half before, when the neighborhood was at the center of a new movement in the arts. I remembered The Kitchen, Nature Mort, and New Math galleries, all now long gone; "Gracie Mansion" before she moved to her current, more fashionable location. I remembered the trendy Japanese restaurant called simply Avenue A, and the little Ukrainian place where Robert Longo and Cindy Sherman and David Byrne used to hang out in the early eighties: the place that served the best blueberry blintzes and borscht in the world and was open twenty-four hours a day. But things had changed. That is to say they'd changed back to the way things were before the "Postmodern" crowd. The area was a real pit again. No incongruous-looking limos pulled up in front of the tiny bohemian galleries that sprang up, it seemed, overnight. There were no longer any galleries to pull up in front of. South of Houston Street, there wasn't anything to attract anyone looking for culture. Sure, the Phoenix was still there on First, and no doubt the out-of-work actors still gathered there to talk about how they wished they had the money to go to L.A. or Chicago. But basically the scene had gone, and any memory of it, too. The Bowery crowd had moved in, no longer threatened by the fashionable youngsters hungry for art and the latest thing in video. It occurred to me that, while I could remember living in the area and walking over to SoHo through Little Italy, now the ever-smaller crowds who attended openings at Metro Pictures, Louver, or Phylis Kind galleries drove down from the Upper West Side and drove back there when the wine was exhausted.

Presently the taxi pulled up in front of a dilapidated old brick tenement on Avenue B and East Tenth, on the east side of the littered and deserted Tompkins Square Park. It had begun to drizzle—a chilling combination of rain and fine sleet—and I damned near slipped and broke my neck getting out of the car. The taxi sped away like he'd suddenly discovered he was somewhere he didn't want to be, and left me to contemplate my surroundings. The courtyard of the building was hedged in by a tall iron fence with a massive padlocked gate. To reinforce the forbidding aspect of the locale, the top of this fence was wrapped around with vicious-looking barbed wire, and some wit—my buddy Pedrolino, likely as not—had spray-painted on the sidewalk at my feet in bold, blood-red letters, *Ich bin ein Berliner*. If I'd been doubtful of the old man's veracity before, I now

felt a complete fool for having come to this part of town by myself—
no matter what Moskowitz had said. What the hell was I doing on
Avenue B and East Tenth? Didn't the Hell's Angels hole up around
here somewhere? Given its shabby outward appearance I could well
imagine what the interior of the building would be like. Probably
smelled of urine and stale cigars. Peeling wallpaper; water stains on
the carpet. And the looming bulk of the once posh but now abandoned Cristodora House with its gaping, paneless windows did nothing to improve the overall effect. Like everything else in the vicinity,
it was a symbol of all that had been resurrected in the eighties only
to crumble again in the nineties. But, well, there I was. And I was
getting wetter and miserabler by the moment.

On a tarnished brass plaque by the gate was a list of names and
doorbell buttons. Room 402 belonged to G. Pedrolino. But I didn't
have to push the button. I heard a noise behind the gate, and there
he stood, beaming happily.

"You surprise me, my friend," he said, and unlocked the gate.
"I did not for a moment think you would come. But I am glad to see
you." He shook my hand warmly and closed the gate behind me.

The old man seemed not in the least concerned with the
appearance of the place, if indeed he even noticed it. He led me
through the weed-grown court to the entrance—a peeling, industrial
green–painted steel fire door—threw it open with a flourish, and
bowed me in as if it were the entrance to a palazzo somewhere in
Tuscany.

"Welcome to my home," he said simply.

Through another peeling door and we were confronted with
a rickety old Otis elevator that looked as if it might easily rise up two
or three floors before letting us free-fall to our deaths. But by now
I was committed, so I followed my host cautiously into the little
chamber.

"Lifts are wonderful inventions," he said merrily. "Remember
when the only way to get to the top floor of any building was to walk
up all those stairs?" He batted his eyelashes and smiled. "No, of
course you don't. How silly of me!"

He pushed a button; the grille rattled shut and the gas-chamber-like door slid to. A sudden jerk and the elevator lurched upward with a great groaning of metal and whining of cables. "This really is a very nice area, you know," he prated on, "except in the summers when the Puerto Rican kids knock over the fire hydrants so they can wash their cars. Then the water pressure drops so badly one cannot take a shower above the first floor. But the location is very convenient for me. Why, I can walk to SoHo in half an hour, and there are some lovely restaurants along Avenue A."

When we reached the fourth floor, I followed the old man down the dimly lighted hallway which, as I'd correctly guessed, smelled like the restrooms at the Port Authority bus station. I began to try to think of a convincing excuse that would permit me to extract myself gracefully from the rendezvous and get back uptown to the Plaza where I belonged. But before I could formulate a plausible story we had arrived at Pedrolino's apartment door. There was no number on it, just a single five-pointed silver star.

Pausing before he opened it, the old man turned to me and said in a grave tone of voice I hadn't heard him use before: "Mr. Peters, you must promise me that you will tell no one of the things you see here. Promise me that and you will be forever welcome to my home, wherever that may be. But should you ever break this pledge, you'll find this all has disappeared, and you will never see me or my collection again. Is that understood?"

I remembered Bob Moskowitz's disinclination to describe the collection. I nodded solemnly. "I understand."

"*Bon,*" he said with a bright smile, and threw open the door.

For the second time since I'd met Pedrolino I found myself stunned to the soles of my shoes. For a time I stood gape-mouthed in the doorway, all of my doubts removed and wonder taking their place. On a partition wall facing the door hung a large canvas by Cézanne. It was a work in his mature style—very like the self-portrait of about 1880 that hangs in the Phillips Collection in Washington, in fact. Only this was much larger, and it was without question a portrait of my host. Indeed, he looked to be of about the same age as he was now, and this struck me as curious because thus far the only portraits he claimed were of him—that I'd seen, at least—depicted a far younger man of athletic build.

How long I stood and stared at this amazing image I don't know. But finally Pierrot laughed and, taking me gently by the arm, drew me inside.

"This is not the best of them, I assure you, my friend," he said. "Do come in and make yourself at home. I will fix us a drink and we can relax and chat like civilized people."

To say that Pierrot's collection was astounding would be an understatement. Nothing I'd heard of it so far—which I had in any event dismissed as sheer fantasy (or perhaps conspiracy, on Bob's part)—could have prepared me for the sight that greeted me when I walked into the living room of the deceptively large flat. The apartment itself, while heavily furnished with all sorts of evident antiques, was dusty and cluttered. But the walls would have done a gallery at the Louvre proud: Over a battered-looking chaise longue that was almost certainly a Napoleonic period piece hung another large portrait of my companion, this time by Daumier. A Frans Hals—again depicting Pierrot more or less at his present age—hung over the mantel. On the back side of the partition that hid the front door, a rather frilly, pastel-colored portrait of the clown as a young man in full costume by Boucher, and beside that, in almost absurd contrast, a Rubens. In this picture, Pierrot appeared to be about middle-aged; his jowl rather heavier than I could imagine him having, and he was dressed in typical Flemish fashion with a wide, circular white collar and black satin skintight sleeves with lace cuffs. But it was definitely him—and if proof were needed, the black skullcap left no doubt as to the sitter's identity.

In the presence of all this priceless art, I suddenly found myself very uncomfortable. For an instant the thought crossed my mind that I was for some reason the victim of an elaborate hoax; that all of the incredible paintings hanging about the room were fakes—fakes so perfectly made as to deceive any but the most attentive and knowledgeable connoisseur. Suspiciously, I walked up to the Daumier and inspected it closely. He was one artist with whose techniques I was thoroughly familiar, and one of the most difficult to successfully duplicate. But my fears evaporated after giving it a very careful once-over. There was simply no doubt of its authenticity. Besides the brushwork and signature, I could see the age-browned canvas edge where the picture was out of square with the old gilt frame.

No, it was just a beautiful Daumier—one that any major museum would kill to have.

In something of a trance I whirled slowly in place in the middle of the big room and looked about. Paintings, hung above and beside each other all the way to the ceiling, salon style, fought for space on the walls. Besides the recognizable masters, there were numerous works by lesser hands, many of whom I couldn't immediately put names to. The furniture in the room was uniformly moldy and in need of repair. But it, too, represented a collection I fancy your average antique store owner would have given his eyeteeth for: everything from heavy, Romanesque chests and stools carved with all kinds of arcane mythical figures to French Regency, Queen Anne, and Hepplewhite. The floor was carpeted with an unruly assemblage of threadbare Oriental rugs and, here and there, a faded Medieval tapestry flung down unceremoniously to do duty as a rug. Overhead an enormous tarnished brass and crystal chandelier glowed softly.

Seeing me gazing at this, Pierrot—who had been standing patiently to one side as I bustled about inspecting everything—interrupted my reverie by saying with a tinge of sadness in his voice, "They took away my gas jets in the fifties, you know. It was a great blow to me because, when I had all the gas lighting in here, I could still sometimes pretend that I was back in my old place in Montmartre, with all my wonderful friends."

He shook his head and looked at me with a gloomy expression. "That is one of the great disadvantages to growing so old: you miss your beautiful friends, and they can never be replaced. Never. That is why," he continued, indicating with a sweep of his hand the paintings on the walls, "that is why I treasure these things, beyond their significance as works of art. They're all I have left now, and they are not only priceless, they are beyond any such consideration."

▲

I watched as his eyes grew distant, and a slight shiver ran up my spine. Then slowly, life came back to his face and he smiled. "But I am being a maudlin old man now, am I not? Come, let's sit and have a beer—or tea, if you prefer. If you are hungry I can make some lunch, although I'm not sure what I have in the refrigerator at the moment. I usually eat out, you see." So saying, he beckoned me to follow him and led the way into the kitchen.

This room had an entirely different character from the big sitting room. As I recall it now, in fact, it was downright funny. It was rather small and painted a hideous yellow, with grease-encrusted green trim. Here, hanging on the walls alongside a Modigliani—a nude, not a portrait of my host—a Matisse, and a Grant Wood, were a Peter Max poster for some event at the White House, a small reproduction of a Rothko painting, and a poster of Bob Dylan from the *New Morning* album. Other rock 'n' roll concert posters for Lou Reed, John Sebastian, and the Youngbloods were taped to the refrigerator door with yellowing Scotch tape, and a movie-lobby bill for Ronald Reagan's *Bedtime for Bonzo* was tacked to the cupboards. The place looked, in other words, like the kitchen of just about any dormitory apartment of any college kid in 1969.

I smiled at the incongruous surroundings and sat down at the linoleum-topped kitchen table by the big window, which provided a grim view of the drizzly, desolate park below. As I watched Pierrot bustle about opening drawers and rummaging for can openers and such, my eyes fell on a large framed poster that hung over the sink, next to the Modigliani canvas. It was obviously a poster of some antiquity; an advertisement for the Feerie at the old Funambules. The date 1858 was penciled in the lower right-hand corner. The commedia *saltimbanques* were all in the picture: Pierrot in his white costume and black skullcap; Arlequin, Leandre, Cassandre, and Colombina. But old Gilles Pedrolino was certainly not the Pierrot.

"Paul Legrand," said the old man, who had evidently been watching me as I examined the poster, again displaying that remarkable ability to break in on my thoughts. "One of the truly great ones, and a dear friend. Now, may I offer you some beer or some soda? I'm afraid I'm just out of tea at the moment, but I do have ginger ale."

▼

"Ginger ale would be fine," I said, and took the glass and thanked him. The old man placed a plastic jug of the soda on the table in front of me, and got himself a sixteen-ounce can of Budweiser from the refrigerator. "I don't understand something," I said, when he had opened it and settled himself at the table. "All the other paintings—except for the Modigliani there—are of you. Who is this Legrand?"

Pierrot smiled patiently. "I will tell you a story about the Modigliani later. But Legrand—do you not remember my telling you at the museum about the many Pierrots who played at the Funambules and the Folies-Nouvelles? Legrand was one of the greatest—after Baptiste and Deburau, the greatest ever, but one. Legrand had his own distinctive style, and many of the greatest authors of the time wrote for him—Hugo, Gautier, Bridault. Legrand was one of the first to portray me in a black suit. He was the first to make me a likeable, kindly dolt, too." Pierrot looked thoughtful for a moment. "In fact," he went on, "now that I think about it, I have a great deal to be mad at him for. Once Legrand got hold of the character I almost never stole anymore; almost never committed murder. He tried to make me human. And though he was, as I've said, one of the great ones, he was in many respects the last of the traditional Pierrots, because he had taken the character about as far as it could go humanistically. After Legrand, I became watered down in the hands of lesser players. Even Najac couldn't retrieve me; the audiences had come to expect what Legrand had weaned them for: the pathetically whimsical clown that could be sympathized with and cheered for in his pursuit of Colombina; the personification that now causes me to rebel personally by indulging in cheap stunts like the one I pulled on you on the train."

Pierrot looked hard at the poster. "Perhaps I shall burn it," he concluded, and swallowed his beer in one gulp.

I sipped my ginger ale and watched him as, preoccupied, he toyed with the empty beer can on the tabletop, spinning it on its side. "There have been many thousands of Pierrots," he said at length, "and there are thousands of them still, my friend, though they are, I fear, a dying breed. Even I cannot be everywhere at once, you understand. My dear friend and student Marcel Marceau is just about the only one left of any distinction; and even so, most people do not know that he is a Pierrot; that he has a history. To most of the contemporary world he is simply a mime." The old man suddenly looked sad again. "You see," he said, "I have been replaced by others. The modern world has neither respect nor time for tradition. A comic is merely a divertissement. He is popular or out of fashion depending entirely on the currency of his material, or the newness of his style—which is too often merely rude, if you ask me. There is no art to it. There are the rare few, of course, who are quite original, and whose art will live after them. But the days of the commedia dell'arte are long gone. The movies, the television, have destroyed the tradition—though they did not have to destroy it. I don't personally see why general access to news and information should preclude the continuance of serious art or contribute to the cult of instant gratification. I suppose it all has to do with advertising at the bottom line; with greed. But that is the way of American culture—and by extension, I fear, an increasing amount of European culture, although they haven't capitulated quite as readily as the Japanese: always so eager to be trendy, without a care as to content or intellect; always so ready to embrace the cheap and fleeting at the expense of the worthy and time-proven. Titillation at the expense of thought-provoking entertainment.

"But I have no time anymore to devote to the calling, my friend. I've done my part. I've had my day on the stage—centuries, in fact. Oh, how I remember the fun of those days, back when we used to travel Italy and Germany and France by caravan. Riding with the circus, years on end. The commedia dell'arte was welcome everywhere—that is, of course, until that pompous ass Louis the Fourteenth kicked us out of France. Said he didn't like the way we made fun of him." Pierrot's eyes sparkled gaily. "Well, fuck him if he can't take a joke!" he said, and rocked back in his chair with a peal of laughter—like a prolonged giggle at the top of his lungs.

His mirth overcame him for a time, and I had to grin. He looked so funny laughing, and did it so wholeheartedly that it was contagious. When finally he got control of himself, he frowned, shot a sharp look to the glass in my hand, and asked gravely, "Are you quite sure you wouldn't prefer something stronger—a beer, or a whiskey, perhaps?"

"Thanks," I said, "this is perfect."

He shook his head pityingly and got up to get himself another beer.

"You must miss the stage after all that time," I said, my eyes on the poster. "Don't you ever feel the urge to get back to it?"

"Why of course I miss the stage, my friend. It was my life for a very long time." He sat back down wearing a pensive expression, upended the beer can, and looked at me rather ruefully. "But I have no time for the stage now," he said. "My vocation allows me no time."

"And what *is* your vocation, exactly?"

"Haven't you guessed yet? I tried to explain it to you the other day—and again on the train." He smiled slyly. "But you were not yet convinced of my authenticity, *non?*"

I grinned self-consciously. "No," I admitted, "I apologize. But then I hadn't seen all of this . . ."

"Or spoken to my friend Moskowitz, *hein?*" Before I could respond he smiled and dismissed my surprise with a wave of his hand. "It is not, after all, surprising. So I do not hold it against you. Besides which, as I told you before, I am not a great fan of critics. But if you will bear with me, I will explain." Pierrot leaned back in his chair, half closed his eyes, and raised his forefinger in the manner of a professor preparing to deliver a lecture. But suddenly he opened his eyes wide and rocked forward. "My friend," he said with a look of the utmost consternation, "are you *sure* you do not require a glass of something stronger before I begin?"

"No. Honestly. I'm just fine, thank you."

He gave the jug of ginger ale a long, doubtful stare, sat back again, and began:

"A very long time ago I met a young man who would become world famous—more than a hundred years after his death, that is. It was, I believe, about seventeen-oh-three or four. I can't remember exactly. I was living in Paris. Like many of my fellow countrymen, I had come to the court of the Sun King some thirty years before to practice my trade. I was, of course, chief among my company; Gilles was a name on everyone's lips, and we enjoyed the favor of the king. Oh, how he loved the Italian commedia then! He attended our performances whenever he could find the time away from court. Why, we were even invited to Versailles to play the palace on a number of occasions. Those, as they say, were the days!"

The old man threw his head back and crossed his hands on his chest as if hugging a bouquet of roses. His eyes were far, far away. "But," he went on, the smile fading from his lips, "as he grew older, Louis tired of us—or, more precisely, he grew so vain and so staid in his old age that he could no longer abide our inventive and pointed satire, no matter how funny. In sixteen-eighty-six, our troupe was banished forever from France by royal decree, and we all had to seek other work. Arlequin became a pimp, of course, and Colombina a courtesan to wealthy merchants. I didn't see her for a very long time then, and my heart ached for her smile.

"But I was fit for only one thing, you see: the stage. The stage was all I knew. And as I could no longer perform the mime and comedy as I had been trained for two centuries to do, I was forced to turn to my second resource: music. I had learned to play the lute at an early age—it was, indeed, one of the more prominent talents that set me apart from Arlequin—and so I went to work playing the little stages and circuses around Paris. It was a hard life, and I was forced to take quarters in Saint-Germain-des-Pres, with all the poor artists, jugglers, and musicians.

"You must understand that in those distant days an artist or an actor was a nobody; a trained monkey who performed entertainment, nothing more. If you were not attached to the Salon or the Royal Academy, you were nothing; a mere hack, that's all. And those were the days I suffered most. I had little money and no prestige. And after the glory years of the commedia, that was not so easy to get used to, as you can imagine. So I was quite miserable most of the time.

Of course, everybody else was, too. Louis was growing old, and his iron hand was faltering. His vanity was killing the country by degrees. He chose his generals from the ranks of his most obsequious courtiers, so battle after battle was being lost through sheer incompetence. His statesmen were fools, and his philosophers and court economists morons. France at that period was—what is that charming American expression?—in deep shit.

"In any event, one day I had arranged to stop by the Flemish quarter to have a drink with an old friend from the circus—at La Chasse, a little inn there that served excellent beer. The northerners always did make the best beer, you know. Except maybe for the Germans—but nobody wanted to deal with them, of course. On the way there, I dawdled on the Pont Notre Dame for a while. They had some fine painting factories there at the time, and you could pick up an excellent reproduction of your favorite Rubens or Raphael for little money. Artisans cranked out popular genre paintings and Old Masters for the masses, and sometimes you could even find an original by a minor master for a reasonable price. I had a lonesome space on the wall of my hotel room, and I was looking for something to fill it. Something pastoral and Italian, to ease my discomfort, my homesickness, and lousy turn of luck. If you wonder why a man of my discriminating tastes and connections would frequent reproduction houses in my search for paintings, I can only respond by telling you that, for one thing, in those days the distinction between a genuine work by a master and a fine copy of it was not as great as it is now. Also, we did not have the means to mass-reproduce pictures. It would be some years before the lithograph was invented, and a century and a half before the photogravure came along. Besides which, there were many perfectly competent if undistinguished painters who turned out a rather nice original scene now and then, and I would buy them simply because I liked them. I never confine myself to pedigrees.

"As luck would have it, I stopped at the first shop I came to on the bridge, and there I saw the most remarkable copy of Gerard Dou's *Old Woman Reading* I had ever seen. Flemish paintings were all the rage just then, you see, and this particular image was very popular, and copies of it were all over Paris. So it wasn't as if I hadn't seen the picture before. But something caught my attention about this one, although it wasn't at all what I had in mind when I stopped in to begin with. I mean, it certainly wasn't what you'd call pastoral; quite the contrary. It was simply a picture of a myopic, toothless old woman reading the Bible. Hardly my cup of tea, as you can well imagine. But there was, as I say, something special about this particular copy that stopped me in my tracks; something in the brushwork; in the liveliness of the handling of the flesh and clothing. And I found myself determined to purchase it—all thoughts of a landscape entirely forgotten.

"I had the picture wrapped, tucked it under my arm, and was about to go on my way when it occurred to me that I would very much like to meet the artisan who had made the reproduction. So I asked the proprietor who that might be. He informed me that the author was a young man who had only recently arrived from Flanders seeking a career as an artist at His Majesty's court, and offered to summon him. 'Jean-Antoine!' he called upstairs to the loft where the work was done, 'Antoine, come down here immediately!'

"Imagine my surprise when a boy of no more than seventeen or eighteen years was presented to me—and none too happy at being presented, either. He was terribly thin, had a pale, wan face with a largish nose and long scraggly straw-blond hair, and he stared at the ground as I complimented him on his handiwork. His sullen demeanor finally got the better of me, and, a bit piqued, I admit, I said before parting, 'Well, I've seen better. But this is quite good, my boy.'

"But as I turned to go, the boy suddenly announced in a rather girlish voice, 'Sir, you've not seen better, either. Nor have you yet seen so good a one painted from memory alone!'

"At that I stopped and turned to see the proprietor, far from clouting the boy around the ears for his insolence to a customer—as would have been deemed perfectly proper at the time—smiling down at him proudly. And when he saw my questioning look, he said to me, 'It's all quite true, sir. No one but my Antoine here can paint any of these pictures from memory—and do a better job than the original master at that!'

"I confess I had to agree, and I regarded the youngster with new respect. But I had to get along to La Chasse to meet my friend, so I bid the two adieu, and made a mental note to look in on young Antoine again in the future, to see how he was getting along."

Pierrot stopped in his narrative for a moment to swallow the rest of his Budweiser. This accomplished, he tossed it expertly over his shoulder into the trash can under the window and asked, "Have you ever seen me juggle?"

"No," I replied, frankly wishing he'd get on with the story.

"Pity," he said, threw my glass another doubtful look, and went on:

"It was, in fact, some years before I chanced to meet young Antoine again. And by the time I did catch up with him, he was no longer just a youthful Flemish émigré slaving away in a reproduction studio, but had been apprenticed to Claude Gillot—a cheap, decorative hack, to be perfectly honest, but a man with a good reputation nonetheless. And Antoine had begun to establish for himself a very respectable trade in portraits and—the thing that caught my eye—paintings of commedia dell'arte characters in the theater. It was a testament to his facility with the brush that his pictures had begun to compete with the likes of Jean Jouvenet, Antoine Coypel, and Françoise Le Moyne for sales popularity—especially when you consider that young Antoine was only in his early twenties.

"It could, I suppose, be said to have been mere happenstance that I ran into him again. But as he was to become one of the greatest of Western artists, it was preordained. If I had not met Watteau again by coincidence, I would have to have sought him out intentionally. But as it turned out, I saw a public notice of auditions for a comedy play, and, still being desperately in need of employment, I went to try out. And guess who was painting the scenery and backdrop for the show?

"It was at that audition—which, of course, landed me the leading role in the play—that Antoine and I became reacquainted with one another. He recognized me even though it had been, as I said, some years since our first encounter. As it turned out, he had grown to love the theater, and had a special place in his heart for the commedia dell'arte. So he insisted on having me model for a number of paintings, and I was perfectly happy to accommodate him. And thus we became fast friends—to the end of his short, unhappy life.

"You see, my friend, Watteau was a very special painter—especially for the time. It was perhaps because he was Flemish (indeed he had received his earliest art instruction in Valenciennes, the town of his birth) that Antoine had an eye for so much that was beyond the scope of his coevals—or, at least, deemed unworthy of artistic endeavor. He was, largely because of the consumption that eventually killed him, something of a misanthrope, at least as far as his patrons and colleagues were concerned. And he preferred to spend most of his time alone. At the height of his popularity in seventeen-seventeen, when he had more commissions than he could possibly fulfill, he moved studios constantly, just to avoid being pestered by fans. He became testier and more truculent as he grew older, and withdrew into books for his sole entertainment. But before those days of success, when he needed to get away from the city and the pressures of trying to make ends meet, he and I would wander from the cluttered streets of Paris and into the outlying villages. And while I practiced my juggling and lute-playing, he would spend hours drawing the peasants and beggars; the soldiers coming back from the provincial wars. And he didn't romanticize them, the way so many others did; no, he drew them footsore and weary, ragged and hopeless as they were. But always with a particular grace of line that was his alone."

Pierrot paused and gave me a searching look. "If you want to see truly great draftsmanship," he said, "you must spend some time with the drawings of Watteau. The pantheon of brilliant draftsmen is very small; but you may confidently place Antoine's drawings on the wall with Michelangelo's or Picasso's. And he will only look better in their company. Especially when it comes to the female figure, few artists come even close to Antoine's depictions. And do you know why that is?"

"Go on," I said.

"It's because he loved them, cherished them, wanted them—but could not have them." Pierrot paused for a moment, reflectively.

"No," he said. "That is not entirely true. He could have them sexually—and often did, I should think. In fact he was one of the first artists I ever met who chose his models—other than those he found in the streets, of course—on the basis of sheer physical pulchritude. Not that he was blind to women as individuals; he wasn't. It was something more remote; an impulse much harder to put one's finger on, if you'll forgive the metaphor. Antoine expressed to me on more than one occasion some puzzlement that he had not been born a woman. 'For,' he would say, 'surely they are closer to the earth in every way than we, and an artist must be close to the earth.'

"I puzzled at this for a very long time, not fully understanding what he meant. The female nude had, of course, been possibly the single most consuming subject of artists since they first began to duplicate the world around them. Not simply as a fertility figure or an object of sexual desire. Think about it: woman became for many cultures the very embodiment of the earth itself; the moon, the stars. More than that, she was often cast as the goddess of wisdom. Why wisdom, one wonders, when for eons the world was dominated by men, and the thoughts of the gentler sex were by and large considered frivolous and unfit to be taken seriously?

"I believe that Antoine was one of the first to recognize the fundamental truth at the heart of this conundrum: that woman symbolized all that a man could not be—leastwise not in his own eyes. It was not merely a question of the obvious fact that man could not bear children. That's too shallow a reasoning. No, it was more a matter of her physical being and self-awareness; her confidence in her own body and its every function. Her ability to face even death—at the hands of men, more often than not—with complacency. And more, it was that woman, with the pure plastic lines of her physical self, contradicted the hard edges of a man's perspective on life; the blacks and whites, rights and wrongs, powers and submissions.

"All this Antoine felt keenly. And if his drawings and paintings of women are deemed so intensely erotic—as indeed they are—it is because they are honest. The paintings were staged, to be sure; the element of woman's appeal as an object of desire hinted at rather than bluntly rendered. But his drawings were different. They were sublime, every line revealing the depth of his love—and perhaps jealousy—of their form. When he painted me, he often used me as a metaphor for himself; contentment was expressed by my being surrounded by beautiful women, and lulled by transporting music. More subtle than his inheritors, Boucher or Fragonard, Antoine's depictions of women are unflinchingly honest, while purposefully preserving the myth of their delicacy and restraint. You see, Antoine knew a great deal about women, my friend. They found him attractive—the more so, perhaps, because he was in such poor health. Many of his models, with whom, to be perfectly honest, he frolicked as he worked, attempted to stay and look after him. But he would have none of it. He enjoyed his dalliances, certainly. But the idea of having a woman about full time—someone to whom he would have to be attentive and perpetually considerate—was anathema to him. His work was as all-consuming as his disease. Between the twain there was virtually no room for other considerations. But he more than made up for this lack of a womanly presence in his life by committing to paper and canvas some of the loveliest and most real-seeming females ever depicted. This was his way of coming to grips with his physical and emotional distance from them, as well as a way of paying homage to the awe he felt in their physical presence. Antoine worshipped women as few men have, and if you should doubt that, look—as I say—at his drawings of them. They are a feast for the eyes, a testament to beauty incarnate. Perhaps if he had been healthier, if he'd only had the chance at a normal outlook on the future, he might have married. Indeed, even my darling Colombina, who generally selected her men entirely with malice aforethought—or foreplay, one might say—even she was, I think, genuinely enamored of him.

"But, as I said, Antoine was never very hale. He neglected his health to slave in his studio: perhaps, like others who know they are terminally ill, he realized that he only had so much time to do all that he must leave the world as his legacy—and he left not only a tremendous amount of work, but a profound influence on the painters of the Regency who followed him. And though his fame was eclipsed

▼

by the rise of Modernism in the nineteenth century, no one has ever questioned his position as the father of romantic French painting; the very soul of French Rococo, and the quintessential portrayer of love and the theater. Certainly no one since has been able to paint me the way dear Antoine did. But that was because we understood each other: we understood how close is the connection between the artist and the clown; the sublime and the absurd, if you like. His ill health dictated that our friendship be very short—he was not yet thirty-seven when he died—but it was a friendship that lasted all of his professional life, and continues spiritually to this day. And I miss him terribly sometimes."

Pierrot's voice trailed away, and his expression became drawn and sad. For a second he looked like he would cry, and I averted my eyes on the pretext of polishing off my ginger ale to avoid embarrassing him. "Did you know," he said after a time, his voice slightly choked and shaky, "that Antoine's very last painting was a portrait of me?"

I shook my head.

Pierrot smiled. "Ah, but that would not be so unusual, would it? Except for this: it is the most faithful picture ever painted of me as a young man—and he did it entirely from memory."

The old man shook his head slowly, a slight smile on his lips. "Oh, my friend," he said, "forgive me for being melodramatic. I can be such a bozo sometimes."

4

▼
▲

WHEN I LEFT PIERROT'S APARTMENT THAT AFTERNOON
I had plenty to think about. It wasn't just his incredible collection,
or the conviction that, though it seemed against all laws of probabil-
ity, he was the genuine article. It was his talk; the hints he kept
dropping—veiled metaphors and references that started me searching
for a key to what he seemed to be trying to tell me. There was an
urgency to everything he said, as if it were imperative he communicate
something to me but was unsure how to go about it. So my head was
full of questions, and I walked around Tompkins Square Park in the
dismal grey of an overcast sky and light snow, too preoccupied to
worry about where I was. On Avenue A I flagged a cab back to the
hotel.

The old clown had exacted from me a promise to return the
following evening for dinner and further conversation, and in ironic
contrast to my earlier view of him, I was frankly looking forward to
it. His story about Watteau had affected me strangely; had awakened
questions in my mind I thought I'd long ago put to sleep for good.
I found myself especially taken with the description of Watteau's years
working as what could only be described as a hack. There he was, a
genius, bursting with talent and ideas of his own, consigned to copying from the acknowledged masters of his time—the Flemish, Italian,
and Dutch painters whose work, without the aid of television or
modern mass reproduction, had nevertheless won them reputations
far beyond the borders of their own countries.

I glanced out the greasy cab window at the bewildering jumble of storefronts, shop signs, posters, lights, litter, and people teeming along Madison Avenue. Everybody hustling to make a buck; to get a foot on the ladder; to establish a face or a name on one of those posters or signs. Well, not all of them. Some were just doing their jobs, spinning dough in the back of a pizza shop, or arranging the mannequins in somebody else's department store window. Repairing TVs. Getting by and perfecting a trade.

Had it been such seemingly unrewarding labor that had enabled Watteau to put his genius into effect; had cultivated in him the discipline necessary to harness and direct all that talent? I tried to visualize the Paris of the early eighteenth century as Pierrot had described it. There had been no flashing neon signs, no electric heat in the winter, and the muddied streets teemed with horses and carts rather than smog-belching automobiles. But such technological differences aside—and of course the sheer numbers of people—the atmosphere in the city at the time of the Sun King was probably not unlike that of a busy downtown street in the Big Apple. The conditions in which the young Antoine slaved away could not have been terribly attractive. He didn't even have the luxury of being able to squeeze his pigments ready-mixed from a tube. His taskmaster, no matter how fond of him or impressed by his abilities, would have been virtually in control of his life. There were no clocks to punch at nine and five. There was no nine-to-five.

Despite whatever advances in technology, hygiene, medicine, and societal values, the exigencies of human life remain remarkably constant. The soma and the spirit demand food, shelter, love, and reward. But for men like Watteau, the spirit also demanded art; expression, beauty, and nuance. And the path to such ends was limned in exigencies that had—and still have—little or nothing to do with food, shelter, love or rewards, pecuniary or sexual. So there he was, this young, sensitive man, doomed to die young, securely lodged on the tines of an expressive compulsion. And to wriggle free of the intellectual and emotional fork, the artist found himself bound to labor.

The cab turned at Central Park and deposited me in front of

the hotel. I paid the fare mechanically, and mechanically, too, rode the elevator to my room. There I threw off my coat, perched on the edge of the quicksand couch, and stared beyond the dusking windows. Was a period of apprenticeship—not an uncommon thing in Watteau's day but a rare one in mine—necessary not only to master the technical demands of one's art but also to fully appreciate one's indebtedness to one's predecessors? To be able to visualize what must come next—or at least get some hint of the logical extension of an aesthetic? Obviously, the implications of such a process, if extended exponentially to each successive generation of artists, placed an enormous burden of knowledge and technical training on them. To work one's way through the aesthetic developments of the twentieth century alone would demand a discipline virtually unknown in modern art academies.

But in the final analysis, wasn't such a discipline crucial to the advancement of fine art?

It grew completely dark outside—completely but for the twinkle and rant of streetlights, taillights, and garish advertising. I watched as the tree-jagged edge of the park grew dark against the yellow city glow beyond. In thousands of lofts and dearly rented rooms, thousands of artists were at that very moment laboring away at bringing their concepts to plastic life in paint, plaster, video, and only God knew what else. Most of them obscured and faceless in the advertising glow. Most of them desperately wanting to add a lumen to it. Most of them never would.

I thought of the piece I had to write by week's end; a pronouncement on the state of the arts at the turn of the millennium. What was that? Whatever had happened to the Watteaus of the world—the Malevichs, Kandinskys, Picassos, Klees, Hoffmanns, Bacons, and de Koonings? Whatever happened to the lambent intellectual probings of Morris Graves or Victor Pasmore? It was chilly, noisy, garrulous, and hollow in New York, and the atmosphere was reflected in the art there. Shaking myself out of a blue funk in the darkness, I padded to the bedroom, unfolded my laptop computer, and turned it on. The green digital display signaled READY, and I lifted my hands over the keys to write. And sat there, motionless. Utterly without a clue as to how to begin.

Pushing the machine aside I thought that not even the marvelous old man's enthusiasm for the art and artists he made such a point of talking about could dispel the pessimism I felt concerning the art of my own time. I no longer had the spark of conviction, or faith—or whatever—to propel me into an essay. I thought of a line of Nietzsche's, and said aloud to myself, "Also sprach Zarathustra: To you alone, you bold seekers, tempters, experimenters, and to all who ever went out on the terrible sea of the art world with cunning brushes . . . art is dead. So go into real estate."

But something prevented me from committing such a cynical pronouncement to print. For once I was unsure of my own professional perceptions. And all because of the old man. I knew I needed to talk to Pierrot again.

I turned off the computer and picked up the phone to call my editor. She'd want to know how the work was going. But by the time her secretary answered I knew that I really didn't have anything to say to her, and I wished I hadn't called.

"Eileen Hannahan's office, may I help you?"

"Hi, Cliff. It's Corry. Eileen around?"

"Hi, Corry. Yeah, she's been expecting your call. Hang on."

Expecting my call. Great.

I actually started when the deadness of hold was broken by Eileen's forced bright voice. "Corry? I'm glad you called. I was just about to ring the hotel to see if you'd checked in yet. How's the piece coming?"

"Oh, fine," I lied. "When do you want it?"

"Can you fax it to me Saturday? You're budgeted for Monday."

"Saturday!"

"Yes, dear. Saturday. You know Saturday's deadline for A and E features. Besides, it's New Year's—you have started it, haven't you?"

"Sure. But . . . well, it's a bit of a tall order, that's all. Isn't there any way I could have till Sunday?"

Pause. I could practically hear her eyes roll toward the ceiling.

▲

"Okay, Corry. Carl's not going to like it, but I'll settle for Sunday noon. No later. And I need fifty inches, and you're responsible for the art. Okay?"

"Thanks."

"Get to work, dear." Click.

"Fuck Carl," I said aloud to the dead receiver, and hung up. The punctilious section editor always suffered mild apoplexy when someone was late with copy, despite the fact that copy for the Arts & Entertainment section was virtually always late. Well, he'd get over it. With every critic on the paper writing their end-of-millennium wrap-ups, he'd have to or die of stroke. I was pretty confident I wasn't the only one begging for another day. I was also pretty sure that I wouldn't be able to write a goddamned word until Saturday, and would probably wind up spending the whole night staring at the terminal in my office.

Well, it was dinner time, and I was suddenly famished. Time to head back downtown. I had a curious desire for something exotic—maybe some kind of Middle Eastern food. Ethiopian or something. There was always that little Yemenite place on Second Avenue and East . . . Twelfth, wasn't it? Right in the clown's neighborhood. I had a taste for falafel and hummous. And maybe some good food would help get my mind off of the nagging questions that had begun to make me so uncertain of my thesis.

Fat chance. Heading down Fifth Avenue in the cab I had the misfortune to spot an old Jenny Holzer sign flashing its sophistic political message from the corner of a neon-spangled building. Still, after what must be ten years or more since anyone cared about Holzer. That was this "artist's" legacy: a sign flashing MURDER IS COMMITTED EVERY TIME MEN THINK OF WOMEN AS OBJECTS. Right up there with other signs that said COKE, THE REAL THING, and GE—WE BRING GOOD THINGS TO LIFE, and almost indistinguishable from them. And as we crept along in the jostling traffic other indications of what art in my age had become kept thwarting my efforts to forget about it. The contemporary artist as sloganeer was everywhere in evidence. Blinking and winking and advertised on posters. All of it mechanical, simple-minded, public, and peevish. How different from the personal passions and aesthetic convictions of the Watteau that Pierrot had described to me. Were such obsessive intellects an extinct species now, at the end of the twentieth century? Had the craft and aesthetic aspects of fine art really become concomitants to art's expressed political purpose in the contemporary cultural arena? If they had—and judging by the distressing evidence, that did seem to be the case—then it was hard to argue with the preachers of Endism, the resurrecters of Hegel and the proselytes of Jean Baudrillard. It looked as if, with the coming of the so-called Postmodern age, the cultural vandalism of deconstruction had gained the upper hand, and that theorists such as Arthur C. Danto were right in the assessment that since the 1970s art in America had been replaced with bald philosophy. Art as the well-crafted object was inconsequential and moribund, and cultural reality a mere simulacrum of the corporate advertisers' ideal world.

So where could the old clown possibly fit in with all of this? Was he not, after all, just an anachronism?—a romantic holdover from a bygone age?

It all looked pretty damned depressing.

At the restaurant I secured a small table in the semidarkness by the back wall, where I could watch the crowd; animated groups of Israelis, mostly, talking in Hebrew, laughing, drinking, and having a rare old time. And I watched the snuggling, pinching, and giggling couples strolling up and down Second Avenue, wrapped in their costly furs and Burberry coats, pausing now and then to peer into the restaurant through the big front window before coming in or moving on. Everyone seemed jovial and exuberant in the clear, brisk night. But I was too preoccupied to share in their fun, even vicariously. Didn't they realize that as they were enjoying themselves American culture was going to hell in a handbasket? I ordered my falafel and hummous and a bunch of other dishes I didn't recognize, picked more or less at random from the menu. All of it was good, and before long the food—and a martini—had the welcome effect of making me drowsy, and my mind began to wander back to my glorious morning

▲

on the coast of France a month before, when everything seemed so much less complicated.

Having stuffed myself to repletion, I was about ready to call for my check when in walked an old friend of mine, Benjamin Levy. One of Israel's more prominent artists, Benny was something of a clown himself; a painter of whimsical scenes of dark-suited and bowler-hatted men posed with musical instruments and fantastic birds, and lovely women half-dressed in lace gowns, their breasts exposed, always. Benny loved breasts. In fact he just loved women, period, and one got the impression from his paintings that were it not for women, he'd never have bothered to become an artist.

Benny spotted me immediately, and with a mephitic cigar held in front of him like a challenge to propriety, he advanced on my table with a smile and a crushing hug.

"Corry!" he announced to the entire room. "You're back!"

There was nothing sullen or ascetic about Benny. To him life was indeed a bowl of cherries. There were bad cherries occasionally, sure; but cherries nonetheless. And his voluminous good humor was impossible to ignore. Short and dark-complexioned, with a neat mustache and ever-present black hat and colorful scarf, Benny was never above coming to openings—his or anyone else's—wearing a Groucho nose and glasses, or entering a party with a cigar in one ear and smoke pouring from his mouth. His paintings mirrored this delightfully fun attitude toward life. He saw immediately that I was pensive about something, and after having broadcast our acquaintance, he sat down at the table and said, "Okay. So what's on your mind?"

"The usual. Art."

"Oh, Corry. A bad thing to think about when you are eating. It's bad for the digestion. You need to think about women. Food, sex, art. All the same thing. You got a woman yet?"

I had to smile. Always the same question since I broke up with Fran. "Not at the moment, Benny. I haven't got time for women right at the moment."

"No time for women?" he asked in mock astonishment—again

67

announcing the fact so loudly that there was a perceptible pause in conversation in the restaurant. I knew what was coming next.

"Listen, Corry. I know a nice girl—beautiful. Big breasts. She posed for me last week. Not married. She loves writers. You want me to call her? She's from Israel, and the most beautiful women in the world are in Israel. You need a woman, Corry. To make you less serious at dinner."

"Benny, right now I have to write an essay for Thursday. All about American art at the turn of the century—I mean the millennium. I'm just all at sixes and sevens. A woman would just complicate things. Thanks."

Benny regarded me with mild amusement. Puffed his cigar a few times to thicken the atmosphere to his liking. "Corry," he said at length, "make art, don't think about it! You think too much. It's bad for the digestion also. Women, you don't have to think about them, either. Just love them." He paused, and I knew he was thinking of his beautiful wife, Hanna, to whom he was devoted, all prattle to the contrary notwithstanding. Then he said archly, "Unless you are married to them, of course; and then you must think about them full time." He smiled radiantly and yelled for the waitress in Hebrew.

I had spent many a night at Benny and Hanna Levy's warren-like apartment on West Eighty-ninth, and I'd always loved the place, it being an enclave of dedicated artists of every medium. Scarcely an evening went by without a poetry reading, or a performance of some kind going on. It was a salon of sorts, the kind I imagined Gertrude Stein's quarters in Paris to have been in the early years of the century, when the likes of Picasso and Hemingway and Malraux could be seen there. But it was a different world today, and no one in the "big leagues" of the New York art scene much cared for such things. They were all too busy donning their all-black vestments and hanging out at trendy galleries like Mary Boone, Metro Pictures, and Louver, to sip wine and admire each other's leather jackets.

I picked the last crumbs of food from my plate and debated whether to mention my meeting Pierrot to Benny. Being several parts pierrot himself, he must have been acquainted with the old man. But then again, who could tell. Something like that might also give him further fuel for fun, and it didn't seem like a good idea to risk having a whole roomful of strangers hear about my encounter with a supposedly mythical character. I decided I'd wait until we could talk in private—if we had the chance this trip.

Benny had been watching my pondering face closely with a knowing look in his eye. For a second after I caught his expression I thought, "He knows already." But to my relief—and moments later, consternation—he said, "You are thinking of Fran again?"

"I wasn't. But I am now, damn you."

He smiled gently. "Like I say, Corry, you need a woman. You want to come to my place later and I'll call this model? She is good for you. I'm sure she knows how to make love good." He winked solemnly. "I know. I can tell."

"Thanks, Benny. But I really am exhausted. I think I'd better just go back to the hotel and get some sleep."

Benny shook his head sadly, and raised his palms in a gesture of reluctant acquiescence. "Okay," he said at length. "But you call me before you go back, yes? Maybe we have lunch at the studio, and I show you some new paintings. Chaim Grosz is coming next week, and we can talk art until you are tired of it, and then I'll find a beautiful Jewish girl for you. Okay?"

"I'll give it my best shot."

I paid my bill and, after the obligatory bear hug from Benny, headed back uptown. Now I had Fran's face firmly engraved on my mind again, and for a while I was undisturbed by thoughts of art or American culture or the damned article. I don't know why I checked at the front desk for messages. I wasn't expecting any, and of course there were none. Back in my room I undressed, letting my clothes fall where they might, and climbed into bed. And no bed ever felt so good.

But sleep has its less welcome side, too, and its revelations are not always couched pleasantly. I drifted off thinking of Fran, heady and nostalgic reminiscences of the good times rather than the bad, as it should be. But not far into slumber, something went wrong. An

▼

unpleasant vision I couldn't control, couldn't resist even with the aid of Fran's powerful presence, nudged itself into my reluctant head. And suddenly I found myself in a large, darkened room; a gallery of some kind, perhaps one of those at the Whitney Museum.

On some unconscious level—or *more* conscious one—I tried to account for the bizarreness of the dream that followed. Perhaps it was due to the quantities of Yemenite food I'd consumed. I'd had similar things happen to me after overindulging in Mexican. Whatever the cause, I swiftly found myself participating in an absurd and scarifying performance, wholeheartedly and with idiotic aplomb.

First, a large wall immediately in front of me began to glow at the edges, revealing itself to be an enormous video screen, or in any event a projection screen of some kind. From the center of it slowly materialized a huge, fearsome head. Its mouth was split sideways into a dripping, bloodied rictus, smeared across the terrible face by thousands of needle-thin horizontal lines. I could practically feel them flashing through me like the stings of fiberglass insulation stabbing up under the raw flesh of a thumbnail. Then, out of an unbearably blue light, materialized a little girl; faceless, anonymous, slender, and completely vulnerable. The terrible head faded as all around her myriad small bright screens flashed maddeningly, screaming with a riot of imagery, though there was no corresponding or specific sound other than a distant, high-pitched whining drone. I tried to ignore the smaller screens and watched the little girl as she slowly faded into the jarring blue, only to reappear closer to me. Now, though still indistinct, features began to grow out of her face, and I could see that she was quite pretty—just the right sort of little cutie for a cereal commercial, like the one years ago that used to say, "Give it to Mikey! Mikey will eat anything!" She smiled vacuously at me while, gradually, out of the distant whining, grew another child's voice, chanting a playful, silly little lullaby, the tune to which I dimly recognized, but the words I'd never heard before: *"Don't you sleep now, don't you dare. You're going to hell and we don't care. When Mommy gets home we'll all get clipped, except for you, you're gonna get whipped. And when Daddy gets home he's gonna bring us a bear, and teach us how to rock it in our rockin'*

▲

chair. Then we're gonna rock 'n' roll around the old maypole, gonna shove it in a hole, to bless your soul, cover you with oil and roll you in the soil, get you in the mind, kick you till you're . . ."

And on and on it went, becoming ever more nonsensical and eerily violent, accelerating into a kind of rap song, until the song became almost a picture itself, flashing in the ears. The little girl with the blurred features meanwhile began to grow larger and larger, until she filled the entire screen; then two screens, then three, then four—and soon I realized I was surrounded by literally hundreds of blinking video screens, each one filled with the image of the little girl, growing larger and larger by rhythmic degrees to the beat of the chanted song—

". . . gonna kick you in the head, until you're dead, gonna take you by surprise, poke you in the eyes, gonna stone you on some weed, love you till you bleed . . ."

—until suddenly her face disappeared into one of her blurred blue eyes, and with a faint crackle all the screens went dead.

I waited breathlessly to see what would happen next. Fran tugged impatiently at my elbow, but I shrugged her off and kept my eyes fixed on the giant screen. I didn't have long to wait. A pinpoint of light appeared at the center of all the screens at once, glittered red for a second, then sprang to life in a flash of painful neon orange. Again the hideous head appeared, rent almost in half by the silently screaming mouth. Again there was silence but for the insidious whining that made my very eardrums itch. For a moment it just floated there before me, seeming to mouth something, and then a deep, resonant, disembodied voice boomed, "Now, for the ISMS!"

The voice was so loud and commanding that I took a step back from the screen. The voice boomed, "Hold it, asshole!" I stood still. There was a pause while the indistinct eyes of the head regarded me severely. Then the voice began again.

"Isms," it said, "are crucial, as everyone knows. So we will begin with the first ism. Classicism. Which is followed, as you are aware, by several esques. We are not concerned with esques. The next ism is much later. It is Romanticism. This, of course, is followed by a host of isms, all jumbled up together in no particular order. Cubism. Surrealism. Suprematism. Dadaism. Futurism. Constructivism. Deconstructivism. Expressionism. Impressionism. Abstract Expressionism. Super Realism. Hyper Realism. Minimalism. Neo-Expressionism. Neo-Classicism. Post-Impressionism. Post-Romanticism. Neo-Romanticism. Modernism. Structuralism. Fauvism. Capitalism, Communism, Endism, and, of course, Postmodernism."

The lecturing voice stopped a moment, as if catching its breath, then said, "There. Now you know your isms. Thank you."

The huge head disappeared and everything went black. After a moment the figure of the little girl glowed on again. This time she was sharply defined, and I could see that she wore a blue-and-white polka-dot dress, and had a little pink bow in her hair. She smiled at me sweetly and said, "Don't touch that dial now, Mr. Peters. All of Mom's and Dad's and the kiddies' favorites are coming. Yes, folks, it's time for Art in Your Face!" In mock-serious grown-up fashion she waggled her finger in front of her face, arched an eyebrow coyly, and slowly faded out. Again I waited. The screen went dark. Then the one next to it, and the one next to that, until they were all dark. Then, so suddenly that it made me jump, a sign flashed out of all of them at once, accompanied by a blaring of thunderously self-important music. Like something Hitler might have dreamed up for one of his rallies. FERRELL ENTERPRISES AND THE INTERNATIONAL MONEY ASSOCIATION PRESENT: *The Art of Fritz Drexler,* it said, then, *Where Once There Was a Curtain.*

Fade out. Crescendo of horns and double basses. Then a light, synthesized rhythmic melody. Fade in: The figure of a skinny, bearded, nude young man with a large paintbrush in either hand. I watched as the camera pulled back, zoomed in on his large member—which, given the skinniness of the rest of him, looked absurd—and then pulled back again to reveal that he was standing on a makeshift stage of sorts, replete with several musicians armed with guitars, drums, and saxophones. Behind them hovered a large white screen or canvas, which rippled slightly as the performers moved about the stage. The skinny young man with the brushes—Fritz Drexler, I presumed—bowed to the camera, turned, and lifted his brushes like batons. The musicians snapped to attention. The synthesizer music whispered away, and when the artist lowered his brushes they launched into a loud, slick, and tediously gyrating tune; like a bad Michael Jackson melody. Or maybe a good one. I never could tell the difference. At the commencement of the music the nude artist approached the big canvas with a silly flourish and obscene wiggle of his emaciated buttocks, and with sweeping gestures of his arms scrawled across it in bright blue, *Freiheit macht Arbeit.* This accomplished—with a great splattering of pigment all over the stage and the musicians—he turned back to the camera and pranced proudly back upstage. Lifting his brushes once again, he signaled the musicians to stop playing. Then, in a thick German accent, he addressed the audience—which is to say, me—thusly: "I vas born in oppression, but now am free for one decade. I vas controlled by zee powers of zee great bear, but now am a creative intellect. Now, I can sing my song of freedom. Pleace join mit me." He lowered his brushes once again and the band began playing a melody I remembered from years before; a catchy little riff that was hard to resist. And at the artist's cue I found myself singing mindlessly along:

"Two all-beef patties, special sauce, lettuce, cheese, pickles, onions on a sesame-seed bun. Two all-beef patties, special sauce, lettuce, cheese, pickles, onions on a sesame-seed bun. Two all-beef patties . . ."

On and on it went, becoming an intoxicating chant, while the artist began to bound round and round the stage, flailing his arms, wriggling his hips to the rhythm, paintbrushes akimbo, blue paint spattering everything in sight. The music grew louder and louder, and the artist's gestures more and more frenetic until, with a great shivering and shuddering of limbs, Herr Drexler collapsed to the floor, evidently exhausted. The music stopped abruptly and the musicians gathered round the fallen painter, hoisted him up on their shoulders, and carried him offstage. Fade out.

Again the sonorous, commanding music. The sign flashed on again: FERRELL ENTERPRISES AND THE INTERNATIONAL MONEY ASSOCIATION *would like to thank you for your support of the arts. This program was made possible by us.*" The screens flickered and were suddenly filled with snow, accompanied by a deafening white noise that made me put my hands to my ears. But this soon faded, and presently the room grew dark again, with only the faint greenish glow of the giant screen to give me my bearings. The room became absolutely quiet, and for a long time I stood expectantly in the dark, wondering if it were all over at last. But as I was about to turn away from the screen a commanding voice from overhead somewhere adjured, "Please push the button!"

I glanced about me in the dark, but couldn't see any button to push. I approached the screen gingerly and inspected the perimeter for any sign of controls, but there were none.

"What button?" I asked the ceiling.

Suddenly the giant wall-sized screen flickered to life and the horrible head reappeared. "Push the button, please, Mr. Peters," the voice boomed again. There was an edge of exasperation to it. Again I cast about for anything resembling a button, but to no avail. All the while I was conscious of the mangled face watching me, its dim sockets following my every move. I walked to what I guessed were the corners of the room, searched with my fingers as high as I could reach. Nothing. I returned to the center of the room and found myself whirling in place, growing a little frantic, my eyes locking from one dimness to another, probing my indistinct surroundings for a button. Finally I gave up and asked the head somewhat shortly, "Okay, where is the goddamned button?"

There was an oddly familiar high-pitched, giggling laugh from the horrible visage, and it said, "Right here, dummy."

I looked to the center of the bloodied mouth, and there, right in the middle of the blurred mess, appeared a small green button that said PUSH. I walked up to it hesitantly and reached out my thumb. It took me a second to get up the nerve to push it. Even though I knew the terrible head was merely a video image—or thought I knew it—this was a dream after all, and anything might happen.

I screwed my eyes shut and pushed it.

Instantly there was a deep, percussive *boom* that caused me to back away hurriedly to the center of the room once more. The huge screen went black again, and then, with a great sputtering and popping and flashing of color bars, it resolved into an image of a half-dressed old woman with thick glasses and a shock of white hair hanging diagonally across her forehead. For a moment her head and shoulders filled the screen, and she stared out at me in mild surprise, as if she'd only just noticed she was being observed. The camera drew back to reveal a messy kitchen and a sink full of dirty dishes soaking in soapy water. The woman had evidently been about to wash them, for she stood over the sink wiping her hands with a towel. She was wearing only a loose white, almost transparent, shirt, under which her pendulous dugs hung like wrinkled bladders against her bulbous belly.

The old woman finished wiping her hands, wadded up the towel, and threw it down on the countertop and said, "Hello, Mr. Peters. My name is Alice Neel. I didn't expect you so soon, but please follow me into the studio."

The camera followed her as she padded through a long hallway that emptied out into a spacious, sunlit room. There was a paint-speckled easel to one side, and beyond the disorderly cluster of wicker chairs and low, cluttered tables an open pair of sliding glass doors looked out over an elevated wooden porch, and beyond that, the sea. The artist shuffled over to the easel, propped a stretched canvas against it, and securely clamped it down.

She turned to me and said, "This'll only take a minute. Please bear with me." She plucked a brush from a coffee can on a table nearby, squeezed some paint from a tube onto the glass tabletop, and began mixing it vigorously with a palette knife. That done, she glanced at me over her shoulder and winked. "Okay, bucko," she said, "now we're ready." And she began to paint.

She worked swiftly, and soon I realized that she was painting the horrible head. In barely a couple of minutes she had a remarkable likeness of it smeared across the canvas. She added a quick smudge here and there with her thumb, then stood back a pace to regard her handiwork. For a moment she tottered there uneasily, one hand resting on her hip, leaving a smudge of red paint on her shirt. Finally she turned back to me and said, "Oh, Mr. Peters, that will never do. Let's try again, shall we?" Arching a prominent eyebrow high on her creased forehead, she smiled broadly. Then she went back to work on the painting, and presently the image reformed under her brush, becoming thinner and more sharply defined. The indistinct, hollow sockets sprouted eyes; heavy-lidded and dark and penetrating. The forehead grew high, smooth, and pale, with a distinct widow's peak in the center. The chin grew long and the mouth full and mischievous, and soon I was staring at a startlingly accurate portrait of Pierrot—as real and immediate as, say, a Polaroid snapshot taken earlier that very day.

Again the artist stepped back to consider her work, hand on flabby hip as before, teetering slightly on her spindly white legs. I waited to see if she'd make any further changes, but presently she walked over to the table, cleaned and dried her brush, and set it back in the coffee can with the others. She wiped her hands on her shirt, leaving still more smudge marks, and turned back to the camera. This time she addressed not me but somebody behind the viewfinder. "Okay, Bob," she said brusquely, "I've got to get back to the dishes. Pull in tight and let him take it." With that, she nodded vaguely in my direction and walked offscreen. The camera moved in to focus sharply on the old clown's face. The detail was absolutely phenomenal—not at all like anything I'd ever seen by Neel before, and as the image grew on the screen, I fancied I could even make out the pores of the old man's skin, and the individual silver strands of his hair.

And then with a sudden smile he said, "I'm so happy that you could join us this evening, *mon ami*. Please have a seat. I shall be conducting the show from here."

I was too amazed to respond, so I turned around to look for a place to sit. I didn't have to look long. Just when I was beginning to feel that this was the most complex and confusing dream I'd ever dreamt, yet another odd wrinkle unfolded itself to my astonishment. I was no longer in a dark, empty room surrounded by video screens. Now I stood in front of the first of a row of theater seats. The place was packed. As I looked about me in surprise, noting the high, vaulted and frescoed ceilings, and the curiously outdated apparel of the restlessly shuffling and coughing audience, someone yelled, "Down in front!" Happily, there was an empty seat in the front row. Fran patted the arm of the chair and said, "Come on, Corry. Sit down, dear, so we can get on with it." Obediently I sat down. Now I saw that the wall-sized screen had changed, too. It was still there, but it had somehow been moved back behind a conventional wooden stage, and was bordered with long black velvet curtains.

The lights in the room dimmed, the crowd hushed. A sudden spotlight stage left, and out walked the clown, attired in frilly splendor, skullcap and all. A commanding voice offstage announced, "Ladies and Gentlemen: Gilles Pedrolino!" Thunderous applause and whistles. Pierrot bowed deeply, crossed to center stage, and with a graceful sweep of his hand spun around to present the giant screen. Then, with a puff of pink smoke, he disappeared.

Instantly the spotlight went off and the screen flickered to life once more. Yet again the hideous head appeared, and I could feel that all eyes were fixed on it. It shimmered above us for a moment, and then the deep, mechanical voice boomed, "And now, back to the game!"

In a wink, the picture changed again. It was the middle of a football game, and the camera panned the sidelines. Players wearing the colors of teams I didn't recognize flashed by in the telephoto foreground. The camera hesitated, then backed up, coming to rest on the thickset figure of Mike Ditka, former coach of the Chicago Bears, chewing gum and playing with the change in his pocket. The camera zoomed in on his heavy, fighter's face, and he turned to the audience with a wide grin. "Hey," he said, "glad you guys could come— especially you, Mr. Peters." This caused me to fidget uncomfortably in my seat and glance about me. But all eyes were still glued to the screen.

I looked back to see that the coach was clearly looking right at me. His jovial expression darkened and faded. "We know you, Peters," he said threateningly. "You're a troublemaker, son. And I've been asked to explain a thing or two to you—hey!" he suddenly shouted to someone off screen, "hold the fucking game a minute, will ya? I'm tryin' to talk here! Time out!"

He stood there glaring for a moment, jaw thrust forward, chewing stopped. But the one hand in his pocket kept moving furiously. The occasional blur of passing football players gradually ceased, and a couple of them gathered about him and stared out at me suspiciously. "Is that him?" one of them asked, and jabbed a sausagelike finger in my direction.

Ditka said, "Yeah, that's him," and started chewing vigorously again. "Fucker needs an art lesson, and we're gonna give it him."

At this the audience applauded loudly and several people yelled, "Let him have it, Mike!"

The coach waited for the clapping to die down and focused on me again. "All right, asshole," he began, addressing me as if I were one of his players, "a lot of us are getting sick and goddamned tired of people like you fucking around with the system. Bitching all the time. Talking about art. What the fuck do you know about art? Huh? Let me tell you something, Bub: art's only as good as the money it makes. You wanna see some good art?—buy a goddamned Leroy Nieman print. Shit, I got some signed ones, man. You gotta understand that nobody gives a shit whether something's pretty or not. Nobody needs that esoteric crap. You think what I do for a living is pretty?—or what my boys here do?"

(General murmur of agreement from the audience.)

"Let me tell you what it's all about, buddy," he continued when the susurrations died down. "It's about knocking the next guy on his fucking can. That's what it's about. Period. Same with the art business. It's about knowing the right guys; hanging out with the right people. Kicking some ass. It's about getting the job done—whatever it takes. It's about cash, Peters. *Cash.* Can't you get that shit straight?"

The coach paused and glared at me for a long moment. I wasn't sure whether to say something or just wait. There wasn't a sound from the audience.

Then the resonant voice from the ceiling boomed: "Well? Are you going to answer the man, Mr. Peters?"

I craned my neck back to find that the vaulted and painted ceiling had gone, replaced by the flat, dark expanse of the gallery one. I looked around me: the audience had disappeared, too, and I was back in the darkly glowing room.

"Well?" inquired the voice again.

I looked at the glaring form of Ditka still regarding me distastefully from the giant screen. "Where is Pierrot?" I asked.

The coach laughed out loud, accompanied by a general smirking and chuckling from his "boys." "Jesus Christ, Peters!" he roared, when he'd recovered himself. "Forget about that damned joker, will ya?" Suddenly his harsh voice assumed an almost fatherly gruffness, and his expression softened. "Look, Bub," he said, "I'm just tryin' to explain something to you—for your own good. *This* is art, Peters. And you better damned well get to like it. I ain't got anything against you personally. But you think because all Eastern Europe's a democracy these days, and 'cause they're making their stupid little paintings; because there's that fucking clown poking around town—you think everything's gonna change somehow. Well it ain't. This is the end of the line, Peters. The ultimate. Art don't get any better than this. You don't like it in America?—go and join the fucking foreigners. And don't let the door hit you in the ass on the way out, neither."

With a loud *frritzzz* the screen went dead, and the room became almost pitch-black. I stood still for a time, until I could peripherally make out the glowing edge of the video screen. Then I turned to look around me again, ready at this point for just about anything. But there were no crowds this time; no stage, no clown. Instead, the faint outline of a door had etched itself into the wall directly behind me. I hadn't noticed it before, and I approached it cautiously, feeling for a knob. Could this be the way out of the nightmare?

I located the doorknob at last and inched it around slowly. The latch tongue sprang back with a snap and the door swung inward.

And in walked Andy Warhol.

Like everybody else, I hadn't seen him in quite some time, and it took me a moment to recognize him. He wasn't looking at all well, but then I guess nobody does after they've been dead for thirteen years. His pockmarked face was, if anything, even paler than it had been in life, and his listless eyes looked just as vacuous as they ever did. He was dressed in a moldy black leather jacket and black slacks caked with mud and clay. His transparent hair looked about the same. In one hand he held an unopened can of Campbell's tomato soup, and in the other a large, luminescent blue rubber dildo with spikes on it.

With an expression of mild perplexity, Warhol shuffled past me and into the room. The door swung shut behind him. I reached for the knob to try it again, but it had mysteriously disappeared. Turning round I found the room had grown noticeably brighter, but also that the dead artist smelled absolutely awful, and even though he was now standing some paces away inspecting the big video screen closely, I had to cover my mouth and nose with my hand to keep from being nauseated. I backed up against the wall of lifeless video screens and waited to see what *this* would be about.

"It's about magic, sweetie," he said with a pronounced lisp, and with what appeared to be a great effort turned away from the glowing screen. Evidently he could read minds, too. He straightened up, faced me uncertainly, and continued: "There isn't any, any more than there is a reality for you—in life, that is. The only reality is death. I know. That's why I'm here. There is no magic, no reality, no love. All of them are figments of your imagination. Take my word for it, sweetheart. All there is is sex and money."

"Did Pierrot send you?"

At the question the artist's black, empty eyes crinkled like wax paper at the corners, and his upper lip lifted slightly to expose his blackened and uneven teeth. "You've fallen for that silliness? Oh dear me, sweetcakes! He's the biggest myth of the bunch." He stopped and lifted his hand suddenly to inspect the blue dildo. He clucked softly. "Dear me. It seems to have grown."

He lowered it and again looked at me. "You wouldn't have a can opener with you by any chance?" he asked as something of an afterthought.

I shook my head.

"I didn't think so. Nobody ever thinks to bring them along in dreams. And no one thinks to bury you with one, either. And those, my friend, are two of the ways you can tell there is no god."

For a time he regarded me sadly, then he turned around to face the screen again. Lifting his can of soup high in the air, he addressed the now coruscant blankness in a soft, husky, but commanding tone: "The medium is like really the message. Reality is a dead issue. Fame is the only thing worth being famous for. Magic is bullshit, and enlightenment a joke. Dig me, girl!"

Instantly the screen flashed to life, and the blue dildo flashed in his hand like an argon tube. There was a puff of bright pink smoke, and he was gone.

The cute little girl in the polka-dot dress filled the screen once more, smiled, and began to sing, *"Reach out, reach out and crush someone! Reach out, reach out and just say no. Reach out, reach out and . . ."*

5

▼
▲

AT THE SOUND OF THE TELEPHONE RINGING I BOLTED
from the bed as if stung. It had been a while since I'd had such a vivid
dream, and even when standing wide awake, shivering amid my discarded clothes, I half expected to see the little girl singing from the
TV in the corner of the bedroom.

When I had recovered my wits I picked up the phone.

"Mr. Peters? Plaza wake-up service calling. It's nine o'clock."

"Thank you."

"And Mr. Peters?"

"Yes."

"A Mister Pederolio called for you this morning. He did not
leave a number."

"Thank you."

"Have a good day, sir."

"Thank you."

Click.

Even after the call it took me some while to shake myself
completely free of the dream's scary claustrophobia. But the details
of it began to lose their sharp edges as I showered and shaved and
called down for breakfast. I felt much better when I'd dressed in the
fresh, crisp linen Christa had packed for me, and by the time breakfast
arrived I'd begun to go over my itinerary for the day. Time to get
sensible.

I had to visit the Whitney Museum to check out the latest
trendy establishment young artists, and also Knoedler's and maybe

the Marian Goodman Gallery, to see what was in that month with the hoity-toity dealers. Then I would go to see the old clown. The dream had prompted still more questions, and by now it looked as if only he could possibly provide the answers. What, for example, had happened to the magic? Was it really dead, as Warhol had suggested? And what of the clown himself? He certainly seemed real enough; tangible, flesh and blood, a prankster with consequences that were all too readily apparent. Yet when I thought of the possibility of such a character being real, I had to question the veracity of my own perceptions. Could it be that he, too, was a wishful figment of my imagination—or the invention of some enterprising corporate conspiracy?

By the time I'd wiped the last of the egg from my plate and had downed the last sweet pulpy dregs of orange juice, I was vaguely anxious and doubtful again. I hustled into my overcoat and went downstairs.

Outside it was bitterly cold, and the wind gusted fiercely round the corners of the buildings, slicing right through my heavy clothes and shower-warmed skin. For an unguarded second I wished I were back home, ensconced in my favorite red leather armchair, with a good book, feet propped on the hearth rail before a roaring fire. Oh well. I got into a cab and headed for Madison Avenue.

Before going on to the Whitney, I had the cab drop me at Knoedler's on Seventieth. Holding my breath against the squall that blew down the wind-tunnel street, I dashed from the car to the heavy bronze doors and practically leapt inside. At the howling rush of cold air, the pretty receptionist at the front desk gathered her sweater about her throat and shot me a frosty stare. The gallery was empty, so I allowed myself the luxury of doffing my frozen wraps and leaving them on one of the benches while I sauntered about the rooms. The receptionist didn't look any too tickled with that, either.

Here, as elsewhere in New York, the work consisted mostly of bad drawings, stenciled or lighted signs on walls, video stills and photographs of well-known mid-century works. I didn't recognize many of the names; this was the post–Barbara Kruger, Jenny Holzer,

Bill Viola, Sherrie Levine, and Jeff Koons bunch. There were droves of them, none of whom had any particularly recognizable style or special subject of interest. One enterprising young man had hit on the idea of simply signing his name on sheets of paper and tacking these up on the wall. Asking price for an arrangement of three of these "statements" as the catalogue called them? A cool $34,000. And the guy must've known what he was about, because there was a red dot by them.

In one corner there was a giant, pulsing video screen that continually flashed the face of one of the new popular "zap-music" stars. I dimly recognized the face from posters I'd seen around town, but couldn't put a name to it. Zap-music stars now came and went with such relentless regularity it was impossible for me to keep up with them—even if I'd wanted to. The music had gone the way of the visual arts: it consisted mostly of loud, monotonous high-pitched chirps and bangs. Melody was no longer an issue. It no longer even remotely resembled the rock 'n' roll I'd grown up with in the sixties and seventies. Indeed, it had precious little in common even with the confusing jumble of styles that marked the popular music of the eighties. Like the art on this gallery's walls, it had achieved the awesome stasis of utter conformity. The Beatles and Dylan—like painters such as Kiefer and Diebenkorn—were regarded by the younger generation as Old Masters at best, and at worst as curiosities or the makers of elevator music.

In the opposite corner was a stack of hundreds of tiny, postage-stamp-size video screens—all blank. A recording emanating from somewhere behind it broadcast the sounds of the traffic-clogged streets outside. There was a red dot on the wall by this one, too.

In sum, everything there on the walls of one of the world's longest-standing and most prestigious galleries seemed to validate the inauspicious and depressing reckonings of the characters in my dream. I began to feel distressingly like one of the characters in an old "Twilight Zone" episode I remembered, wherein a honeymooning couple arrive at their destination only to find themselves in a kind of ideal little township where nothing is real or alive; even the squirrels on the trees are stuffed. If I recalled the point of that skit correctly, it turned out that they'd somehow wound up as the pets of giant, anthropomorphic aliens.

As I put on my coat again I found myself entertaining the notion that contemporary art was unwittingly serving the ends of a monstrous plot—either that or conducting its own honeymoon of specious reasoning and self-indulgent media manipulation. I nodded to the still frosty young woman on the way out and headed up the street toward the Whitney, not at all thrilled at the prospect of viewing an entire museum exhibit of such stuff. But a job's a job.

I wended my way through the forest of scented and two-legged fur-bearing creatures on the fashionable avenue, and soon found myself under the darkly frowning façade of the institution that had become arguably the most influential force in the American art world—outside of dealers and corporate collectors, of course. From the banner hanging outside to announce the show I deduced immediately that it would be vain to expect to see the work of anybody I respected—Moskowitz, for instance, or John Torreano, Big Al Carter, Robin Rose, or Wesley Kimler. These were all artists of deeply private aesthetic drive. The exhibit was ominously titled "The Refigured Future: The Politics of American Art in the 1990s," and the rubric was buried in small type between the big blaring monikers of the corporations that had sponsored it. It looked as if every major communications company, oil company, and international marketing firm in the U.S. had put up money for the show, and were all jostling with each other for the lion's share of the credit.

The minute I entered the lobby bookstore and paid for my $35 ticket, I was alerted by the irritating high-pitched whine that I was in for more video work. In fact the entire interior seemed to pulse with a faint bluish glow. Sure enough, when I stepped out of the elevator on the fourth floor, my eyes were dazzled by a barrage of blinking screens. Loud and furious zap-music in about five different keys bellowed from every available corner, creating an absurd and vaguely frightening cacophony, like the carking babble of a thousand mechanical complainers. Here and there bewildered and intimidated people inched hesitantly around corners, some with their ears covered. Others were evidently trying to focus on one particular strain of music and move to it. But that was impossible.

I didn't stay long. There was really no need, as I'd dreamt it all before. The only substantive difference was that everything in the Whitney had a pointed political agenda. It was a compendious assortment of campaign advertisement artists in the making; the best and the brightest of the media hype-sell upstarts. Not a single drop of paint had been expended; not a single object cut or crafted. Pictorial or spatial concerns were not at issue here. No, this was the ultimate exegesis of the Postmodern axiom: engage the audience at whatever cost—evidently a euphemism for *intimidate it*.

I fled the gallery in under twenty minutes, lighted a cigarette, and burst out into the cold air. The freezing wind felt positively bracing after the agitated darkness and blinking screens of the gallery, and I decided just to set out walking downtown. It was a long walk to the Cedar Tavern on University and Eleventh, but I felt so restless I was up to it. And nearly an hour later, out of breath and sweating despite the frigid atmosphere, I crossed Union Square and plunged into the welcome darkness and cozy smell of stale beer and cigarettes of the bar. And after downing a pint of rich Newcastle Brown ale I felt much better; better to know that there were still places—even in New York—where people appreciated intimacy, elbow-smoothed wood, and well-made beer. I ordered lunch and wolfed it down in a fashion Pierrot would have envied, and then it was time to see the old clown himself. I paid my tab and caught a taxi to the run-down apartment on Avenue B.

As if he'd had somebody following me to report my every move, the old man was standing behind the gate as I pulled up. And when the rickety elevator door had closed behind us he turned and said to me with a mischievous grin, "So, *mon ami,* did you sleep well last night?"

"We need to have a little talk about magic," I growled.

▲

"*Bien sûr,*" he replied with a chuckle and a slight bow. "I thought perhaps we might."

▼

▲

"Oh, I wouldn't say it was gone, exactly," Pierrot said mildly, as he put a match to an after-dinner cigar. "I suppose you might say it was in hiding. Just not here; not any more."

He paused for a moment, and sucked vigorously to coax an even red glow from the tip of his pungent-smelling stogie. "There!" he said at length, "Delicious. Absolutely delicious. Now, where was I? Oh yes, magic. Well, *mon ami,* mystery—or rather the lack of it in these technologically advanced times—is only a small part of the reason for its elusiveness today. You see, more than mystery, magic requires faith. Demands it, actually. And artists in this country, like so many others of its thinkers and creative people, have been wrestling with a crisis of faith for quite some time now. Thay have, in other words, lost that vital sense of what it means to pursue truth and beauty for their own sakes: to reveal the world as only an artist can do. More importantly, they seem to have lost their sense of reality. And how can one possibly dabble in magic if one doesn't understand the nature of reality?"

I confess that this rhetoric baffled me completely. "Maybe I'm a bit slow on the uptake today," I said, "but I fail to see a connection between magic and reality. I'd have thought the two were mutually exclusive."

"Ah, a grave mistake, *mon ami,* if a predictable one. But let me try to explain: for many years now, we have lived in a society that has increasingly been defined by the exigencies of capitalist enterprise—the very things so many Postmodernist writers, painters, and poets have made the sole focus of their work: media saturation with the saccharine but apocryphal images of American life concocted for us on television, billboards, magazine advertisements, and so forth. Many intelligent men, such as your philosopher friend Baudrillard and others, claim this saturation has become so complete that there is no longer any such thing as a reality that exists beyond our perceptions of what it *should* be. This is to say, what we are shown and told it should be, *is*. In other words, our experience of the world is so completely governed by this mass manipulation that we have lost the ability to discern what is truly real. Do you follow me so far?"

"Of course. I've read Baudrillard—and Derrida."

"Bon. Then I must tell you that in my opinion it is the cultural authority granted this sort of reasoning—which is ultimately equivalent to hopeless pessimism—that has led to the kind of cultural emptiness and stasis you see about you now. Including the failure of contemporary American art.

"I will tell you now, and you must accept for the moment that this is so—no matter what your view of this theory—that there *is* indeed a reality. It is reality that lets you know beyond the shadow of a doubt that you have a toothache—regardless of what is being sold you on the television; regardless of how many items in your home are made of plastic; and regardless of what circumlocutions and dissemblings your politicians are spouting on the radio. It is reality that makes you fall in love when the time comes, or causes you to lust after a beautiful woman. It is the reality of your flesh and blood and the blueprint of your genetic makeup; the reality that determines your joys and sorrows, victories and defeats. Reality is the cardinal nesting in your wisteria; it is tornadoes and earthquakes, stars, sunsets, and time. And it is unperturbed and unswayed by all the artificialities with which contemporary society bombards us every day. Am I being quite clear?"

"Certainly. But I still don't see what all this has to do with magic."

The clown struck another match to his cigar and chuckled heartily. "It's really quite simple, my friend. Reality *is* magic. What could possibly be more magical than life itself? I am here. You are here. We see essentially the same things about us, regardless of our philosophical opinions; we hear them, feel them, taste them, smell them. Two men may speak of loving a woman, and both understand the feel—the magic—of flesh to flesh, the wonder of a kiss. Granted, we are not here for long; even my great age is but a blink in the history of this young planet, and hardly a flicker in the vast age of the cosmos. Yet we are here, now—which is why corporations take advantage of the fact so they can sell us things. And all the myriad wonders of the world about us are here, too. The world is not an illusion, although illusions are part of its complex reality. If you want to see the purest and most compelling form of magic, watch a bud develop on the twig of a tree in spring. Spend a few weeks just watching, until it unfolds completely into a bright new leaf, pulsing with life. Or watch a baby being born. I assure you that such exercises can only reaffirm your faith in magic."

The old man sat back in his chair, his eyes on me fiercely. His cigar had gone out, but he took no notice.

"And now," he said after a moment, "here is where art comes in. You recall I told you how Watteau expressed the artist's need to be closely connected to the earth; to life. That is because the very nature of the artist's work dictates that he be firmly grounded in reality. It is his purpose to be, just as it is the purpose of a mathematician or a physicist to be. It advances nothing to replicate that which is patently false to begin with. The nature of reality is for everyone such that—believe me—even the very dumbest person in the United States knows full well the difference between the antiseptic life he sees giggling on the television sitcom, and the stains on his trousers or the dust balls under his bed. It's entirely true, of course, that many people conduct their entire lives on the chilling assumption that the things in life that really matter can simply be purchased: that it is a primary function of life to be able to own an expensive car, or buy fashionable clothes. But even these unfortunates know exactly what reality is— even if it sneaks up on them only in the form of an audit by the Internal Revenue Service.

"But the artist, of all people, has a special relationship to reality because he makes objects; creates tangible, experience-able products. I speak here of the bite of the saw, the buttery consistency of fresh paint, the rasp of a file on metal. Of the arts, music is perhaps the least tangible, and therefore most abstract, of the lot. Yet it exists when it is being played, and it can be crudely written down on paper, and perfectly captured in the memory. At the same time painting, of all the arts, is possibly the most complex. And the painter is a person who in many respects must be the most deeply connected to the reality of his materials and methods than any other artist. Because he must be competent to make of them an illusion, and that illusion must say something of reality. Do you follow me?"

"I believe so. But I'm not sure I understand why American artists should have lost this sense of reality—or of faith in the magic of reality, as you put it. It seems to me they ought to be the ones least deterred by the media bullshit—not suckered by it."

"Oh, they haven't all lost it, of course. Only those whose purpose is to become well-known and wealthy have succumbed to the illusions of plastic American society. There are literally thousands of artists working here who have a very keen sense of the magic of reality, and it shows in their work. Unfortunately, pecuniary reality dictates the course of the successful ones, and the market is defined and orchestrated by the same forces that bring you the television commercials. By and large, most of the more prominent American artists of today have, on their roads to fame and fortune, misplaced for the time being that most important impulse: the sheer love of making objects or pictures. Why your average four-year-old has more sense of this expressive dynamic than most of them. And the artists have bought into another dangerous philosophy: the Marxist notion that art must be political to be viable."

"But isn't all art inherently political? Can an artist—an intelligent person with his eyes and ears open—ignore the societal realities around him?"

Again the clown chuckled and, leaning back in his chair, puffed hard on his extinguished cigar. He lit it again and blew a great blue cloud of noxious smoke toward the ceiling.

"I assume," he said then, "you have heard of Daumier, Delacroix, Géricault, Caravaggio, and Goya?"

"Of course."

▲

"These great painters, Mr. Peters, were exceptionally political men. Mary Cassatt and Frida Kahlo were politically active women. Intellects that clearly saw and cared very much about the social ills about them. And they painted some very political images. However—before you protest, *mon ami*—yes, there is a huge difference between them and the artists of today. These artists were craftsmen first, political intellects second. They understood that art is by its very definition the mastering of a craft. They knew how to paint. They were first and foremost aesthetes; masters who observed carefully the world about them, and learned from the masters who had preceded them. They were, in other words, firmly grounded in reality. A talentless or unschooled artist can no more make a great painting of a political subject than a talentless or untutored writer can make a great novel of the same material. And no matter what his politics or ethical backbone, an untrained violinist simply cannot play the Tchaikovsky Violin Concerto. Great poets are not judged solely by the content of their poems; they are first recognized as great wordsmiths.

"It is, to be sure, a large burden to place on the shoulders of any artist to demand of him that he be both aesthetically and technically accomplished, *and* that he have an intellect capable of recognizing the problems with the society of which he is a product. But there you are. This is the charge, and it must be met if the artist is to have any hope of leaving his mark on history, or of significantly influencing the social climate of his own times.

"Goya is a very good example of the importance of this dynamic, and I'll tell you a story about that—if you have the time."

I glanced out the window. It was dark outside, but for the sickly yellow glow of the city's billion lights against the lowering clouds and sodden air. Our reflections in the grease-fogged window looked pallid and insubstantial. Dinner had been interesting: Campbell's tomato soup and grilled peanut butter and horseradish sandwiches, washed down with ginger ale and beer. It was a mystery to me how the guy had managed to live so long on such an appalling diet—or hadn't yet choked to death bolting his food. Yet he'd shoveled it all down with such a volley of lip-smacking you'd have thought

▼

it had been a gourmet meal especially prepared for us by Paul Prud-homme or Wolfgang Puck.

And like a fool I'd forgotten the Rolaids.

I downed my glass of lukewarm ginger ale and looked at my watch: eight o'clock. Pierrot watched me closely, his brows raised like twin diacritical marks against his pale forehead, waiting.

"Tell me a story," I said, and wedged a cigarette in my mouth.

6

PREPARATORY TO BEGINNING HIS TALE, PIERROT topped up his glass with brandy and raised it to his lips. But he stopped drinking abruptly and, bidding me stay where I was, jumped to his feet and disappeared into a darkened room that led off from the kitchen. For a time I listened to him rummaging about, and presently he returned to the table with a triumphant expression on his face. Under one arm he carried an old canvas and in his hand he held a small, elaborately decorated gilt box. The back of the canvas faced me, and I saw that it was covered with curious inscriptions in pale red, barely legible against the dark brown of the ancient material.

The little box he set carefully before him on the table, and then without a word he turned the painting around so I could see it. It was another portrait of himself, and it was obviously a Goya. It was executed in the master's late style; at a guess I would say sometime in the early 1820s, when the artist was a very old man of declining popularity, who would shortly exile himself to France to spend the last of his days. It was the period when Goya's prodigious ability had begun to fail him, due to poor eyesight as much as anything else, although I knew that he had suffered several serious illnesses in his later years and was, according to contemporary accounts, weak and unsteady. His paintings of this period are often indistinctly rendered, their colors predominantly mellow, pastel hues. And this work was no exception. Still, it was a powerful picture for all that.

Needless to say I'd never seen the piece before. It was the most unusual of the portraits of the old man I'd yet seen—or rather, the young man. Like so many others, Goya had portrayed a Pierrot barely in his thirties. Yet, again, it was obviously my host across the table; there was no mistaking that chin, full mouth, and heavy-lidded eyes— or that idiotic grin. And this was perhaps the strangest thing about the portrait, for Goya had painted my companion with his head and hands clamped in stocks, and on his head, rather than the customary black skullcap, he wore a strange-looking, tall conical hat. Though split down the center like a greatly elongated pope's mitre, it resembled nothing so much as a fanciful dunce's cap. Over the clown's left shoulder hovered a large brown bat or owl (it was hard to tell which), and over his right was draped a wicked-looking cat-'o-nine-tails. The implications were obvious—and yet Pierrot was grinning like an ass.

The old fellow must have read my thoughts from the expression on my face, though I didn't count it such a feat considering the subject of the painting.

"The Inquisition," he said simply, and a slow, faint smile spread to his face. "Very few of us escaped their clutches in those miserable days of the so-called Enlightenment. But Francisco did not paint that particular image from life. I had long been free of the torturers when I posed for him in Paris, in the summer of 1824. We decided that it would be suitably macabre if I were smiling in such a situation. He was merely painting from the memory of the time he'd seen me in the stocks in Madrid back in eighteen-oh-eight—the year Carlos the Fourth abdicated to José Bonaparte. And believe me, I counted myself lucky to be in the stocks. It was of course quite painful to be whipped for two days, and certainly nothing to grin about. But it could have been much, much worse. In fact, that was the closest I ever came to, shall we say, missing dinner with you this evening. Many of the others arrested with me were taken out and summarily shot. Others were garroted in front of their families, or forced to hang from chains with their arms and legs doubled up behind their backs until they starved to death. Women were sometimes impaled on sharpened sticks rammed up between their legs, and a favorite sport for the men was to hang them by their testicles until they ripped off from the weight. So, as you can see, a flogging in the stocks was practically a slap on the wrist by comparison. Let's say it was rather a bad time for some clown to be in Spain. It was the year of the beginning of the Peninsular War—the Spanish War of Independence. While the French troops were executing people left, right, and center, the Spanish Loyalists were committing atrocities of their own against the French, French sympathizers, and innocent citizens. Brutality was in the air, as it had been since Fernando the Seventh had had a hand in government. And after the war—after the French withdrew—and he reassumed the throne in eighteen-fourteen, things got worse. It was Fernando who resurrected the Inquisition after Carlos had banned it. But that is water under the bridge, as you might say, and anyway by that time I had been safely back in Paris for many years. Suffice it to say that things were bad enough while the French were in occupation. Almost any reason could be fabricated—by either side—to persecute anybody. There was no rhyme or reason to it. You could be tortured and your possessions confiscated just for being a Jew, or a mendicant, or for being a *brujo*—a witch. And anybody could be branded a witch, if he were intelligent enough. Me, I was a foreigner. I was not at that time a French citizen, but I was perceived as such. This obviously made me suspect to begin with, and the years I had spent on stage ridiculing both Fernando and Carlos had not made me terribly popular with Loyalist authorities."

The old man grinned broadly. "I have never been very popular with authorities of any sort. It's rather a matter of pride with me. *Pour Dieu et Mon Tort,* you might say, has long been my motto. But then I am charged with certain duties also, and have always done my best to prosecute them to the fullest in spite of the troubles they've sometimes brought me. In this instance, however, though I cannot prove it, I suspect that my dear enemy Arlequin had something to do with my predicament. You see, while I had stuck to the stage with Leandre and Colombina, he had been busy as usual playing Lothario to various wealthy señoritas around town. And I know for a fact that he had been seeing one of the Osuna girls, so he certainly had some court connections. It wouldn't surprise me at all to learn that he'd concocted some story to get me into trouble. I am sure I made him uncomfortable with my antics on occasion; Arlequin, you see, took a very dim view of lampoons, especially where they might have compromised him with the husband of some young woman he was trying to screw. And of course it is part of my job to compromise that *petit con* whenever possible. Please excuse my French."

Pierrot paused for a moment to set the remarkable portrait against the wall so that we could both see it as he talked. He took a deep swig of brandy and pushed the gilt box against the wall next to the painting.

"And what's in the box?" I asked.

"Ah, the box." He held my eyes for a while, as if trying to satisfy himself that I was not in fact a soldier of the Spanish Inquisition. His slender fingers toyed abstractedly with the little gold clasp on the lid. "We will discuss the box later," he said at length. "Actually, it is for you. But not just yet.

"Now, where were we?"

"In the stocks."

"Ah yes, the stocks. In Madrid. And that, *mon ami*—as ignominious a position as I'd been in since being banned from Louis the Fourteenth's France—was where I first encountered the great Goya. Or saw him rather. We exchanged no words. Our eyes met as he passed me in the square on the way to the Prado Palace carrying a bulky sketchbook under his arm. I recognized him immediately from his self-portraits: a short but burly man with heavy blue jowls and unruly black hair, and a dark, scowling expression. He reminded me very much of Beethoven—though the composer was a much younger man, not yet in his thirties when I met him in Vienna some ten years earlier. In fact the resemblance was striking—the more so when you consider that Goya, too, was by that time nearly deaf as the result of fever, and equally a genius. I was familiar with several of his folios of etchings, the *Sueños* and the *Caprichos,* and had admired his work very much. But, despite his liberal leanings (which he did not exactly broadcast to the king), the artist was a painter to the king's court, admired and respected by the French and Spanish alike. He was a great and famous man, and I was a mere actor; a no-account, and I'd had as yet no opportunity to make his acquaintance.

"But he looked hard at me as he walked past, and he recognized me—probably from the stage, or from the commedia posters that were often posted around town.

"In any event, I watched the great man trundle off into the crowd, pausing once to look back at me before he disappeared, and I knew the day of our meeting was yet some time off. I remember feeling quite miserable that he had not stopped to talk with me. But he was a busy man then—the more so because of the political upheaval Napoleon had visited on Europe over the past miserable years. Goya was not a deep thinker in political terms. But he was deeply moved by the misery that events had wrought on the people around him. And he was ever a man of two vocations; his work for the court—the paintings and portraits on grand themes with which he kept bread on his table—and the huge folios of etchings and smaller paintings he made for himself. Since he'd met the philosopher Jovellanos some thirty years earlier, he had worked feverishly on the folios, producing more work than you'd have thought possible in a lifetime—let alone three decades. Few artists in history have produced so much work of such outstanding merit: Picasso, Rembrandt . . . the list is short, *mon ami*. Jovellanos had honed the artist's sense of urgency concerning the social ills about him, and had helped refine the literary aspect of his work."

Pierrot paused to refill his glass from the bottle of brandy. After he had refreshed himself with a snort, he went on. "It isn't generally known, but one of the greatest tributes Goya paid his philosopher friend—besides painting his portrait—was to use him as the model for the sleeper in the famous etching *The Sleep of Reason Breeds Monsters.*"

I raised my eyebrows at this pronouncement. "I thought scholars generally agreed that the sleeper was Goya himself."

"Perhaps. But look at the evidence of the works: both the portrait and the etchings for *Sleep of Reason* were based on a sixteen-ninety-nine engraving of the poet Quevedo dreaming at his desk. Just compare Goya's poses; clearly, in *Sleep,* Jovellanos has fallen asleep at his desk after having sat so long for the painter. Did you never notice how tired he looks in the portrait?"

"Monsieur Pedrolino," I laughed, "I hate to break this to you, but I know for a fact that the *Sleep of Reason* studies were executed in seventeen-ninety-seven. The portrait of Gaspar Melchor de Jovellanos was painted a year later. Besides, in the drawings for *Sleep,* the subject is sitting over a copy of one of Goya's earlier works—a self-portrait tradition—and leaning on an engraver's table."

The clown fidgeted with his cigar. "Really?"

"Really."

"Oh."

For a moment his face went blank, and the corners of his mouth twitched slightly. He took another slug of brandy.

"My dear Mr. Peters," he said finally, "that is an alarmingly studied way of shattering someone's pet theory."

"Sorry."

"*De rien.* I shall try to stick to the facts from now on. As I said, it wasn't until almost twenty years later that I finally met Goya. He had arrived in Paris, fleeing Fernando's revenge against the Spanish Liberals—it was a hatred he'd nursed for years as a prisoner of the French. The artist was nearly eighty; sick and almost exhausted. Were it not for his friend the priest—José Duaso y Latre—who nursed him in hiding, I doubt he would have made it. But as it was he arrived safely and took rooms at the Hôtel Favart on the rue Marivaux. Of course I heard immediately that he was in the city, and I went round to see him the minute I found out. It was sad to see him like that. I barely recognized him as the bulldoggish, vital man I remembered from Madrid. His hair was grey and straggly, and his heavy jowls had given way to soft folds of pale flesh. But his eyes were still fierce.

"Goya spoke almost no French, but my Spanish was good and he seemed delighted to have someone to talk to. He was a very lonely man—especially since his wife, Josefa, had died twelve years previously. Most of his old friends were dead by that time, too. Jovellanos had been killed while fleeing the French in eighteen-eleven. But he remembered me from the stocks, as I knew he would. And even though we had not spoken then, the memory made for a lively reunion. Francisco wanted to visit the Louvre, of course, and it was my pleasure to escort him there—the more so because in the presence of all the great paintings he seemed to regain some of his old fire and vigor, and by the time we came out—after several hours—he was quite rejuvenated. I wanted to hear his opinion of some of the Italian pieces in the museum, but he was so deaf that you had to shout in his ear with a horn, and the guards took a rather dim view of that.

"But when we got back to his rooms at the hotel he grew talkative, and we spent the next several hours reminiscing. I was particularly interested in how he had come to paint the ominous "Black Paintings" on the walls of his home, the Quinto del Sordo, and the series of works dealing with witchcraft he had executed for the Duquesa Osuna's boudoir. As Goya was one of the leading figures of the Spanish Enlightenment, it had long struck me as odd that he would have taken such a lively interest in the occult. Of course," Pierrot said with a wink, "I also wanted to know something of the circumstances surrounding the *Maja Nude.* But then, who wouldn't? He had risked a great deal to create these masterpieces—he had even been summoned before the kangaroo court of the Inquisition to answer to obscenity charges concerning the *Maja,* and I believed he must have had a very compelling reason to have risked his neck in such a fashion.

"The old artist was not at first inclined to discuss these paintings. 'That was so long ago, señor,' he said. But I persisted and, with the aid of a little wine, he began to open up. It was magical listening to him talk. He had a deep, whiskey voice, and as he sat in the large, silk-upholstered chair in the hotel room, with the window at his back overlooking the jumbled, cat-studded roofs of Paris, he could not have seemed more out of place. Though it was the middle of summer, it was overcast and dreary outside, and the soft light falling through the window drew a spectral, flickering edge around his hunched frame and seemed to make a halo in his hair. It is hard sometimes for old people to re-create in their minds the splendor and vigor of younger days, because age robs them of their associations by discrediting romance and dulling the keenness of curiosity. Yet Goya seemed to be able to call his life before him vividly, perhaps because he had

▼

captured so many moments of it in pictures. And as he began to talk he seemed to grow younger before my eyes; his back straightened and his chin jutted forward assertively.

" 'I have never asked pardon for anything I painted, señor,' he said. 'I always made the pictures my gut dictated I should make. Even official commissions. I did not flinch from painting into them references and allegories to let my viewers know precisely how I felt about my subjects. And there were many I painted, my friend, in whose presence I wanted to spit on the ground. But then, a man must eat, must he not? It has never been easy for me to be a court painter. The royal are so vain, so white-complexioned. The lack of dirt under their nails has always bothered me. People who can at a word inflict death and misery on thousands are often, I've noticed, appallingly clean; like slick worms under river rocks.

" 'I always much preferred to paint the poor; the vendors in the marketplace, the whores, the blacksmiths, and the inmates of the prisons. These had something to say with their very bodies. There is so much to read in the great rough, brown hand of a knife-grinder, or the full breasts of a pretty demimondaine. Simple, hardworking people who live their lives lustily, content to feel themselves live and breathe in the world; the workman to feel his calloused hand on the soft breast of his woman—or of a whore; and she to have it there. It is all a matter of being alive, you see, and monarchs are too often dead before their last breath rattles in their chest.

" 'You ask about the "Black Paintings" and the witches for the Alameda. The witches were mostly inspired by the plays of Zamora. And the subject was suggested by the Duquesa herself. She was a vain and self-important woman, but lovely for all that. There was a sensuality about her that few men—including myself—could resist. And she used her position to satisfy her sexual cravings, which were legendary. She once had me paint her a Priapus, and posed nude herself as the worshipping young maiden before a nude stableboy whom she helped to maintain an immense erection by licking him until I thought he would go mad. I don't know if she actually believed in or practiced witchcraft. I rather doubt it. But she always kept a copy of *Auto-de-fe* on her dresser, and loved to repeat stories about witches and vampires she heard from the country folk about her home.

"'I do not myself place much stock in witches, but I have always been intrigued by the idea. There is something fascinating about the grisly; the horrifying. And I must say that many of the country people in Spain still believe quite fiercely in such things. But then, religious people are often the most susceptible to such fantasies. It is, I suppose, because if you believe strongly enough in the reality of goodly beings, then you must also believe in the bad. For myself, I cannot say that I believe terribly in anything but reality; and that contains more than enough great good and great horror to satisfy any intellect. If there is evil in the world, it is the evil of ignorance, and it is the sworn mission of those in power to cultivate the ignorance of others, for the smart monarch knows that to educate the masses is to lose control of them. And the wise know that that is what must be.

"'I say I do not place much stock in witches. Yet I will admit to having had a certain fascination with the more erotic aspects of the occult. I know very few artists who haven't. There is something that appeals to the artistic temperament in unrestrained perversity. I cannot claim to know what impulse that is, but I would venture to guess that it is a consequence of social or religious repression and conditioning. The notion of having illicit sex with a hooded woman under the coalfire gaze of the Great He Goat, for instance, as awful as that may sound, has its gut appeal. One might even fantasize about killing her; taking the sacrificial athame and slitting her throat, as the Scythians of the Russian steppes are said to have done. That is even more perverse a concept. But there you are: one may entertain the notion and never hurt a fly. There appears to be, in other words, a large difference between such fanciful cruelties and banal, sordid fact. The atrocities committed both by José Napoleon and that son of a *puta*, Fernando, caused me to weep in the street, and to vomit over my drawings. I know that I could never bring myself to kill an innocent man in cold blood. War? That is another question, as is the defense of honor. But there is no honor in killing one's countrymen for the sake of power, or for the sake of specious religion; no honor in keeping them poor and hungry and miserable. Of course, there is no honor in the contemplation of fucking a woman before the devil, either. But there is a place for fantasy. And if we were to condemn fantasy of any kind, we should have to police the very mind. And as that is patently impossible, the only way to control people's fantasies—their hopes, beliefs, and perceptions of truth—is to kill them. So I opt for the fantasy. If the occult be part of that proposition, then I opt for that, too.

" 'In any event, I rather enjoyed painting those pictures. But what you call the "Black Paintings"? They were not a matter of enjoyment; they were an exorcism. When I painted those horrible visions I truly believed in the devil, for I had seen him. I had by that time, Pierrot, seen twelve years of war—or at least the effects of it. I had smelled it in the market, and tasted the salty sourness of blood, even as you felt it through the sting of the whip. I had on occasion returned home at night to find that my shoes left bloody footprints across my carpet. In eighteen-twelve my darling Josefa died. That was the devil's quietest victory over me. I had been unfaithful to her, yes. But I was cursed with hot blood and too much imagination. That, of course, excuses nothing. But I loved her all the same. I had seen the horrors the French committed at the hill of Principe Pio; common laborers and their wives and children lined up against a mud bank and shot by soldiers—for no particular reason, señor, other than they did not smile or offer the occupying army words of welcome and praise. I had to cover my nostrils at the stench of bowel and flyblown blood. I saw the heads of babies shattered by bullets. All this I witnessed, and for a time my mind was simply too numb to do anything with the imagery. I started to make some etchings for *Disasters of War* a couple of years later, but they were unsatisfactory. And then my wife died, and suddenly my inner vision cleared. Within two years I was able to paint the *Third of May*. I don't know why that is. Perhaps there is a limit to the amount of horror a man can tolerate before he forces himself to see it clearly; to try to do something about it. And what could I do? I am merely a painter. And a paintbrush is

▲

a poor weapon, for all the learned philosophers' defense of the pen. Words may at least rouse men to anger and action. But a painting? No. A painting is something to cry before; something to contemplate in the quiet spaces of the heart. To a degree, I suppose, it may shock or titillate. It may certainly arouse passion and desire. But it cannot win wars, nor move people to violence. I have often pondered this fact. Jovellanos urged me for years to "get involved with your brush!" And I tried to do so. Alas, Gaspar was a poet; a philosopher. And in the affairs of men, the poets have the power to move countries. Painters do not. The greatest politicians have always been poets in their way—or at least great orators. And I have been a creature so designed to the art of the eyes that I have even been robbed of my hearing. Were an orator to communicate to me, he would have to shout his words in my ear, and wouldn't that be an absurd sight! And I have come, señor, my friend, to doubt the powers of my art. At least where expressions of outrage are concerned, it would seem tailored to the deaf alone; and the sense of smell is keener.'

"For a long moment the aging painter gazed beyond my shoulder, and I could see that he was fighting with some deep emotion. Naturally I poured him some more wine. As the afternoon moved to evening, a stray ray of sunlight slipped out from under the clouds and shot over the windowsill and through the rich crimson-colored liquid in his glass, and Goya's eyes fell upon it. A merrily wavering spot of brilliant pink appeared on the white tablecloth, and suddenly his eyes grew teary with a brilliant smile.

" 'But maybe that's it,' " he said thickly. I was almost alarmed at how shaky with emotion his voice had become. 'Yes. That's it. You see, señor, I could paint that glass of wine; that needle of light, to make you cry, too. That I know. Blood is far too dense to allow light to illuminate it. And it is not red, in any event: it is brown, and soon black. My brush has always felt most keenly the touch of the edge of blown glass; the play of light and shadow on a wall; the silky shimmer of silver satin, or the soft edge of a woman's thigh—like the bloom on a fresh-picked Bordeaux grape. That, I believe, is what paint was made for. The pen and the stylus are different. Curiously, I have often

▼

found it far easier to convey violence or horror with the crisp line and velvet blacks of ink than with the brush. Perhaps that is why the "Black Paintings" are so black. Black is a color one tends to avoid in painting. It is a tyrant. It forces the rest of the painting to compensate like colored glass in a window, restrained by the lead borders. There is very little black in nature; even the deepest night is a shade of Prussian blue. Only carrion birds are truly black. But living flesh is translucence itself. You inquired about the nude, Maja? I will tell you the truth, señor. The picture was painted entirely from memory— that is to say, hope. She would not pose nude for me. Not her. Oh, I knew her body, as few had known it. And I can feel the sweetness still. But that was always in the deep blue of night, between the satin coverlets of her sumptuous bed. By morning she was covered again; wrapped in the decencies expected of her. And I, señor, donned my decencies, too. And then we pretended we were very fine friends indeed, as if God himself were watching from the ceiling. Is that not curious? Perhaps not. We were satellites of different circles. But I will tell you this: never again after her sudden death did I ever feel so alive as when her gentle hands were about me, or her lips coaxing my very being out of its shaking shell.

" 'How, then, does one translate such things into paint? When I was called before the Office of the Inquisition, I tried to explain. I called as witnesses the statues of Michelangelo and the sensuous nymphs of Caravaggio. I made a bid for the artist's sacred duty to faithfully replicate God's precious gift of human flesh.'

"Goya grinned impishly. 'They didn't believe any of that for a second, of course. But none of them were willing to argue the point because it was too embarrassing for them. You see, señor, there was not a man among them who did not empathize with what I said, and all of them had a woman to hide. And anyway, they had to shout their questions at me at the top of their lungs, and none of them wanted questioning of that nature to be heard all over the courtroom and the rest of the grounds. I could hear them better than I let on, of course. But why not make the best of a bad situation, eh?'

"Goya positively beamed at the memory of his old strategy,

▲

and it was a pleasure to see him so tickled. And to think it had been caused by a wayward beam of light through a glass of wine. The old man must have caught me looking at the glass and shaking my head in wonder, for he said suddenly, 'Let me tell you a story about that, señor—about why such light, such transparencies, are special to the painter. Or at any rate to this painter.

" 'This, I suppose, is a story of contrary purpose, but it serves to illustrate a point. For quite a few years during the War of Independence, I had been making many drawings and etchings of horrible things; grisly and terrible sights I had seen, mostly around Valencia. And when I wasn't busy with those, or filling commissions, I was making satirical drawings. Especially I targeted the friars and priests, and other plagues of the church.

" 'One day, I think it was the winter of eighteen-oh-nine, I decided I needed a break from such visual tirades. So on an impulse I began to work on a painting of a nude. There was a blacksmith down the lane who agreed to pose for me, and I decided to paint him from the back, raising his hammer as if about to strike an anvil. The painting was a release for me, and I worked on it on and off for almost a year before I realized that it was a bad painting. I was just too preoccupied with what was happening all around me. And when I had a spare moment from painting the portraits of vain politicians and noblemen, I had so much anger pent up in me that I had to get it out in the drawings. So one night I gave up on the painting. There seemed no point in continuing it, so I painted it out and, in a somewhat nationalistic mood, began to do a sketch of victorious Spanish troops routing the French from the land. It was very impulsive, that oil sketch. And very dramatic. Wains and cattle rushed helter-skelter through a deep valley under lowering clouds and the smokes of war. I completed the entire reworking in a matter of hours and, tired and dissatisfied, decided to go down to a local bar to have a glass or two of wine.

" 'As it turned out, I had far too many glasses of wine and, being on occasion prone to belligerence, soon found myself in a heated argument with the very blacksmith who had posed for me. He was many years my junior, and I had been in ill health for some years. But wine, as you are aware, has many remarkable powers. It can, among other things, make you taller, stronger, quicker, and healthier than you have any right to suppose you are. So in the heat of passion I actually raised my fist to that huge, young man. Of course I had considerable standing in the community at the time, and the black-smith was actually a decent enough fellow—even if his politics were in need of repair—so he did not attempt to hit me back. Instead, he gathered me up in his arms so I could not move and said quite gently, "Señor Goya is going home to bed now, isn't he?"

" 'As I was in no position to argue, and as the wine had suddenly abandoned me to a remarkable appreciation of dimension and the perspective of the floor from a considerable height, I agreed. So the blacksmith—who later became a good and faithful friend, who helped me avoid the authorities when I was in dire peril—the black-smith carried me home. At the door we shook hands, and I promised him I would never again be so foolish as to start a fight with someone so much bigger than I. But when he left me, and I returned to the studio to take a last look at the picture before going to bed, I was stunned to my shoes. There he was—in the painting; looming over the little scurrying soldiers like the giant of the Prophecy of the Pyrenees. The image was absolutely shocking, and I began to suspect that I had been given some very bad wine indeed that night. Unable to believe my eyes, and too drunk to keep them open much longer anyway, I went to bed.

" 'But in the morning the figure of the blacksmith was still there, and I realized what had happened: the first painting had not yet been fully dry when I'd painted over it, and it had bled through the pale blues and lead-white greys I had made my sky of. What to do now? I looked at the picture a long time over several cups of strong coffee, and it dawned on me that the Colossus of the Pyrenees was exactly what the painting looked like: the spirit of Spain itself when threatened by attack. It was perfect; divine providence if you will. So I set to work refining and changing the giant figure. I also changed my French soldiers into frightened country folk, fleeing in all directions from the monstrous apparition that had appeared from the mountains—little known to them—to defend them against the hostile French.

"'And so, señor, this is the true story of the birth of *The Colossus.*'

"I thought the story over for a time before I perceived the moral in it. 'So, Francisco,' I said, 'no matter how hard you tried to make an unpolitical painting, it wound up being political after all, *non?*'

"'Yes, it certainly looks as if that is the case,' he said. 'But truthfully, señor, I only wished to make a great painting.'"

7
▼
▲

I LISTENED TO THE STORY ATTENTIVELY. THE OLD painter's message, at least according to Pierrot's spin on the story, was clear: craft before content. Yet there was a question the story did not address. A question raised by the state of contemporary society—a state Goya could not possibly in his wildest dreams have imagined.

"But what would he have said now?" I asked. "How do you think Goya might have responded to, say, the mind-boggling blitz of advertising imagery in Times Square? Wouldn't the work of someone as sensitive as Goya be influenced by all that? I mean, slick visual propaganda is everywhere today—in every forum; politics, sales, entertainment. When I think about it, is it really any wonder that modern artists are so influenced by it all?"

Pierrot got to his feet and began pacing slowly back and forth across the kitchen floor, marshaling his thoughts carefully before responding.

At length he said, "It isn't enough to mimic what you see about you. You must somehow make art out of it. That is the point." He stopped his pacing and gave me a searching look. Then he returned to the table and sat back down. "You are proving to be more of a problem than I anticipated, Mr. Peters," he said finally, with a slight shake of his head. "But I shall try to answer your question. It may, however, be a rather lengthy answer.

"There is obviously no question that such pervasive influences need to be addressed. The question is, *how?* But let's look at this another way. Let's leave Goya for a moment and see if we can't define some sort of contemporary context in which to express the values he and his kind have always stood for.

"Over the years I have developed something of a theory that I call for convenience the 'theory of imposed systems.' It is a concept that rather ambitiously attempts to cover all things human—an attempt to explain why we are the way we are. But here, I think, it may have a special application to contemporary American art. Simply put, the theory runs something like this: as I'm sure you know, the nature of the physical world is essentially entropic—in other words, it tends inexorably to disorder, at least on the level of experience at which we humans must operate. Now, in order to facilitate our existence in such a world, humankind has attempted to both understand and manipulate nature. To that end . . ."

"This isn't an answer. It's a lecture."

"Please, Mr. Peters. Bear with me. Now . . . where was I? Oh, yes. In order to understand and manipulate nature, we have imposed artificial disciplines of one sort or another on her: cause-and-effect reasonings such as physics, quantitative systems such as mathematics, communication systems such as language, and others. Along with such systems evolve sets of rules, and by applying these rules we try to thwart the inevitability of entropic decay by attempting to predict and, ideally, avoid it. So the biological urge to survive is ultimately at the root of all epistemological enterprise. There is no such thing as knowledge for knowledge's sake. Furthermore, in order to communicate what we call 'knowledge,' we humans have also imposed categories, identities, and names on the various entities of which our world is constituted. But the trouble with taxonomy is that every name carries with it an ascription of value or connotation of good or evil—no matter how subtle this may be. So even our systems of oral communication are inherently flawed. Indeed, one could with some justification say that the fate of Mother Earth was sealed with the invention of the noun."

"This is all very interesting," I broke in impatiently, "but I don't see what it has to do with art."

"Patience, *mon ami*. I'm getting to that. Now, to sum up:

▼

because we know the world to be disorderly, we impose intellectual disciplines on it—imposed systems—in order that we might to some extent control our own destinies. So, too, in its own way, does every creature under the sun, if only by virtue of the biological equipment nature gave it to survive on the planet long enough to procreate. But we humans have taken things a good deal further than most of our fellow creatures. We have decided that everything can be dealt with systematically, and so we apply the concept not only to nature but to human affairs as well. And this is where politics and economics come in. It is also, by extension, where the role of the artist in society is defined.

"Politics, no less than any other imposed system, is a convenient abstraction, designed for the purpose of overseeing the welfare of the race—or of the privileged few, depending on your perspective. The cosmos at large neither recognizes nor cares whether we ascribe to a communist ideology or a capitalist one. They are both axiomatically just two ways of achieving for humans what certain trees achieve with cyclic boom years in mast production, and bees achieve by swarming: namely, creating the right environment for the successful procreation of the species. The only criterion in the long run is whether or not the system does what it was intended to do. But the problem with all systems—natural or artificially imposed—is that, due to the entropic nature of the world, they eventually decay. Think of them, if you will, as spinning spirals that eventually spin into themselves until they vanish in a vortex of their own making. The process can never be halted, only adjusted and to some degree maintained until it becomes obvious that the system is no longer viable as a means of protecting its intended beneficiary. In nature, of course, evolution and periodic extinction see to it that natural systems which prove ineffective simply disappear, to be replaced by new, more efficient ones. So, too, do humans' imposed systems eventually spin themselves out and disappear as they become inviable. Therefore politicians and philosophers spend an inordinate amount of their time on earth tinkering with systems; trying to maintain or alter them in accordance with what they perceive as being necessary for the preservation of the race—physically, ethically, and otherwise.

▲

"And here, at last, Mr. Peters, is how art relates to all of this. Remember that the artist is the only intellect that need not name a thing or assign it a value in order to describe it. The artist is therefore in a unique position to inform us about the nature of the systems in which we live. The artist is the outsider with the clear vision. And that makes him essential to society for this reason: a system that is not working cannot be repaired or altered from within. This is a maxim; it is the maxim responsible for revolutions, be they violent or peaceful, physical or intellectual. It is the nature of an imposed system that people working within it can only perpetuate it or perish with it. But when a system has reached a critical point of decay, it *must* be replaced. If a political system, for example, reaches this critical point, it festers into decadence and then anarchy, both of which herald the death of a system, and, by implication—if not in fact—the death of those who depend on it. But to see a system clearly enough to figure out what is wrong with it, one must step outside it. Think of it this way: if you have the misfortune to be caught within the eye of a hurricane, you cannot see its shape nor can you avoid its consequences. So we send up satellites and weather planes that can see the telltale shape of the system forming and warn us of its approach. It is not, of course, a one-hundred-percent fail-safe means of avoiding hurricanes, but it is better than being caught in one without warning.

"And so in this regard, the artist, wittingly or unwittingly, can function as a kind of weather plane; a sensitive barometer, if you prefer, of the climate and health of a social, political, or cultural system. The point is that his work would do this anyway. It is not necessary for the artist to deliberately go out and appropriate from the system; indeed, it is a grave mistake for him to do so, for then he is in fact contributing to the system. Reinforcing it, participating in its perpetuation. The artist, in other words, is by nature and necessity apolitical, while his work cannot help but be political and be viewed in a political context. The artist's clear vision, and the fact that he does not need to name or value things in accordance with the system's nomenclature or established values, makes it inevitable that this is so.

"And so you see I have come back to your question at last. Asking if Goya would not be influenced by the barrage of advertising and other aggravating social phenomena today is the wrong question. Of course he would be. How could he not? The question is rather how would an artist of his stature respond to it? How would such things be reflected in his work? They surely would, because they are there. But it is a matter of the aesthetic agenda, not a consciously political one, that ultimately determines what constitutes great art. The magic inherent in the craft of art must always come first. The individual vision of the artist, else he becomes merely another cog in the vast machinery of the system, hastening its demise. The reason, Mr. Peters, that Postmodernists failed to reinvigorate the stagnating fine-art situation in late-twentieth-century America was because they attempted to do so by working within the system that was the cause of its decline in the first place, and to make matters worse they lost their vital appreciation for the making of objects; their respect for the craft of art. Appropriating or mirroring the products and symbols of a system only strengthens those products and symbols by investing them with cultural authority. Once that happens, the system happily reappropriates them to keep the system going. Perhaps worse than this is the penchant of artists today for appropriating the symbols of older, completely failed systems. Trying to reinvigorate a troubled culture that way is a bit like trying to repair a new automobile with antique parts.

"The artists, of course, would argue that they need to 'engage' the system to make a living in it. The fact is that that has nothing to do with the making of art. Art is not about making money. And great artists have never had an easy time of it unless they were fortunate enough to live long enough to reap the benefits of their honest labor. That is simply the nature of the beast.

"So forget your Baudrillards and Foucaults and Bartheses! Philosophy does not produce paintings. Painters do. And if a painter is simply out seeking status or money, he will never be an artist, only another cog in the system. It takes courage to be an artist, my friend; to look at reality clearly; to form one's own opinions. To make magic. And perhaps what artists in America are most in need of today is courage. I can assure you that were Señor Goya alive today—a severely hypothetical were—he would not have the courage of his convictions tempted by anything so insubstantial as a crack at the Whitney Biennial. Nor, I think, would he fail to see the danger in blatant appropriation and mimicry."

The old clown stopped for a moment and frowned in concentration. He attempted to reignite his cold cigar, puffed at it for a moment, and gave up. Then he looked up at me wide-eyed, and said slowly, "Do you know, perhaps there is something he might be expected to do under these circumstances: reintroduce metaphor to contemporary art. It is an element that appears to have gone by the wayside, and it is a very important one in the arts. It is through metaphor that art can express some of its most profound observations, while not directly engaging the apparatus of a pernicious system. Hence such pictures as *Saturn Devouring His Children* and others. And metaphor can communicate on a universal level that the specific contemporary image cannot, because it appeals to a set of perceptions, truisms, and likenesses that we all share to some degree, the world over. At this point, from the perspective of the twenty-first century, human existence seems bound in a finely woven net of numbers, chips of silicon, and Styrofoam bubbles; a kind of synthetic hell—an inescapable cage of technological horrors that threatens to cut human beings off entirely from the magic of the natural world. Think of the potential for metaphor in such a description. But where do you see it today?"

The clown stopped abruptly, the question mark over his left eye. His great black eyes were so penetrating that I avoided them self-consciously, shifting my gaze to the kitchen window. I tried to penetrate the greasy streaks and reflections in the blackened panes to see into the park. But I knew that even were the window wide open on a sunny summer day, I'd see no magic down there—and precious little of nature, either. And above the pitch darkness hedging and concealing the miserable little patch of rotted earth, the sullen glow of the city reached up like mad fingers.

"It all has to get back to nature somehow, then," I said.

"Must it?"

▼

"I wish I knew."

I looked at my watch. It was getting late and I was suddenly terribly tired. I thanked Pierrot for the dinner and the conversation, once again promised to see him the following evening, and went back to the hotel. If I had dreams that night, I don't remember them.

8

▼
▲

THE NEXT EVENING, AT MY INSISTENCE, THE OLD MAN
and I went out to eat—my treat. After peanut butter and horseradish
sandwiches, I thought it best not to tempt the clown to even more
inventive cuisine, no matter how well intentioned. I'd had another
long day of disappointing art reconnaissance in TriBeCa, SoHo,
and the midtown galleries, and the last thing I needed was indiges-
tion. So we had an excellent meal at a little Indian place in the East
Village and afterward headed back to Pierrot's apartment for more
conversation.

As I was still mulling over the substance of our last session,
and as I'd been thinking about Fran again during the day, I thought
I'd broach the subject of the clown's own life, about which he'd so
far said very little—aside from his occasional references to Colombina. And it was she, in particular, I was interested in. Who was this
beautiful, legendary creature who always stirred the old man to emotional reminiscence? And how did she figure into his lifelong preoccupation with art?

When I brought the topic up, his first response was a prolonged and moody silence, punctuated by the gulping down of huge
shots of brandy. We sat in the kitchen again, and during this period
of evident hesitation, I found myself again examining the characters
on stage in the old Funambules poster: the Pierrot with his lute,
Leandre seeming to sneak offstage into the darkness, and the black-
masked Arlequin pawing at the dove-white breast of the lovely
Colombina. Glancing at the old man from the corner of my eye, I
realized that he was pondering the picture, too.

Finally he burped, then uttered a huge sigh. I turned my attention to him, as he seemed about to speak. But first he poured himself another generous brandy.

"It all has a great deal to do with the moon, of course," he said at length, and picked his teeth thoughtfully with his fingernail. "It always has. Indeed, it is only to be moon-mad that I live so long. Moon-madness stirs the memories and keeps my hopes alive. Can you understand that, *mon ami?*"

"I think you're getting just a little ahead of me there," I replied. Moon-madness?

At that, he rocked back in his chair with an unexpected loud laugh. "Oh, my friend," he said, "I'm so sorry. Of course you would not know. Sometimes I presume far too much of the young." Rocking forward again, he withdrew a cigar from the folds of his white coat, and practically sucked his cheeks down his throat trying to light it. "There!" he exclaimed when he had created a satisfactory reek in the kitchen. He fixed me with his darkling eye, and gracefully laid one long, bony hand across the little gilt box by Goya's portrait.

"The moon-madness," he began again, "is what keeps me forever pursuing my Colombina—no matter how often she spurns me. But I will tell you how I first met her." He flung a glance at the little box, half closed his eyes, and intoned:

"It was in fourteen-fifty-seven . . . no, no wait. It was fourteen-fifty . . . yes. Yes, it was fifty-seven after all. I remember because I had gone to see Piero della Francesca's *Invention of the True Cross* at the San Francesco church in Arezzo earlier that summer. He had just completed it, and as he was making quite a name for himself, I had to hurry to Tuscany. Yes, of course. How silly of me to misplace the date. Oh, how she would laugh if she knew!" His eyes opened suddenly. "You must swear never to tell her I forgot, Mr. Peters."

"I swear."

"*Merci, mon ami.* So, it was fifty-seven, and I was still a young man—very young indeed, in fact. Barely thirty . . ." The old clown's eyes closed again and a satisfied smile played on his lips. His eyebrows tilted on his forehead in an expression of sweet memory. "Ah, my friend, she was beautiful! But I get ahead of myself. I had returned to Frankfurt, where the troupe was playing at the time. We had been on tour for several years, working our way north, following the streams of peasants and priests fleeing the constant feudal wars in the Italian principalities and states to settle in the green lands along the Rhine. We'd played successfully in Cologne, Konstanz, Meersberg, and Heidelberg, finally arriving in Frankfurt in the autumn of fifty-six. It had been a long, hard journey, for at that time the dense pine forests extended down to the banks of the rivers, and paths through it were few and dangerous. Besides the constant threat of wolves and brown bears, there were robbers all along the way, lurking deep in the black forests, waiting to attack just such defenseless-looking troupes as we. More than once, Arlequin and I had to defend our actors against the ruffians with magic—something neither of us liked to do. We were supposed to reserve that for the stage, you understand. It didn't take much, of course—which is a good thing, because we didn't have much. I am quite good at disappearing when I'm in good shape, and that rascal Arlequin can make a pretty mean fire jump out of his fingers. It was enough, at any rate, to put off the robbers, who considered almost anything out of the ordinary to be the very work of the devil. You could absolutely petrify them with a magnifying glass, for example.

"Wolves were rather harder to deal with—for me, at least. You see, although I could disappear relatively well at the time, I couldn't cover my smell, or silence my footsteps. So it was a pretty useless sort of magic to pull on wolves. They just sniffed me out and chased me. Luckily I am also very good with animals. Perhaps it is because they recognize in me a kindred spirit, I don't know. But I always managed to charm my way out of wolfy situations without too much trouble. But the woods were dark and lonely, and it was a relief to arrive in a thriving metropolis—although Frankfurt was at the time nothing like it is now. Most of the old buildings were lost during the various wars since then. But the downtown area of what is now the Römer Platz used to be so lovely. We played nightly in the square in front of the Hoch Haus, just blocks from the Main River. The townsfolk would bring in wagons of hay to sit on, and a great bonfire would be built. Brewers would arrive with huge barrels of fine dark beer, and vendors would set up their tents around the stage. On holy days especially, it was a joyous scene. Parties of field-workers would ferry across the river from Sachsen Hausen, a little community of ceramists and artisans just to the south. And the Bürgermeister himself would often come out to watch the shows. I doubt if any one of us ever ended a performance entirely sober in those days. Leandre, poor soul, was particularly susceptible to the lures of the hop, and many's the night I had to wander down the dark, crooked streets to the wharf to find him.

"It was just one such evening that I met Colombina for the first time. There was a full moon up, and it had been a particularly riotous night. We had given a good All Saints Day performance, if I do say so myself, and afterward Leandre, as usual, wandered over to the brewer's cart to get on intimate terms with a fresh batch of Heffe Weizen. And I can't say I blamed him. There was nothing like it in the world; rich and deep brown, sweet and intoxicating. I confess a penchant for the stuff myself, but nothing to match Leandre's obsession. In any event, he had disappeared once again, and as I had a good idea of where he liked to go when he wandered off to the river, I elected to go get him. Now Frankfurt was a trading center at the time, but it was a very small town by modern standards. I seriously doubt if there were more than two thousand people living within the city walls, and at night the little winding walkways that led down to the river were very dark. Being as they were paved with rough cobbles, it could be treacherous to walk without the aid of a torch, and I was in the habit of taking one with me when I went searching for Leandre. But this particular evening the moon was so incredibly brilliant that I left without one. It is hard, *mon ami,* to explain to someone— anyone—of the last two centuries what it could be like under a full moon back in those days. We had had no experience of electric lights—or even of enhanced oil lanterns with mirrors. At night, the sky was dark. And if you were under the canopy of the fir forest, or wandering the alleys of a village between the irregularly spaced houses, it could be absolutely pitch black. But when the full moon was up, it was like daylight. Sometimes it could be so bright that you couldn't look directly at it. It hurt the eyes. And everything would be bathed in an intense blue light. That was the only real difference between night and day at such times; all colors were converted to various shades of blue or bright grey. The firelight of human dwellings looked positively red by comparison.

"But that night was such a night. The moon was absolutely blinding, and I felt confident that I could find my way through the maze of streets down to the Main. Well, I somewhat overestimated my ability to see in the dark that evening. Another consequence of an unusually bright full moon was that it made shadows that were blacker than ignorance. And I got myself lost on the way. To this day I don't know quite how I accomplished it. I knew perfectly well which way the river lay. But I took what I thought would be a shortcut down to the wharf. I know that it started out in the right direction, at least. But before long I realized I was heading east—parallel to the river, and I could find no way back south. And I had on only my stage outfit of billowy cotton and a light leathern vest I'd thrown over it as an afterthought. So before long I was positively freezing, especially once I got down near the water. The air down there was always moist and chill.

"So there I was, stalking cautiously along the cold stone cobbles, like a pale ghost in outrageous makeup, one hand extended to keep contact with the walls of the houses to my right—which way I knew I must turn eventually if I were ever to reach the riverbank. And as the sounds of merrymaking from the town square diminished and then completely faded behind me, I began to greatly fear that I would never even find my way back should I decide to turn around. I don't know how long I crept along, stumbling now and then on an unusually irregularly placed cobblestone, but it must have been nearly forty minutes. For when I finally detected a passage between the houses leading off to the right and turned down it, I came out hundreds of yards above the wharf I was aiming for, and staggered into a fallowed field of dense high thistle and dock. In no time flat, *mon ami,* I was cut, stung, and stabbed almost to ribbons; my clothes were never the same—and finding a seamstress capable of sewing so elaborate a costume was a chore in those times, I can tell you. So hissing and cussing to myself, I ouched my way through the thorny field down to the riverbank. And there, lovely and heartbreaking in the silver moonlight, I first spied my wonderful Colombina.

"I did not know who she was, of course. All I knew immediately is that I had never seen a woman so beautiful. I had never imagined a woman so beautiful—and, believe me, there were plenty of lovely ladies in Naples, where I was born. But to understand how incredibly lovely she was, you must understand this: in the fifteenth century very few people indeed escaped the ravages of scurvy or smallpox or other common—and often fatal—diseases. Those who lived to be twenty and more generally bore the scars of a bout with some illness. And life was hard to begin with. A man or woman of twenty-five or more would have passed for a forty-year-old today, most of the time. Not even those souls fortunate enough to be born into nobility could entirely escape the rigors of life then, and they were by comparison well fed, well housed, and had their own personal leeches to look after them. The average cover girl so common on fashion magazines of today would have seemed a goddess to people then. Yet my Colombina was more lovely still. Not even today is there anyone of her beauty in the living world. So you may imagine how stunned I was to see her sitting on a wide, flat rock by the broad, murmuring river in the moonlight that night. At first I thought her an apparition; or that I had had some poisonous meat earlier that day (I'd certainly not had much to drink that evening because I had to play the lute on stage).

"I had to have been making a great deal of noise in the field, what with all my stumbling and cursing and so forth, but she appeared not to have heard me for some reason. So I crouched down amid the prickly thistles and watched her for some time, hardly able to convince myself she was real.

"Oh! How can I possibly explain the magic of that moment? The only time since then I've ever felt anything like that kind of

▲

breathtaking excitement—almost fear—was when a friend and I stalked the last wild unicorn in fifteen-fifty, in the wilds of the Camargue fens in northern Portugal. But even having that rarest of wonderful antelope step silently within a pace or two of our reed blind could not compare with the enthralling, interminable hour I spent crouched in the weeds watching Colombina for the first time. I even forgot the cold, though I was shivering mightily, and bit down on my finger to keep my rattling teeth from giving me away.

"Her skin was so pale it seemed almost translucent in the moonlight, and her hair so black that it had blue and purple highlights. She wore a close-fitting dress of shimmering green satin, so her figure seemed to shift and fade against the moonlit shimmering green of the purling water. Over this she had on only a patterned leathern bodice, and about her white throat a velvet choker. And even from a distance of some yards I could see that the skin of her face was flawless.

"Curiously, as cold as it was by the river, she seemed not to notice. And she sat as still as Andersen's statue, with one slender hand held to her throat, eyes lost in the endless convolutions of the river's surface. But what she was doing there at that hour, risking the wolves—both the grey and those of the human variety—I had no idea.

"To this very day I don't know, nor has she ever offered to tell me. Perhaps it was merely destiny; kismet. For until I saw Colombina by the banks of the Main, I had been a happy and happy-go-lucky youth, with women aplenty in every town, and no thoughts of lasting love; no dreams of possession. But from that night forward I have had no real peace, for I have never been able to get her lovely face out of my head. And to this day, when the moon is full, I feel compelled to do the most idiotic things. It is something I cannot resist, and no longer try to fight. There comes a time in every person's life, *mon ami,* when he realizes that true magic cannot be resisted; that there are feelings and longings in the world over which we have no control. Such it is with artists—of any kind: that sense of needing to do, to be, to make something we have only the vaguest notion of, yet know

▼

beyond a shadow of a doubt we must spend our lives striving for. This is the true magic. For some, the compulsion comes in the form of an urgent poem, of which only the merest suggestion of a cadence or an expressed emotion is available to our waking senses. For others, it is the perfect combination of color and form; an image so profound that even in our dreams we are afraid to look fully at it, lest, like Perseus looking in the face of the Gorgon, we become forever stone, unable to accomplish another vital or meaningful thing in life. For the composer it is perhaps the unearthly melody of such astounding beauty that anything else he contrives through the strictures of his art must seem rude and inadequate. Indeed, perhaps, only the very deaf are privileged to realize such melodies on paper, and when translated by the wooden and brass instruments of mortal musicians, we listeners are only privy to the crudest approximation of the glorious music that played, say, in Beethoven's head.

"For me, this impulse took the form of Colombina, and in centuries of searching, and ages of trying, I have neither witnessed another woman as beautiful nor succeeded in merging my soul with hers. And that is the most desperate feeling; the knowledge that no matter how hard one tries, one can never, ever *be* the object of one's desire. The best one can do is to serve it the best way one knows how—and that sometimes is a self-destructive impulse, unavoidable and irreversible.

"So there I was, crouching in the cold damp weeds by the river, suddenly aware that I was face to face with my dearest hope and mortal nemesis. Now the question was, what to do about it? Should I get stiffly to my feet, dressed as I was in my ridiculous stage costume which was, in any event, dirtied and torn almost beyond recognition; with my face painted a glowing white and my hair slicked back with bear grease in order to hide it properly under my skullcap? Likely as not such a move would have scared her right off the rock and into the river to her death. It was, you understand, a bit of a pickle to be in, as at that point I wasn't even confident that I could successfully make a retreat without her seeing me. So for a while I was forced to sit and watch, biting down on my finger and feeling my knees gradu-

▲

ally lock into a position from which they would likely never move again. There are few things in life sillier than some clown dumbstruck in the presence of a woman—though it happens every day of course. But as it turned out I didn't have too long to wait for the resolution to my dilemma; the business was taken out of my hands by that other nemesis of my life, my colleague Arlequin. The little shit. Pardon my French.

"Actually, to be fair, before Colombina happened along, Arlequin and I got along famously. He was always something of an egomaniac, forever trying to upstage the rest of us. But offstage he was quite a companionable fellow; quick-witted and possessed of a wry sense of humor. But when Colombina appeared on the scene . . . Suffice it to say that the muse is no less alluring to those who are not charged with the duty of serving her than to those who are. And Arlequin, who had come wandering along the waterside looking for me, even as I had set out for Leandre, was immediately smitten. And being a low-down, conniving poseur and philanderer—that is to say, much better with the ladies than I—he went boldly right up to *my* vision, sweet-talked her for a moment while I crouched nearby plotting his death, and presently waltzed away with her. And that, my friend, was the beginning of both a cancerous longing and a lasting animosity. It became the stuff of countless skits and mimes, of course, and served as the model for many an epic tale. But what the writers and storytellers do not know is that to this day the struggle rages on—the eternal triangle, if you like, between love, necessity, and impotence. And with every passing day the resolution seems if anything further away. Great age is of no particular palliation where affairs of the heart are concerned. Neither is wisdom. And that, my friend, is why I am not, for example, as troubled about the state of the arts today as you are. The arts concern a state of the heart. In the grand scheme of things, they occupy a position rather less noble than the act of copulation, yet nobler than the concept of an eternally loving god—which is in itself a manifestation of that uniquely human need to order or re-create the world about us. And it is telling, is it not, that the art of so many men is concerned with the grand themes:

glorious battles and ensanguinated heroes, while the art of so many women confides itself to the infinitely more important issues of pro-creation and the nursing of new life? Few male artists indeed have managed to advance an aesthetic *and* remain true to their most inti-mate convictions and self-awareness. It is just such a rare worldview that marks the work of Watteau, Dürer, Vermeer, Rembrandt, Klee, or Modigliani as remarkable. Such artists had their own Colombinas to serve, while at the same time having to deal with their own Ar-lequins. It is no accident that my colleague has played nearly as prominent a role in the work of male artists as I have. He is the metaphor of the phallus; the Priapus in constant search of one pur-pose. And the difficulty from my perspective is the realization that his is the more important role. I am but a dreamer, in charge of dreams and the maintenance of them.

"Of course one can argue, too, that men make art because they need a surrogate for their lack of ability to bear children. But that would seem wrongheaded reasoning. Men were not designed to bear children, so how could they possibly need to satisfy such an urge? No, I cannot and will not believe any such convenient explanation. It simply does not make sense. But what then are we left with by way of explanation?"

I waited for the answer, clutching my empty glass and staring at the little gilt box under the old clown's hand.

"Well?" he asked suddenly.

"I was under the impression you were going to tell me."

"Certainly not, *mon ami*. I would never presume to state as a fact something I have each passing year less and less understanding of. All I know is that I have my Colombina, but that I do not really have her at all as long as Arlequin lives to pursue her with his dart in his hand, and she is willing to be seduced. I have only a dream, and a little bit of magic. And that is more than sufficient."

The old man stopped and regarded his empty glass with a self-conscious smile. "Well," he said at length, "perhaps not more than sufficient, after all. I do not yet have the heart of my Colombina, and sometimes it looks as if I never will. When I am being honest with myself—which is as seldom as I can possibly get away with—I admit that dreams and magic are not everything. A man needs love. Perhaps it is that art needs love. Or perhaps art itself is a surrogate for love rather than for fertility. But that would be curious, too, for so many of the artists I have known have done their very finest work when they were in love; Picasso, indeed, could scarcely work if he wasn't. But then, artists tend to be if anything more idiosyncratic than most people. Still, love is in the artistic equation somewhere. But, as I said, such things are a mystery even to me, and if I fully understood them I would have my Colombina eating out of my hand."

Mechanically, he reached behind him and grabbed the bottle of brandy. He poured himself a full portion and raised his eyebrow in my direction.

"What the hell."

"I drink far too much, of course," he said casually. "But that is also a consequence of my trials of the heart—inexcusable, of course. But I will tell you how I first came to drink heavily." The old man looked at me with such a sad expression that I again thought he was on the verge of crying. But instead he smiled. "Have you ever been in love, Mr. Peters?"

Love was not something I generally spent a great deal of time thinking about. But the question always recalled painfully one woman in particular, and Pierrot had a way of making almost every ordinary sensation more vivid; every memory more poignant.

"I see that you have," he said, stretching across the table to pat me on the arm reassuringly. "Then you know the awful, unbearable pain of it when you are rejected, or when things simply will not work out. It is the same with almost everyone on earth, and quite likely always will be.

"That first night, when Arlequin waltzed off with my Colombina, though she had not yet even seen me or, as far as I know, been aware of my presence so near at hand, I felt that I would die for jealousy. And since that night he has always found a way to confound my every effort to woo her. But let me start at the beginning:

"It wasn't until the next day that I had a chance to introduce myself to her. By that time, of course, the bastard had already had his way with her. I could see that in the looks that passed between them as she watched him during rehearsals that afternoon. The knowledge made my heart ache, for I knew full well that Arlequin would never love her as she should be loved. To him she was merely a toy, and the moment she was out of his sight he would be chasing the very next pretty thing that came his way. Arlequin was the original Don Juan. To this day—and he is fully as old as I—he cannot seem to resist the chance to impose himself on women. It makes him especially happy if he can seduce someone else's wife or girlfriend. It satisfies his sense of conquest, I imagine. But be that as it may. There are many such people in the world, and he is the father to them all.

"I could hardly keep my mind on my part that day, with that lovely dream of a woman sitting coquettishly just in front of the stage, all fresh and happy looking. That, I suppose, was what made me the most miserable. How could she possibly be happy about having spent the night with that monster? And Leandre, who was in a mean-spirited mood, as he always was when recovering from a hangover, read my feelings in my face, and took it upon himself to tease me mercilessly about her every time I came offstage. That only made me more embarrassed than I was already, so when Arlequin got around to introducing us during the break, I could scarcely look her in the face. And to make matters worse, I somehow managed to spill an entire flagon of beer down my shirtfront, thereby ruining my sec-ond—and only other—outfit. And my, did that make her laugh merrily! Yes, she and the others had a jolly good time with that one. And I became so completely flustered that, in trying to get away from them, I backed into the tent-string which held the canopy over the stage in place, bringing down the entire works."

Pierrot smiled broadly and shook his head. "It was, I suppose, quite an amusing incident, now that I can look back on it after several hundred years. But I assure you, *mon ami,* that I have never in my life been so thoroughly miserable. It was everything I could do to keep from turning and running away. As it was, I made a halfhearted attempt to pick up some of the canopy, then with a bow said to Colombina, 'So good to make your acquaintance,' and turned stiffly around and walked away. I could hear the lot of them laughing and giggling behind my back as I once again headed for the river down the narrow, crooked streets. When I got down to the wharf, I walked out to the farthest end of the pier, and feeling a hopeless and lonely fool, I sat and cried until my eyes were so swollen I could barely see.

"As I was sniffling and drying my face on my sleeve—which also turned out to be a mistake, as my makeup had run all over my cheek and of course only made a further mess of my poor costume—as I sat there so miserably, a strange-looking little man came along the wharf, carrying a large wineskin on his back. On impulse I waved him over. In spite of my shabby appearance he recognized me, and he gladly came and sat down beside me.

" 'Why, Herr Pantaloon,' he said, 'whatever is the matter? You look as though you could use a draft of my fine wine. It is from my very finest barrel, and I was bringing it to the Rathaus for the Bürgermeister's table this evening. Would you care for some?'

"To be honest, I had up to that point never much cared for wine. It always gave me headaches. But at that moment I think I would have swallowed horse urine if I'd thought it would make me feel less of a fool, or remove Colombina's face from my mind. So I accepted the merchant's kindly offer. In fact the merchant was evidently quite thirsty also, and so, between the two of us . . . Suffice it to say that the Bürgermeister had to make do with a lesser vintage that evening, and the commedia had to make do without Pantaloon. But I'm sure they got by just fine without . . ."

"Pantaloon?" I interrupted, "I thought your name was Pedrolino."

"Pardon? . . . Oh, yes, yes. My friend, I have been many things to many people over the years and have played many parts. Pantaloon, Punch, and Pagliacci are just a few of them. At that time I was playing Pantaloon—or had been until that evening. I must say that it was very good wine, and in little time at all both the wine merchant and myself were so intoxicated that neither of us could stand too steadily—much less walk. And it did ease the pain for a while. That is, until I killed him, of course."

"Until you killed him!"

▼

"Why yes. Not intentionally, you understand. I had staggered with difficulty to my feet, in order to piss into the river. The little merchant was also desperate for relief about that time, having consumed nearly a gallon of sweet wine. It was all I could do to keep myself from falling into the water. It was quite dark by then, and I could barely see to direct my piss so as not to do it all over the little fellow. But he kept grabbing my leg in an effort to hoist himself up also. Finally he gave me such a mighty tug that I lost my balance, and in trying to regain it, I kicked out with my leg, knocking him off the pier and into the river."

"My God. Didn't you try to save him? Or get some help?"

"It would have been quite hopeless, *mon ami.* I was too drunk even to see him. And there was absolutely no possible way I would have made it back to the town square in the dark in that condition!"

"So what did you do?"

"Why, I cried for him, of course," said the clown, looking as surprised as if I'd just asked him why he didn't fling himself out the kitchen window. I wasn't sure how to respond to this news at all. It certainly didn't appear to be of any particular consequence to my host. Finally I asked, "Didn't anyone miss him later?"

"Not really. I'm sure his wife wasn't very happy that he never returned home—if he had a wife. But the Bürgermeister might well have thrown him into the river himself, had he found out what happened to the wine he had ordered. So I didn't let it upset me too much. After all, I said he *fell* in. The wineskin was beside me, and I saw to it that not a single drop was wasted. But that is the way of things sometimes: you have a good time, somebody gets killed. There is an old Parisian saying, *'A une fesse qui dit merde à l'autre.'* Do you know it?"

I shook my head.

"It means, 'One ass says shit to the other,' and it expresses such things quite succinctly. In any event, I woke up the next morning—which is to say the next afternoon—stiff and sore as I had never been before. And standing over me with disapproving looks on their faces were Arlequin and Colombina. Can you imagine? After a night like

128

that? After all I had been through the day and night before, and after my poor little wine merchant had drowned in the river? If I had looked a fool the day before, imagine what I must have looked like then. You can see that my relationship with the love of my life did not get off to a very smooth start."

Pierrot threw me a rather bleary look and swallowed the remainder of his brandy. "Well, my friend," he continued, again reaching for the nearly empty brandy bottle, "at that point, even so gentle a soul as I began to lose my temper. Looking up after such an experience to the censorial expression of my colleague in the presence of Colombina was simply more than I could bear. And that is why I first came to kill Arlequin."

"You killed him, too?" My queer but gentle old companion was beginning to sound more and more like a casual serial murderer, and I glanced around the room to see if there were any weapons of any sort hanging from the walls or standing in corners.

"Picture this, if you would," said the old man, closing his eyes and spreading his arms as if revealing an elaborate stage. "Pierrot, sore and stiff from a night on the cold hard wood of the pier by the river, his head screaming as if a thousand harridans were ripping at his brains with ragged fingernails, staggered to his feet. Over him, lips pressed tightly together, eyebrows drawn and hands on hips, stood the dark figure of Arlequin. Beside him, radiant in shimmering white silk, stood the lovely Colombina.

" 'Were you aware that there was a performance last night?' said Arlequin in a tone of voice that would have offended a twelve-year-old, much less a fellow actor.

"Pierrot, feeling small and filthy before the beautiful woman, looked down at his scuffed and soiled trousers. He examined his sleeves and blouse, studiously avoiding the eyes of the diamond-clad man, who as usual looked snappy and clean; every hair in place. Especially, though, he avoided the soft, clear eyes of the woman. His misery and jealousy now compounded by pain, he suddenly decided that for once in his life he was not going to stand humbly and be berated by someone whom he at that moment abhorred. He wanted

▼

to go back to the caravan; wash up, change clothes, and be left alone. But so accustomed was he to keeping his feelings hidden behind an expressionless mask that neither Arlequin nor the woman could see his agony; his embarrassment. Arlequin was by nature something of a bully to begin with, and now that he had a lovely damsel to impress, his demeanor was doubly offensive.

" 'You ass!' he hissed. 'Do you know that the Bürgermeister attended the play last night, and that the rest of us had to improvise? Without our principal player? Without our musician? Do you know what fools we felt?' Arlequin's face grew florid as his voice grew louder. 'And, you idiot, you would pick the night that the Bürgermeister's specially ordered wine failed to arrive! We are through in Frankfurt. Do you understand that?'

"With that, the belligerent fellow grabbed the downcast, ragamuffin clown by the collar and shook him. His other hand strayed to the hilt of his dagger. Little did he know the depth of his folly in doing that. He could not possibly have known the rage born of hopelessness that welled in his colleague's breast; the anger that flared in his sad, aching mind being so treated in front of Colombina.

"With the fury of absolute desperation, the clown lunged for Arlequin's throat with one hand, while reaching for the dagger at his side with the other. At this violent turn, Colombina stepped back, her eyes wide, her hand to her mouth. Arlequin struggled to free his knife from the clown's grasp, but he found himself surprisingly unequal to his strength. The clown had always been the gentle one; the one who always backed down or went out of his way to avoid contentious situations. But now in actual combat, the blustering Arlequin was dismayed at the fiendish strength in those slender, bony hands; the iron will of that lanky frame. Now he looked into the dark, round eyes of Pierrot and saw there for the first time murderous intent. No fear and no gentleness. And the diamond-bedecked poseur was afraid.

"As the clown inexorably drew his knife from its scabbard, Arlequin clung to it frantically, until the keen blade cut deeply into his curled fingers. Then, with a scream of pain, he let go the dagger and pushed the clown away with his good arm. For a moment the

▲

two rivals stood gasping and staring at each other. Pierrot held the knife in his hand, blade downward, his knuckles growing white about the hilt. His knees shook with the anger in him, yet he held back—held back until Arlequin, face twisted in rage and prideful spite, yelled, 'You stupid, impotent little prig! Do you honestly think the troupe needs you? Why, you're a nobody. You think you'd have a chance with this woman here? You're a fool and an ass, Pierrot, and I will tell the world so from here on in, I swear it!'

"At that, Pierrot lost his restraint. Arlequin had cut him to the very quick, and he fancied he felt the mocking eyes of the woman upon him. With one vicious blow, he plunged the dagger into the bastard's breast. A look of utter shock came over Arlequin's face—almost comical, it was, so blank, so disbelieving. Then, as his warm blood gushed over the clown's white wrist, and he jerked spasmodically sideways and slid to the ground, Pierrot suddenly became aware that Colombina was giggling. Yes, giggling like a little girl. Arlequin made a frantic grab at his trouser leg before the blood welled in his throat, but the clown turned in amazement to look at the beautiful woman. Sure enough, there she stood, her eyes watching him merrily, girlish dimples flickering on her cheeks. Dumbstruck, he looked down at his lifeless companion; his own blood-clotted hand holding the wicked steel.

" 'Smartly done, my clown,' said Colombina with a gay little laugh. 'Now catch me if you can!' And with that, as if they were playing a game of maypole, she gathered her skirts and tripped off over the water meadow toward the town; her shimmering silk dress making her seem like a vision of a wood nymph dancing about a fairy ring."

His narrative finished, Pierrot's eyes started open again, and a smile formed on his wide mouth. "And that, my friend, is how it all got off on the wrong foot."

I didn't quite know what to say to him, so I asked if he had another cigar.

"Certainly," he replied cheerfully. "I always feel so much less offensive if someone else is smoking also. Here."

The old guy was so full of stories that by this time I was finding it hard to sort them all out. As I lighted the thick cigar my eyes again fell on the curious little gilt box by the clown's elbow. What on earth could it contain?

"So, what did you think of my little tale?" he asked with a self-satisfied and amused expression.

"I'm not sure what to think of it," I answered honestly, and puffed my cigar vigorously. "But two people in twenty-four hours is impressive. What happened to you after that?"

Pierrot shrugged. "Oh, nothing, really. You know—they came and cleaned up the mess and asked us to leave town."

"It doesn't bother you that you killed two people?"

"Goodness, no. Why on earth would it? The audience loved it every time."

"The audience?"

"Why of course, *mon ami!* What would be the point of going to such trouble if there were no audience?"

"But I thought . . ."

My question was interrupted by a loud and prolonged ringing of the door buzzer. "Excuse me," my host said, "but I do believe that's him now."

"Him?"

"Of course," he said mysteriously, and got to his feet. "Please come with me. It's important that you meet him, and you may never have the chance again."

With that the old man strode into the living room. I swallowed the last of my brandy and got up to follow him. Ahead of me I heard him open the front door and greet someone who had a deep voice. They spoke in rapid French, and the sound was too muffled to make out anyway. Feeling awkward—and just a tad tipsy—I hovered by the settee and pretended to examine the Daumier portrait under the dim yellow lights of the chandelier. For a while the two whispered to each other behind the partition. But as I shifted my weight uneasily from foot to foot the voices grew louder and louder, until the deep voice I didn't know broke out over the conversation

132

with a loud, stern *"Non!"* The next instant, one of the most remarkable-looking men I've ever seen came strolling into the living room as if he owned the place, stopped in the middle of the floor, and said to me with a scowl, "Monsieur, I must demand that you give it to me at once."

His rudeness and brusque manner gave me pause enough to scrutinize him closely. Tall and barrel-chested, he looked to be about sixty years of age, but with shiny black hair and thick black eyebrows. Under his fashionably baggy, knee-length coat, he wore a black cotton shirt decorated with Keith Haring's squiggly stick figures, and a pair of loose black baggy trousers. His face was deeply tanned, as though he had just emerged from one of the trendy tanning studios downtown, and he carried a fancy cane. In net effect, he looked like a fashionable, 1990s version of a Sherlock Holmes villain—Dr. Moriarty goes to SoHo, that sort of thing. Under any other circumstances I might have been tempted to laugh. But in the cavernous gallery of Pierrot's apartment, with all the period furniture and fine paintings staring from the walls, the man cut an imposing-enough figure. And his eyes were piercing—not unlike the old clown's, I remember thinking.

Before I could explain that I didn't know what he was talking about, Pierrot whisked around the corner of the partition and laid a hand on the stranger's burly arm.

"Please, Arlequin," he said in soothing tones, "this man is my guest, and this is hardly the time to make a scene."

9

▼
▲

TO SAY I WAS CONFOUNDED WOULD BE PUTTING IT mildly. There I was face to face with yet another character of the commedia dell'arte—and by all accounts the blackest of the bunch. And little did I know then that the fun was only beginning.

The forbidding, dark man turned when Pierrot addressed him, and shot the old man a look that would have withered cactus. Withdrawing his hand, the clown suddenly assumed the most obsequious, pleading attitude; twining and untwining his fingers like a little boy asked to explain why his brother has a bloody nose. A shadow of utter disgust crossed Arlequin's stern face, and he turned back to me. Never before have I seen such penetrating eyes: black as obsidian; calculating and cold. Not being able to think of anything else to do at the time—and partly, I guess, because the man's confrontational attitude got my back up—I held out my hand stiffly and returned his chilly stare. (I don't know how well this came off, because in the back of my mind I couldn't help but wonder what on earth the "it" was he had demanded of me.)

"Peters," I said, as manfully as I could manage, "Corry Peters."

He hesitated a moment, evidently caught off guard by the gesture. Then, with a sharp glance at Pierrot, he took my hand and gave it a perfunctory squeeze. "Arlequin," he said gruffly, "Camille de Corazon d'Arlequin, at your service."

He released my hand abruptly and I put it in my pocket, and looked uncomfortably at the clown. His mobile countenance clearly told me that he too was trying to think of how best to relax the tension in the room. Finally, Pierrot said brightly, *"Alors!* Well now, how nice that you two could meet at last. You know, Arlequin," he nattered on, busily pretending to tidy up, "I've just been telling Mr. Peters here all about you. Haven't I, *mon ami?"*

"Yes, indeed," I said, forcing a smile in the brooding man's direction. "Sounds like you two have had some interesting times together."

Realizing that he was for the moment outflanked, Arlequin allowed a slight smile to creep across his thin, tight lips. Faintly arching a dark eyebrow at the old clown, he shrugged his big shoulders, removed his fashionably baggy overcoat, and tossed it onto the couch. Then he sat down beside it heavily.

"I don't suppose, *mon vieux,"* he said to Pierrot with a sigh of resignation, "there would be any possibility of my obtaining a glass of brandy?"

This caused the old man to stutter in his busy bustling and throw me a rather desperate look. But before he could think of an adequate circumlocution, Arlequin—who obviously knew our host's every expression—raised his eyes to the ceiling and asked, "Well, what *have* you got to drink, Pierrot? Or did you ask me here simply to sit about with a stranger with nothing even to wet my lips?" He glanced at the heavy gold Rolex that adorned his hairy wrist, and tapped on it with his finger impatiently. "My time is not entirely without value, you know."

"Now, now, *mon mieux,"* said the clown, starting for the kitchen. "Let's not get hasty. I'm sure there is some sherry. Just let me get some glasses." He stopped in the doorway and turned to me. "More ginger ale, *mon ami?"*

"Oh, no thanks," I said, and caught a startled look from Arlequin as Pierrot disappeared into the other room. "I've already had more than enough bran . . . That is to say, sherry," I explained.

Some people have a presence that is just naturally disconcerting, and this man was one of those. I found myself trying to imagine what there might possibly be about him that a woman would find in any way attractive—unless, of course, Pierrot had been making all that up. But so far as I could tell he was just a cold fish; downright hostile. And it took every bit of diplomacy I possessed—which isn't much—just to try to seem congenial. Meanwhile, he sat there and scowled at me.

After an awkward silence, Arlequin said suddenly, "So, Mr. Peters, you wish to visit Hokusai. May I ask why?"

"What?"

He lowered his eyelids patiently. "I asked you why it was that you wished to visit the master Katsushika Hokusai."

As I opened my mouth to explain that, once again, I hadn't the faintest idea what he was talking about, Pierrot practically leapt back into the room, singing, "Oooh, just a little suggestion of mine, Mr. Peters. Not to worry. Arlequin—here. Please have some sherry and I will explain. You see," he went on, perching himself birdlike on the arm of the settee while Arlequin watched him like a cat, "I thought it would be just the thing for my friend here—to help him with his research." He shot me a quick, pleading smile. "To help his research on the book he is, you know, researching. Isn't that so, *mon ami?*"

Arlequin looked from one to the other of us suspiciously. "Exactly what sort of book is it you are writing, Mr. Peters?" he asked presently.

"An art history," I said, to a surreptitiously approving nod from the clown. "Pierrot suggested I study the, er, Japanese artists as well as the, um, Europeans I was, er, studying."

I hadn't a clue what I was getting myself into, of course. But Pierrot evidently had something in mind, and by this time I was too intrigued not to go along with him. I tried to smile brightly.

Arlequin regarded his sherry glass thoughtfully, then said, "I don't know what you are up to, Pierrot. But very well. It can do no harm, I suppose. I now understand why he has it. However," he said to the clown, suddenly stern and threatening, "he must give it back the minute we return. Is that understood?"

"Why of course, Arlequin!" Pierrot said.

At this point mystification began to get the better of me. "Would one of you please tell me what this *it* is? I don't mean to pry, but it would be nice to participate in this discussion—and I wouldn't mind knowing where it is you're taking me to. In case you hadn't noticed, it's nearly one in the morning."

The two characters exchanged a quick look. "Just one moment," Pierrot said, and got up and went back into the kitchen.

"You must understand, Mr. Peters," said Arlequin, rather less testily this time, "that it is not easy to see Hokusai. He has been dead for over a hundred and fifty years. So it will take the combined powers of my colleague and myself to get you back."

"Get me back?" Understanding the situation seemed hopeless, and in exasperation I almost yelled, "Back from where?!"

"Damn it, man!" Arlequin barked in reply, "do you or do you not wish to meet the master?"

Pierrot darted back into the room quickly, carrying the little gilt box. "There there, Arlequin," he soothed, "Mr. Peters has not yet had the situation explained to him. But by your leave I shall do so now."

The dark man sat back again and moodily sipped his sherry.

"Now," said the clown, coming over to me, "I told you earlier that this was for you. And so it is." He handed me the box.

"For the time being," Arlequin interjected.

"Yes, yes. For the time being, *mon mieux,*" said Pierrot. "Now, *mon ami,* the box may *not* be opened, but while we are away you must keep it with you at all times. Do you understand? You let it go at your dire peril."

I took the heavy little box—surprisingly heavy for its size—and hefted it in my hand. "I understand," I began, "but *where* on earth are we going at this time of the morning?"

"To Edo, of course!" Arlequin said brusquely. "Where else would you expect to meet a Ukiyo-e master?"

In response to my startled look, Pierrot nodded at me solemnly. "You see, Mr. Peters, I simply could not do it all by myself. Some things are just too strenuous for a man of my years. But with

Arlequin here, it shouldn't be much trouble. So," he said, and sprang to his feet, "if we may get started?"

He beckoned me up and held his hand out to me. With a grudging sigh, Arlequin also stood up and took Pierrot's other hand in his. "This is positively the last time, *mon vieux,*" he said to the clown. "Positively."

I hesitated a moment before taking the old man's proffered palm. I'd never even attended a séance before—which was what this business had begun to look like. I felt silly, I guess.

"Come now, Mr. Peters," Arlequin said sharply. "We haven't got all night, you know."

"Just hold onto the box, *mon ami,*" Pierrot said, "and you will be fine. Come."

Like reaching for a red-hot poker, I extended my shrinking palm toward his. The moment we touched . . .

When at last I opened my eyes, I had to clutch the clown's hand hard to keep myself from pitching dizzily to the matted floor.

"He is okay, this one?" inquired a soft, mellifluous voice with a gentle edge of concern.

"He's just fine," I heard the gruff growl of Arlequin reply.

I opened my eyes. And blinked them shut again quickly, for brilliant, watery sunlight poured into the airy room through the thin rice-paper panels that surrounded us. But in that brief initial glimpse I was amazed to see that we stood within an almost empty room, apparently constructed almost entirely of bamboo. Pierrot and Arlequin stood beside me, and in front of us stood a small, singular-looking Japanese man. I don't think I'd ever before thought about what Shunshō's most illustrious student might have looked like, but upon opening my eyes again to inspect my surroundings, I found him to be quite unlike anything I might have expected. Katsushika Hokusai was short and barrel-chested, with a round face and large humorous eyes. He had long, glossy black hair gathered into a sort of bun on his head, and his skin was so fine and smooth a twelve-year-old girl would have envied it. He was dressed in a long, pearl-grey, unadorned kimono, and he stood smiling at me, hands clasped on his ample belly, a long-handled *sumi* brush held like one of Pierrot's cigars in his teeth. The artist's figure was silhouetted against an open vista of a tidy, well-tended garden, a low stone wall, and beyond that a roadway along which men and women bustled singly and in little groups, some of them stooping under the weight of various containers and bundles tied to the ends of stout bamboo poles slung across their shoulders. Beyond the roadway were open rice fields being tended by women with their white kimonos gathered and tied about their waists; some of them bent to plant their slender, grasslike bundles in the ankle-deep water, others in the farther distance prodded huge black water buffalo along with thin sticks, their encouraging voices now and then wafting musically back to us. The bright, clear air was redolent of jasmine, and some small warblerlike bird sang a gently grating, chattering song nearby, above the distinct tinkle of running water. Behind Hokusai, and facing out at this lovely panorama where two of the large translucent panels had been slid open, stood a low lacquer table of sorts; besides ourselves, the only object in the room. On it were a neatly arranged assortment of brushes of various sizes and thicknesses. A square of mulberry paper had been wetted and stuck down to the lacquer's shiny surface. And beside this stood a small ceramic bowl of water, a *sumi* ink-stone and a long brick of the caked ink, decorated with a colorful *hon*.

But what most struck me about the place was that, behind the small, pleasant sounds just mentioned, there loomed a profound silence which made everything about us—sights and sounds—as sharp and clear as crystal. The place was, in a word, enchanting.

I quaffed a deep breath of the refreshing air, and turned my attention to our host, who removed the brush from his mouth and, putting his hands together in a gesture of greeting, bowed deeply.

"Welcome to my home," he said in that gentle, liquid voice I'd marked before.

"Thank you," I said, and stopped with my mouth open. "Are we speaking English or Japanese?" I asked everyone in general.

"What is 'English'?" the artist inquired, a puzzled expression skewing his fine features.

Pierrot cleared his throat. "We are speaking Japanese, of course, Mr. Peters." Then, in an aside, he muttered, "Perry won't get here for another thirty years or so yet."

"Oh. Well, it's very nice to meet you, Mr. Hokusai," I said, in what sounded like English to me. It was a curiously satisfying sensation, as I'd always envied people who could speak the tongue.

The artist grinned broadly and clapped his hands once. Instantly, a lovely young woman in elaborate dress entered through one of the side panels that served as the walls of the airy room. Behind her I could see a corridor of dark, gleaming wood. She deftly slid the panel closed behind her with her foot, and with a backbreaking bow glided into the room carrying a large tray laden with teacups and an ornate teapot. This she set on the floor next to the lacquer table and, with studied grace, folded herself down beside it and began to prepare tea.

"Please, gentlemen," said Hokusai, "some refreshment."

We followed him to the low table and seated ourselves cross-legged on the floor around it. Only then did I notice with something of a shock that I was no longer wearing the corduroy trousers, heavy sweater, and jacket I had put on that morning. Instead I had on a handsome kimono of heavy blue silk, bound at the waist with a broad black sash or cummerbund of sorts. After inspecting my own attire carefully—under the curious gaze of our host—I looked about and noticed that Pierrot and Arlequin were similarly attired. Something about Pierrot's long, pale face made him look particularly incongruous in the outfit, and he evidently knew it, too, for he threw me a self-conscious smile. Arlequin, meanwhile, looked quite dashing in his kimono, and all his attentions were concentrated on the lovely courtesan, who blushed under the intensity of his gaze.

When the tea had been served, first to Hokusai, who held his cup in both hands, murmured some silent words over it, and then by gripping the lip rotated it several times, we all took sips of ours.

▲

"Well, my friends," said the artist to Pierrot and Arlequin, "it is good to see you again. How long has it been?"

"Several years, I should think," said Pierrot, and downed his tea in one gulp as if it were brandy. The attentive woman instantly poured him another.

Hokusai smiled broadly at me, and for the first time I saw that the corners of his eyes were alive with a network of fine wrinkles, and that there was the faintest trace of a mustache on his lip. How old was he, then?

"I see you have brought me another student," he said. "It's good that you could come in the spring. Many artists prefer the cold contrasts of winter; the cranes stringing across the white sky, and the frosted buds of the cherry. These are noble subjects, to be sure. But I have always preferred the spring, and the blush of new life." He glanced at Arlequin, who continued to keep his eyes glued to the courtesan. "And the women are most beautiful in the spring, too. Is that not so, my friend?"

Reluctantly, Arlequin withdrew his attention from the woman's face and turned to Hokusai. "To the lovely ladies," he said, and for the first time smiled. He looked quite nice when he smiled, I thought, and I wondered why he didn't do it more often.

The tea was thin and green, but oddly aromatic, and its vapors in the room combined with the jasmine to form a complex, almost intoxicating atmosphere. I drank the liquid down and looked at the old clown, who was watching Arlequin's wordless seduction of the young lady disapprovingly. "Pierrot," I said, "what is the year?"

"It is eighteen-oh-eight, Mr. Peters. And it is the second week of May."

"Third," Hokusai corrected him gently.

"Third," Pierrot repeated, with a deferential nod.

1808. Then the artist was forty-eight years old. Yet, except for the tiny crowsfeet, he didn't look a day over twenty-eight. And he still had forty years of work ahead of him. I set my empty cup on the lacquer table top gingerly, and reached to roll up the voluminous sleeves of my kimono with my other hand—and realized I didn't have

141

the little gold box. Quickly I looked up to Pierrot. But as usual he caught the observation before it was released.

"In your pocket," he said with a knowing grin. Sure enough there it was, making a heavy bulge in my gown.

"So," said Hokusai in a businesslike tone of voice, "how may I be of service to you, Mr. Peters?"

Seeing as how I hadn't even known until—I think—a matter of minutes before that I was going to see him, I obviously didn't have the foggiest idea of what he could do for me. But Pierrot stepped seamlessly into the breach.

"I believe," he said, "that Mr. Peters could best be served by a drawing lesson. A lesson such as only you can give, master."

The artist bowed his head slightly at the compliment. "Very well, then. He shall have his lesson." He clapped his hands again sharply, and the young woman, who by now was gazing steadily into Arlequin's cobralike eyes, started to her feet quickly, bowed, and left the room through the opening. Arlequin's eyes followed her out of sight. Then he too got to his feet and, on the mumbled pretext of going out for some air, followed her around the corner of the building.

Pierrot shook his head slowly from side to side in disgust, but the artist only smiled and said to him, "Not to worry, my friend. Fumiko can look after herself. And if she can't? Well, she has been well trained in the gentle art. It is, after all, what she is here for."

"He is a vulgar man," said the clown sorrowfully, and poured himself some more tea.

"He is lusty," said Hokusai. "And now, Mr. Peters; would it be convenient for you to join me in a little walk—to find a suitable subject for our lesson?"

"Sure," I said, and got stiffly to my feet. It had been a while since I'd endured the lotus position, and a walk sounded like just the thing to get the circulation back to my legs. And it was such an unexpected pleasure to suddenly find myself in Japan almost two hundred years earlier than I had any right to be, on a beautiful spring day. The bitter cold and sooty gloom of New York seemed barely a memory already, and I couldn't wait to see what the countryside had to offer.

"Excellent," said our host. "Then if you will excuse me for a moment, I will go get a roll of paper and some mats—and, of course," he said with a wink, "I shall have something a little stronger sent in for Pierrot-san, to enjoy while we are out."

At this, the old clown's eyes fairly brimmed with thanks.

▼
▲

Looking back at Hokusai's residence from the slightly elevated vantage of the dusty grey rutted road, I was surprised to see how large a complex of buildings it was. The bright, spacious room we had been in was but an addition to a veritable warren of one-story cubicles, all linked by a raised walkway that wound in and out and over a lovely rock garden with a gravel pathway that had been carefully raked seemingly hours before. Roughly following the path and the walkway was a stream of clear water, evidently diverted from the irrigation ditch that fed the rice paddies across the road. I stopped to admire this panorama, and Hokusai, nudging my elbow, said sadly, "It is a beautiful home, is it not? But I will be leaving it soon."

"Leaving? Why?"

He smiled hesitantly. "I am, alas, a man of uncertain fortunes, Mr. Peters. I have had already too many wives, and yet I never seem to learn. I owe my lord a great deal of money, and my last wife still more. This will be the third home I have had to abandon to pay my debts. I am, unfortunately, a restless man, and I have succeeded in giving away thus far most of what I have worked for in my life. And each time I resettle, I build my own floating world in which to work." The merry, rotund little man had a distant, pensive expression on his face as he took me gently by the elbow and urged me on. "You are, of course, aware that I have managed to make myself unwelcome in virtually every school I have ever been associated with. It is because of my inability to remain faithful to any discipline whatever for longer than I feel I can derive some intellectual sustenance from it. The moment I begin to feel that my brushes are becoming dry, I shoot off in another direction—and it is never one of which my erstwhile colleagues approve. They are all about style. My master, Shunshō, was a brilliant and talented man. A Ukiyo-e master of the first order. And yet, I had to break with his teachings, because I found the venerable style to be about surface; detailed and graceful, to be sure. But detailed and graceful surface, nonetheless. I found, perversely perhaps, that I needed something more than courtesans and the trappings of royalty and the ceremonies of the privileged to make my eye break with empathy. The stylized landscapes and perfect birds in perfect skies left no room for spontaneity; no room for the happy accident of the hesitant line; the sure but searching stroke. There were too many other possibilities cleft to my innocent eye. And I was one of those with the misfortune to be born with a brush in my hand. And when that is the case, one's brush is prone to wander where the pundits have it it should not. And my brush wanders far from the conventions of styles and schools, my friend. It wanders happily into bedrooms and rice fields; bathhouses and printmakers' sheds; it wanders to the monkey-trainer's table and the fishmonger's toilet. Worse yet, it wanders with no set purpose; no set design, other than that it strives to make each and every line carry volume and grace—and truth, above all."

While the master talked, I let my eye wander before us, up the winding road past the rice fields terraced greenly up the sides of the soft hills, and to one side of these, across the uneven paddocks where the sling-horned buffalo grazed in bovine complacency to the distant glint of water. The sky arched overhead in cerulean peace, barely diluted with downy clouds like fine fibers of cotton strayed into a woodblock print. By the roadway a host of weeds and wildflowers grew thickly, and here and there a stunted, wind-wrecked pine hunched over our path, casting a thin, irregular shadow of pale violet. A constant if desultory stream of people passed us going in the other direction, and at the sight of the artist they bowed and muttered, "Good day"; and he managed to smile brightly at each and every one, while keeping up a train of conversation with me.

▲

When we had walked for quite some distance, I became aware that we seemed to be making for a sharp, wooded escarpment, up to which the road led in a broad arc ahead of us, snaking into the blue woody shadows with a glimmer and a gleam. Looking back behind us I was surprised to see how far we had come, and I commented to Hokusai that, though I was aware we had been walking for fifteen minutes or so, the distance we had traveled seemed out of all proportion to the time we'd been on the road. At this he smiled knowingly and said, "It is an illusion caused by a peculiarity of the terrain hereabouts. For many years I, too, was often puzzled at the ambiguous distances that I sometimes saw in a painting I had completed only the day before, when I knew I had represented as accurately as possible the view before me. Some objects I knew to be quite close appeared quite distant; and far-off things seemed too near. In fact my home is much nearer than it looks, and if you look carefully, you will see that it is a trick of perspective caused by the size of that hill there behind it. It is an unusually large hill, far bigger than those immediately around it, so its presence disturbs the cozy order of diminishing size we expect—or are taught to express in our representations of things. But there you are: that is precisely the reason I have had to divorce myself from so many schools of thought. Nature simply does not do as we should like it to. The world about us is a mass of inconsistencies; indeed, that is the only consistent thing about it. And the artist must learn that true beauty lies not in the comfortable orderliness he often may be inclined to bring to his pictures, but in faithfully capturing the essence of its beautiful inconsistencies. It is good that you noticed the phenomenon. It will make it easier for you to understand the lesson we are about to discover together."

With that, the little man turned and began fairly bounding up the steepening road, and I panted to keep up. Soon the dark, blue-green pines closed overhead, and the air grew heavy with their sharp, sweet scent. For another ten minutes or so, the artist led me on into the woods, his eyes to the front, evidently heading for some specific point. Small birds called back and forth to each other from deep in the shadowy foliage, and an occasional bright shaft of sunlight smote down to the needle-carpeted floor like a theater limelight, and in it, tiny particles of dust and minute insects danced in crazy spirals or settled on the gilded ground.

Suddenly my guide plunged off the road to the right, making for what was evidently a break in the trees. I stumbled after him, unaccustomed to walking on uneven ground in thonged wooden sandals that didn't seem to want to stay under my feet. Presently the wood did indeed give out, leaving us atop a high, bare cliff, sucking in our breaths quickly at the loveliness of the panorama before us: far below, in shades of jade and water green, stretched an Oriental land of counterpane; the tiers of terraced rice fields randomly folded between soft low hills, riven here and there with snaking white roads and dotted with little clusters of thatched-roof houses. We looked out over a wide valley—or rather down it as it sloped to the glimmering sapphire sea, just discernible on the low horizon.

"It's glorious," I exclaimed, momentarily hoping the master didn't expect me to try to reproduce such a landscape.

"Yes," he replied, "it is one of my favorite views in all Nippon, and one of the reasons I decided to build a home nearby. Yet it is not what I brought you here to study. Come with me."

With a sigh of relief, I followed him a little way along the cliff edge till we came to a wide, flat stone that jutted out over the giddy valley. In contrast to the generally blackish color of the surrounding cliffsides, the large stone was of a warm pinkish-brown hue; as if it had been placed there for our benefit by a giant hand from the sky. And yet it had obviously been there for eons, for in the center of it, its twisted roots buried in the matrix and causing irregular fine cracks to radiate across the stone's surface, stood an ancient, thrawn, and wind-polished bare tree. Judging by the nubs of limbs that still studded its trunk here and there, it had once been a pine tree of considerable girth, although it had been bent bowlike by the wind. Not a patch of bark remained on it, and any needles it once bore had long ago reverted to earth and been carried away by the rains.

Hokusai stopped and surveyed the scene critically for a moment through narrowed eyes, then, walking a little to one side, he unrolled the mats he had been carrying and spread them on the ground. He sat down cross-legged on one of them and bid me come sit beside him on the other. When I'd made myself as comfortable as possible on the hard seat, he handed me something wrapped in soft cloth.

"Here," he said, "are your tools."

I looked at the bundle uncomfortably. Although I had done quite a bit of painting as a student, I had never been very good at it, and I hadn't so much as touched a paintbrush in almost thirty years. Perhaps, I thought, now would be a good time to tell him that I was not an artist, only a critic and admirer. But there was no need.

"Do not look so terrified, my friend," he said with a gentle smile. "I expect nothing of you at all, other than that you watch and listen. When you have watched me for a while, I suspect you will feel tempted to try your own hand. But do not expect too much of yourself either. The point here is not to learn to draw in one afternoon, but to learn to see; to learn to understand what I am after."

Hokusai unwrapped his own little bundle, and withdrew a long, soft brush, a roll of paper, and a corked ceramic bottle of water. These he laid out on the mat before him, and from his pocket took a *sumi* stone and a cake of dried ink. I followed his every move attentively as he splashed a small amount of water from the bottle into the shallow "well" of the sumi stone; then, holding the cake of ink flat against the sloping surface of the stone, he ground the ink into the water smoothly, every so often stirring the darkening liquid briskly with the tip of the cake and adding more water. When the ink was of a consistency to his liking, he took up the long bamboo-handled brush, and holding it almost perpendicular with a grip somewhat reminiscent of the way a violinist holds a bow (only with the brush end down), he set it to the surface of the pool of ink, allowing the pointed tip to wick up the liquid into the bundle of hairs. When the brush was loaded with ink, he unrolled a sheet of mulberry paper with his other hand, holding one end down firmly with the tip of his foot.

"Now," he said, speaking more to himself than to me as his eyes wandered over the surface of the sculpted tree, "the thing one must remember about the art of the brush is that perfection resides in the *attempt* to capture the essence of the subject, rather than in the finished work. No painting is ever truly finished; the artist merely decides that the attempt can go no further."

The artist's hand hovered hesitantly over the paper, now and again seeming to feint in one direction or another before coming back to the center. Following his gaze, I tried to determine what aspect of the tree he would begin with. But for the longest time he simply sat there, tense, with a look of excruciating concentration on his round face.

Finally he sat back, took a deep breath, and laid down his brush. "No," he said suddenly. "This will not do. A moment please." With that, he got to his feet, letting the sheet of paper curl sharply back to the roll. He approached the old tree as if he were stalking a wild animal that might at an incautious movement start up and fly. When he reached it, he straightened up and stood before it for a full minute, motionless. Then, with the quick flash of a smile, he returned and sat down once again.

"I have painted this tree a hundred times or more," he said, picking up his brush and resetting the paper before him, "yet every time the attempt grows harder. Perhaps it is that the better you know a subject, or the more deeply you understand it, the harder it becomes to describe it. I do not fully understand why this should be, but experience has taught me it is so. Even a tree as venerable and solid as this one can prove to be a mirage; as if it does not truly exist until I put it here on the paper. Yet that obviously cannot be so, and the longer I look at it, the more it resists my efforts to capture it."

I had begun to wonder how by merest propinquity I could ever hope to absorb so subtle and complex an aesthetic, and was about to ask Hokusai why he continued to return to this particular tree, when with a quickness and surety that was marvelous to watch, he suddenly set the brush to the paper and in several graceful movements put the old trunk right where he wanted it. With pauses between his darting marks on the paper, he completed the entire study in a matter of a minute or so, set down his brush, and regarded it with an expression of utter distaste. I craned my neck to see the image clearly.

"That is beautiful," I said, frankly in awe of the picture—not to mention how quickly it was made.

"It is not successful," he said. "I will have to try it again."

I could hardly imagine anything being more successful, lest Rembrandt himself were to suddenly appear with his easel and oils beside us. But I kept that thought in check. The way things had been going it wouldn't have surprised me if the old Dutchman were to do just that.

"I don't understand," I said. "It looks to me like a lovely work. Why is it not 'successful'?"

Hokusai smiled and rolled the painting back onto the scroll of paper. "Here is where your lesson begins in earnest then."

The artist placed his hands flat on his knees and gazed at the tree as he spoke. "Have you ever heard of Kōetsu Honami?"

"No, I don't believe so."

"Then you have a great deal of study before you, as there is not time right now for me to tell you about him in proper detail. Suffice it to say for now that he was one of the greatest of all our masters. He lived more than two hundred years ago, near Kyoto, where he was a sword master to the court, as had been some six generations of Honamis before him. They are yet, though the court of course long since moved here to Edo.

"Kōetsu created a village of artisans at Takagamine, to the north of Kyoto, and dedicated the last years of his long life to the making of pottery, the study of The Way of Tea, the practice of Buddhism, and the making of books of calligraphy and painting. The dishes and pots from his hand are unsurpassed, save perhaps by some of the works of the Kenzan masters, and you would better understand what the art of painting is about were you to take the time to study them. It is important to understand that Kōetsu was an amateur—a self-professed amateur—in all but the care and craft of the sword and the art of calligraphy, a field in which his work was admired even in China. But for myself, I have seen few paintings more beautiful than those that decorate some of his dishes, nor any man-made objects more lovely than some of his tea bowls. And though the quality of his lacquer works is disputed even today, he was in fact a master of that craft also.

"I recommend Kōetsu to you, my student, because in him you will discover both the evenness and the uncertainty that are necessary to art. He failed often, and his failures are utterly superb. I wish only that I could fail in such a fashion. But I fear my hand has been spoiled to some degree by my association with Ukiyo-e; with the floating world. I spent too many long years illustrating and decorating in a discipline that valued the symmetrical composition over the accidental perfection. The older masters of the grand age, particularly the masters of Zen, understood the need to appreciate the world for its accidents. They knew how to see themselves in the context of nature; unnamed, un-self-centered, and unafraid. Kōetsu himself must have also been a Zen master, whether he acknowledged it or not—and it would have been in his nature not to—because when I look at some of his paintings I see where the polished discipline of his aesthetic has been cracked; where he has allowed his brush to veer from the anticipated line; the blossom that would balance the composition.

"You ask why my painting was not successful? Think about it. You have seen the work, and it is not necessary to see it again. But look at the tree. Do you see how it is not graceful? Can you see how, from this angle at least, the curve of its back breaks the line of the stone's surface unpleasantly?"

Obediently I looked, and tried to see what the master was talking about. I compared the distance from the ground to where the line of the stone's rounded edge met the twisted trunk; and above that, where the rest of the misshapen tree hung over like the writhen torso of an old, old man. True enough, I thought, when you focused solely on the tree itself from our low perspective, its presence in the field of view was rather lopsided; like a hasty or inexpert snapshot; an unintentional exposure.

"I see," I said, "how this particular point of view might not be the most advantageous for getting a balanced picture of the tree's actual shape. I mean, it doesn't look as graceful from here as it did from over there, where I first saw it."

"Precisely. And that is why I chose this position, as I have many times before. And yet my drawing, no matter how carefully I prepared myself for the attempt, is a balanced diagonal across the paper; the horizon, indicated only with a faint wash, far higher than it is seen from here in actual fact. The painting, in other words, is a deliberate device."

"But isn't every work of art a deliberate device? Isn't that, in fact, what makes it art?"

"No, my friend. What makes it art is the discipline. And the discipline is self-imposed in an effort to achieve harmony. But it is important to recognize, as a look at Kōetsu's pots would show you, that harmony is not always in accord; more often it is merely in acceptance."

I was beginning to find that Hokusai was fully as good at talking in riddles as Pierrot himself. But then I had in fairness been forewarned. "I'm not sure I understand," I said.

The artist laughed merrily. "I did not expect that you would. You have not spent as many years attempting to paint this tree as I have. And there are some truths that can only be known through patient experience, for there are no words in any tongue that can fully describe them. That is why we use metaphor, both in language and in the arts. There is simply a limit to human consciousness, and the longer one strives through one's art to describe the nature of the world or nature of beauty, the more one becomes aware of the fact. So one is forced to fall back on models; to describe, as it were, through association. But even that is an imperfect means, for everyone brings a different set of experiences to any metaphor. And thus we see that the human mind is just like nature; indeed it is an integral part of it. That is a concept of Zen—but also of all great art.

"Painting is fundamentally about process, not about message. But perhaps it would be easier to explain it to you this way: there is an element of the Tea Ceremony called *Wabi*. It is difficult, if not impossible, to describe the term precisely. But roughly it is this: there is a need in every human mind to feel at one with the world around it; to be in harmony with the very reality of things. *Wabi* is a concept that stresses a cultivation of solitude; the solitary contemplation of one mind as itself in relationship to the totality of physical experience, all prejudices and preconceptions removed in as far as that is possible. My attempts to paint this tree are essentially my own form of *Wabi;* an effort to understand that tree as it truly is, not as training and habit would have it be. My brush can make only the merest metaphor of what I experience when looking at that tree, yet the noble effort is to make the metaphor as accurate as possible. It is ultimately a hopeless task, of course. Only the tree can truly be itself or reveal its true self to the eye; and even that is misleading. But I am a painter, and as the nightingale must sing, so must I paint."

And on that cryptic note, the lesson was evidently over. The little maestro got to his knees and began carefully stowing away his things. I had not even unrolled my packet, and I offered it back to him.

"Keep it, student, as a gift. You may wish to use it someday, when you find an old tree of your own to challenge your perceptions."

I thanked him and got up to roll up the reed mats. These Hokusai insisted on carrying under his arm. "Now," he said, turning his back to the tree without a further glance, "I will take you the other route home, so you may see something of Edo, where the Emperor, son of the Shinto gods, keeps his court."

I followed the little man as he agilely skipped down from the cliff edge back into the deep green woods, and wondered how it could be that the most famous of Japanese artists—to Western eyes at any rate—the man whose print *The Wave* had had such a profound influence on Degas and Lautrec and had inspired countless imitations that continued even into my own time—how could this great man be so self-deprecating? There was something in his attitude toward his work that seemed almost regretful; as if at heart he dearly wished he were anything but a painter; as if, indeed, he felt as though he had no choice whatever in the matter.

We worked our way down to the road again by a slightly different path that brought us out on the other side of the escarpment, clear of the woods. Now on either side of the way grew dense, shoulder-high thickets of delicate maples and azaleas, under which low canopy a veritable sea of bright green ferns rippled gently. But soon this foliage, too, gave way to rice paddies again, beyond which I now saw the city in the near distance. Once again we began to encounter people on the road, some of them farmers and laborers; others obviously well-to-do merchants, dressed in finely decorated kimonos of lively colored silks, wearing elaborate caps and hairdos. Soon the intoxicating scent of jasmine and leaf mold began to give over to the sharper smell of cow manure, drying fish, and pungent soy. As we entered the first narrow, winding streets on the outskirts of the city, these odors became almost overpowering, to the point where I had difficulty resisting the urge to cover my nose and mouth with my hand. But my guide seemed entirely unaffected.

The streets were crowded and noisy, alive with the cries of fishmongers and artisans, awash with shopfronts displaying colorful fabrics of all sorts, and countless items made of iron, ceramic, and bamboo. Occasionally we passed a teahouse from which the refreshing scent of green tea wafted temptingly, and at other times the smell of incense and sandalwood mitigated the general miasma. Once, upon rounding a corner, we were almost bowled over by a troupe of scurrying men wearing wide round straw hats and carrying between them a kind of carriage of intricate lacquer-work and gilt. Large, rose-colored peonies decorated each of its doors, and as it passed, people stopped and averted their eyes.

"Who was that?" I inquired.

"The Emperor's daughter, I expect," Hokusai replied, "although it might also have been some emissary to the court. Come, we'll take this road here. It is quicker, and I want to get back before Pierrot and Arlequin have the chance to start a fight." He shot me a quick grin. "The last time they got to fighting, they nearly ruined an entire house."

With that, the artist turned left abruptly and plunged into the crowd that had closed behind the passing carriage. He must have had a little New Yorker in him, for I was amazed at how freely he used his elbows and shoulders to shove his way through the press. I

▼

followed suit, and in a few minutes we were back out by the watery green fields, the cloying smells of the city receding. I was surprised to see how little time it took to get back to Hokusai's home. What had given me a false impression of its relative isolation was that the large hill the artist had pointed out to me effectively hid the sights, sounds, and smells of the nearby city, and once one rounded the hill on the road, one felt as though one were a hundred miles out in the country somewhere. It was a unique and envious setup for a man who both valued his solitude and needed to be near the center of commerce, and I felt sorry for the poor guy that he had to abandon it. But there was little chance to ponder such things any more deeply, or to put any more questions concerning art to the master, for we no sooner rounded the hill than the sounds of a heated argument reached our ears, and Hokusai, a look of panic on his gentle face, broke into a sprint toward the house.

10

▼
▲

"THIS TIME I WILL RUN YOU THROUGH FOR GOOD, YOU sniveling little moron!" I heard Arlequin yell as I dashed into the room behind Hokusai, who stopped suddenly and stood aghast at the sight that met us.

In a corner of the room cowered the old clown, his arm raised to fend off an impending stab from a long and wicked-looking samurai sword clutched in both hands by Arlequin, whose face was flushed with fury, and whose eyes practically started from his head.

"Yoo hoo," crooned the clown from under his arm, "we have company!"

"Good!" Arlequin retorted without turning his head. "Then they are just in time to witness a justifiable homicide!" With that, he drew back his arms and prepared to lunge with all his might at Pierrot.

"Wait—please!" yelled the artist.

"Wait?" responded Arlequin with a sneer, but momentarily staying the blow nonetheless. "I've *been* waiting for over five hundred years to have done with this miserable clown!"

"Yes, yes, my friend," said Hokusai, warily walking toward him, hands held out, palms up, "but please do not dishonor me by spilling my friend's blood in my home. You would force me to commit *jisatsu.*"

At this Arlequin turned his head and lowered the shining blade somewhat. "Suicide? Why? It would not be your fault."

"Yes, Arlequin. But such a thing would be too great a smear on my honor, and custom would demand it. So, by killing my friend you would be killing me also. And I was not aware that you, my guest, held me in such low esteem."

Arlequin lowered the sword still further, perplexity overcoming his anger. For a moment he stood undecided, glancing from Pierrot to Hokusai and back. The old clown kept his arm held right where it was.

"Okay," said Arlequin at length, "I'm sorry, maestro. I certainly meant no harm to you. I'll take him outside and kill him on the road where he can bleed to death in the dirt."

"Is it really necessary to kill him?" I said, a bit surprised at my own boldness. The last thing I wanted was for the bully to turn the sword on me.

"Yes, it is," exclaimed Pierrot with a sudden giggle. "I tried to cut his dick off."

"What!" said Hokusai in disbelief.

"Well," said the clown accusingly, and lowered his arm a little to glare at his assailant, "I caught him trying to bugger your maid."

"I did no such thing!" screamed Arlequin, again raising his sword furiously.

"Did too!" taunted Pierrot.

"Did not!"

"Did too!"

"Okay, now you're dead meat, asshole!"

But before the razor-sharp blade could reach its mark, Hokusai leapt forward with amazing quickness and grabbed the bigger man's thickly muscled arm. "Help me, please," he shouted over his shoulder to me, and in a somewhat less-than-enthusiastic fashion I shuffled warily across the room to grab Arlequin's other arm.

He struggled like a crazy man, but the three of us somehow managed to wrest the weapon from him without anyone getting slashed or stabbed. But no sooner had Pierrot got the sword in his hand than he pointed it at Arlequin. "Okay, *mon vieux*," he declared, "*now* I shall cut your balls off!"

Again Hokusai and I had to dive into the fray, which this time sent us all tumbling to the floor, crack into the fragile rice-paper wall, and through it onto the gravel path outside. I smacked my head sharply on the gravel as I fell, and must have passed out momentarily, for when I came to my senses and stood up, aching in every joint, Hokusai was holding the sword high over his head and shepherding the two insult-hurtling characters back into the house.

Once we were all inside, Hokusai called for an assistant, who entered the room with a terrified expression on his face and took the sword from his master as if it were a snake that might turn suddenly and strike him. "Restore it to the armory," commanded the artist, and shut the sliding door behind him. Then he surveyed the room with a look of dismay. His beautiful lacquer table had been overturned, its effects scattered across the floor. There was a gaping rent in the wall where we had fallen through, and the other panels were slashed here and there where Arlequin must have chased the clown around the room. In all, it was a pretty embarrassing situation, and I, for one, felt like a complete fool. Yet there was no sign of contrition on the faces of the two antagonists, who continued to glare at each other— or in Pierrot's case, make idiotic faces and animal sounds.

Finally Hokusai turned to me with a rueful grin. "You see what I mean?" he said. "It is always a pleasure to see these two arrive, and a greater one to see them depart."

Hearing this, Pierrot got ahold of himself long enough to say, "I'm sorry."

Then Arlequin also bowed his head and growled something of the sort. An uneasy calm settled on the group, and I stood a little aside fidgeting nervously and wondering what was to happen next. I was beginning to feel quite tired, and I had begun to wonder how—if at all—we were going to get back to New York, 1999. At length, though, Pierrot answered the question for me.

"Well," he said to Hokusai brightly, "I guess we'd best be getting back now—before we do you any further harm."

"You're not going anywhere, *con,*" growled Arlequin, "until your friend here returns the box to me."

I reached into my pocket and felt it sitting there heavily. I'd almost forgotten I had it, but I was more than willing to hand it over if it would ease the tension and expedite our leaving. But as I was drawing it out, I suddenly remembered Pierrot's strenuous caution not to let go of it while we were away. So I stood there holding it in my hand, undecided.

When Hokusai's eyes lit on it, they widened suddenly. "You are holding the secret, then?" he exclaimed in surprise.

"The secret?" I said.

Pierrot stepped forward quickly and laid a slender hand on the artist's shoulder. "Patience, maestro," he said in a whisper, "there is not time, and he knows not what he holds."

"Ah, so," the artist responded, and exchanged a knowing glance with the clown.

"Well *I* damned well know what he holds," thundered Arlequin, taking a step toward me, "and I demand to have it back. Now!"

"Arlequin," said the clown, moving to block his way, "you know perfectly well he cannot get back without it. You will have to wait till we return."

"To hell with him! Let him stay here." Arlequin moved to try to step around Pierrot, but Hokusai also moved to block his path.

"I think," said Pierrot, throwing a curious look at the artist, "that perhaps my colleague needs to calm down before we can resolve this matter to everyone's satisfaction. I don't suppose, maestro, that there are any geisha in the immediate vicinity? It would, I believe, be just the thing to encourage an attitude adjustment in Arlequin here."

At the mention of the word, Arlequin's ears pricked up— almost visibly, I thought.

"But, my friend," Hokusai stammered in amazement, "I thought . . . ?"

"Yes, yes, I know," said the clown with a wink at me, "but I fear I have been unjust, and have misunderstood my companion's motives. He has hot blood, you see, and I am beginning to think that only the touch of an experienced woman can cool him off."

"It couldn't hurt," muttered Arlequin approvingly, but also looking at Pierrot with disbelief.

"Well," the artist began, evidently baffled at the change in the clown's attitude, "I suppose I could send my boy to the city for one. It is not far, after all."

"Good, good," Pierrot exclaimed delightedly, "and while he is on his errand, I can see to the cleaning up."

I confess that even I was mystified by the old man's sudden change in humor, and I slowly inched the gilt box back into my pocket, fearful of another sudden outburst from one of the men.

But there was no need to worry. "Very well, then," said Hokusai with a shrug, "I shall send Tomiko." He clapped his hands twice. In a trice the little assistant returned to the room, glancing fearfully at the two sworn enemies. "Did you tend to the sword, Tomiko?" asked the artist.

"Yes, master," said the young man with a bow.

"Well, you will need to take it to the sword master to have it wiped and seen to tomorrow. But right now I want you to go into town and fetch the prettiest woman the geisha house has to offer. Tell her she will be well paid, but that I want her to come immediately. Is that understood?"

"Yes, master."

"Go then, and be quick about it."

With another deep bow, and a furtive, fearful look at the glowering Arlequin, the young man turned and shot out of the room as if he were being chased by a samurai. Arlequin suddenly smiled happily, but when he looked at me, I saw that his eyes were still cold and threatening. "Do not go too far with that box while I am entertained, my friend," he said coolly through his grinning teeth.

"I hadn't planned to go anywhere," I returned, as coolly as I could.

The big man bowed slightly to each of us in turn, and strutted out of the room whistling the cancan. As soon as the sound of his footsteps disappeared down the gravel path, Pierrot stuck his head through the torn panel to check after him. Then, going to Hokusai with a cunning look on his face, he said, "Quickly, maestro! You must follow him and see that he is kept busy. We must go now. There is not a moment to waste."

"But you are going to *leave* him here?" Hokusai blurted, and ran his fingers nervously through his hair.

"Oh, don't worry about Arlequin," the clown said reassuringly. "He won't stay long. In fact, as soon as he has finished his carnal tryst with the young lady, I'm sure he will be more than anxious to come after us." Pierrot turned to me—and then, on an afterthought, back to the deeply puzzled looking artist. "But I beg you, maestro, don't let him have a sword!"

All this was beginning to sound mighty odd. "Pierrot," I said, "I thought we couldn't make it back without Arlequin. Where are we going to go, then?"

"Don't worry, *mon ami*. Don't worry," said the clown with a hearty laugh. "I was lying through my teeth. I can get us back perfectly well by myself. I simply thought I could kill two birds with one stone by begging Arlequin's assistance; introduce you to the master here, and get rid of my nemesis for a time. Oh, he'll get back eventually, but it will be much harder for him without the box, and the effort should keep him occupied for a while—long enough, I hope, to allow me to track down Colombina in Europe. And don't fear, Katsushika," he said, suddenly turning back to the exasperated artist, who was staring at the ceiling with a tragic look, wringing his hands. "Just tell the bastard that we've gone into town to visit Hiroshige. I guarantee he'll leave in search of us immediately."

"Oh, Pierrot-san," said the artist with a shake of his head, "I honestly do not know why I like you."

"Ah, well," said the clown with a great grin, "nobody does. But there you are." He extended a bony hand to the little man, who took it fondly, although the tragic look lingered on his brow.

"I will go and see to Arlequin, then," he said with a bow. "I would however greatly appreciate it, my friend, if the next time you come, you would leave him behind. He may drive me to suicide yet, for want of peace and quiet!"

"Thank you, master. And I assure you I will never trouble you with him again."

The artist stepped over and shook my hand also. "It was good of you to come," he said. "Do not forget the tree. When you learn the secret you carry, you will understand it better and, I hope, understand our friend here, who long ago mastered the Zen of the world."

"Thank you," I said. "I won't forget." In my pocket I clutched the box, feeling its surface with new interest.

"Well then," said Pierrot, *"On-y-vas!* Take my hand please, Mr. Peters."

With a last look at the Japanese master, I put my hand in the clown's, and . . .

▼
▲

Of course I don't have a clue how such tricks work, but if it has anything to do with aiming, Pierrot's aim was quite bad. I wound up on my knees on the icy pavement outside the building, the old man nowhere to be seen. I stood up carefully, checking myself for possible injuries. But I had none. I was back in my corduroys and jacket, the little box was in my hand as it had been before we left. I looked at my watch—and suddenly panicked: it still read just ten minutes to one. And it was pitch dark out. Had I lost a whole day? Could we really have been gone that long? And where was the old man? I gazed up and down the street anxiously. It was bitterly cold outside, and I'd begun to shiver violently after the spring warmth of Edo.

As I was about to trot to the corner to look up Tenth Street, Pierrot's voice rang out from somewhere above me. Looking up I saw his head framed in the kitchen window.

"Are you all right, *mon ami?*" he inquired.

"Yes," I shouted up, "but it's a bit chilly out here."

"I'll be right down."

In a few minutes he was opening the gate, apologizing profusely for his "miscalculation." When we reached the apartment at last, Pierrot fetched me a warm blanket, had me sit on the couch, and headed once more for the kitchen. He returned a moment later

▼

carrying a glass of something, which he handed me and said, "Drink this down. It will warm you up."

Obediently I took the glass and tossed the contents down in one gulp—and practically choked to death.

"My God!" I sputtered. "This is brandy!"

"Of course, my friend. It is the best thing on a cold night."

"But I was expecting sherry, Pierrot. I thought you were out of brandy."

"Oh, I only said that for Arlequin's benefit, *mon ami*. I am *never* without brandy. But it will be a very cold day in hell, as they say, before that shit gets any of it." He smiled at me broadly and sat down across the room on the couch. "I have hoarded this liquor for several centuries, you see. It is some of the finest ever produced in the Armegnac region, and Napoleon would have had me shot if he had ever suspected I was the one who spirited it away—if you'll pardon the pun—for it was his favorite vintage. It is good, no?"

"Yes," I replied, finally beginning to get my breath back. "It's good, but it's pretty potent, too." Still, I began to feel the liquid warmth spread through my body pleasantly. When I had relaxed somewhat, I again turned my attention to the box. Pierrot watched me as I inspected it closely in the dim light of the sitting room.

"I understand your curiosity," he said after a while, "but you will know the secret soon enough my friend. For now, please, just leave the box on the table there beside you. It will not disappear, I assure you, and you have no need of it right now."

Reluctantly I did as he asked. But, as you can imagine, my head was full of questions. I looked at the old man, who looked back at me with his eyebrows raised in anticipation of questions.

"How did you do that?" I asked finally.

"How did I do what, *ami?*"

"How did you get us to go back in time to see Hokusai? You know what I meant."

"It was magic, of course, Mr. Peters. You should know that."

"But were we—was I really there? Or was it all just a dream?"

"Have you ever had such a long dream in so short a time?"

162

Evidently he had seen me looking at my watch. "That doesn't answer my question," I persisted.

"Of course not, *mon ami*. But I cannot answer all of your questions, now can I? It is sufficient, I think, that you should have had the experience. And I hope it was an enlightening one."

I thought over some of the things Hokusai had said to me about his reason for painting, and smiled. "It will be in time, I hope," I said. "To tell you the truth it may take me a while to figure out what my 'lesson' was all about."

"Well, that is not surprising, Mr. Peters. After all, it will take the master himself nearly another forty years yet to figure it out himself. And he has—that is to say *had*—a better grasp of the business than all but a very few of the great ones."

I thought about this for a time—Hokusai's curious reluctance to claim any particular talent or accomplishment for himself. But I was too tired to consider it in any depth just then.

"You may, of course, stay here the night if you wish," said my host.

"I believe I could fall asleep right here," I said. "It has been a pretty long day."

"Very well, then, my friend. But there is a guest room just through there, next to the bathroom. And I will put out some clean towels for you." He stood up to go.

"Thank you," I said. But then another question hit me. "Pierrot," I said, getting up to follow him, "can you visit the future, too?"

"Please, Mr. Peters. You have not been listening to me. Of course I cannot visit the future. There is no future to visit, other than the guesses of your mind. How can I visit what hasn't happened yet? Didn't I tell you that time's arrow travels in one direction only?"

"But . . ." I began stubbornly. "Oh, never mind. Lead me to a bed."

"Certainly, my friend. This way, please."

I threw the mysterious little box one last, lingering look, and turned in.

11

THE LAST DAY OF THE CENTURY DAWNED FINE AND cold, but I missed that part of it because I slept until about eleven o'clock. I opened my eyes to an unfamiliar ceiling, and lay staring at it perplexed for some time before I remembered that I was at the clown's apartment. I climbed out of the soft, deep, comfortable bed slowly, shivering at the chill. By grey daylight I could see that I was in a little room, absolutely packed with curios of various kinds, and, like the rest of the place, jammed with paintings. Among these was a rather nice portrait of Pierrot by the German painter Ludwig Kirchner, and beside it one by a hand I didn't recognize until I stood up to look at it closely. It was an Arthur Dove in pale greens, browns, and soft pinks. On the bedstand, under an old frayed and tarnished lamp, was a little dusty silver frame, the glass so dirty I couldn't see through the glare on its surface. I picked this up and wiped the face with a corner of the coverlet, and gasped. It was an old photograph of the most beautiful woman I'd ever laid eyes on. Surely this had to be Colombina. The shot had caught her in the act of tossing her head of shining black hair playfully, a brilliant smile illuminating her sweet, girlish face. Her eyes were huge and dark, her nose and mouth finely sculpted as in ivory. She was dressed in a heavy coat whose style was rather hard to pinpoint: it might have been something worn at the turn of the century, or it might have been a garment I could see on Park Avenue that very morning.

I spent a long time looking at the remarkable picture, at last comprehending the old man's glowing description of the woman who so dominated his thoughts. But what did she look like now? If she were as old as the clown, how would those classic features have altered with age? Contemplating that was depressing, and I put the picture back on the bedstand and began to dress.

When I walked out to the kitchen, I found that my host had been up well before me—if indeed he'd been to sleep at all. The counter was littered with dishes left over from what looked to have been a large and hearty breakfast: the smeared, golden crusts of dried egg yolk, scraps of toast, jam-covered knives, and half-eaten links of sausage. The old man sat at the table reading the newspaper, a pair of square, wire-rimmed spectacles perched on his long nose.

"Bonjour!" he bellowed as I entered the room. "I trust you slept well?"

"Like a log, thanks."

"May I make you some breakfast? I have some excellent Brown 'N' Serve sausages and plenty of eggs."

"Thanks, but I think I'd settle for a cup of coffee."

"Bien sûr, mon ami. It is there on the counter."

I helped myself to a steaming cup, and sat down in the chair by the window. Patches of floral-patterned frost crept in from the corners of the streaked panes, through which the park appeared hazy and derelict. A solitary bag lady ambled aimlessly round and round the public restrooms in the center, pausing now and again to jabber to herself or to flail wildly at some invisible attacker. Not the most inspiring scene to wake up to in the morning.

Looking beyond the boundaries of the park and up past Avenue A, I saw that the streets and sidewalks were oddly empty and quiet. A sense of expectancy in the air was palpable. But somehow it wasn't the usual New Year's Eve spirit of bottled-up fun and tipsy goodwill. As I raised the cup of hot coffee to my lips, I was suddenly reminded of the entirely different atmosphere of Hokusai's beautiful bare room, and the delicious smell that came in from outdoors, and the delirious scent of the green tea. But had I actually been back in time to old Japan, or had it all been a dream, conjured with the use of some drug in my drinks? I glanced at the clown, whom I discovered to be watching me intently with the merest hint of a smile on his broad mouth.

No. There was no use in pursuing the subject further.

"I like the Kirchner portrait of you very much," I said instead.

"Yes. It is a good one," he replied brightly, relieved, I suspect, not to have been asked anything further about the "journey." "Did you also like the ones by Bonheur and Cassatt?"

"I don't think I saw those. There was a lovely pho . . . a rather attractive Dove."

"Oh, dear me. I forgot—I moved them into my room last year. Let me fetch them for you. They are two of the best."

He got up and bounded into the other room, and presently returned with two lovely paintings. The Bonheur, dated 1898—the year before her death—was one of the most singular pictures of the old fellow I'd yet seen. Vaguely reminiscent of some Watteaus I was familiar with, the clown was posed with his head thrown back playing a flute, reclining against the back of a large but cuddly looking lion. He was dressed in a shimmering costume of gold satin, with a row of big fluffy buttons down the front, and instead of the skullcap he wore a wide-brimmed hat with a long golden tassel. It was a classic Bonheur in every respect but for the subject depicted: the lion was painted as only Bonheur or perhaps Landseer could have done it, and the whole picture had that sort of luminous, translucent quality all of her best works possessed.

Pierrot smiled fondly as he looked at it with me. "Rosa was such a stubborn character," he said, and shook his head. "I was terrified of the lion—who was actually quite tame, of course. But she refused to paint me if I wouldn't pose with him. She had several of them, you know, out at her château at By. In fact she had several of just about everything. The woman was completely crazy about animals, and visiting her studio could be a trial indeed, as you were forever getting chased about by playful rams, or inspected in the most embarrassing sorts of ways by monkeys and wolves and god-knows-what-else. Still, she was a great painter; one of the best ever, and she had few rivals even among the best of the men. The critics were not always fair to her, because her attitude and individuality threatened them exceedingly. She was quite assertive of her individuality, and smoked cigarettes—practically a crime in those days for a woman—and she wore trousers most of the time, for which she had to apply for a permit from the police, if you can believe it. And she cropped her hair short, which actually made her look remarkably like Lord Byron—although no one ever told her so of course. She had a very agile tongue, and was probably pretty good with her fists, too."

The clown set the Bonheur against the wall on the table where the Goya had rested previously, and turned the Cassatt around so I could see it. "Ah, Mary, dear Mary," he said sadly. "One of the loves of my life."

This painting was as wholly different in appearance as Cassatt was from Bonheur in temperament. Executed in flat, thin washes of color—pale pinks, mauves, and earthy greens—she had painted the old man sitting against a gallery wall, with the corner of a Degas pastel of ballerinas over his left shoulder. In this image, Pierrot was dressed very much as he was that very morning; in a loose white shirt and white trousers, his hands crossed loosely on his knee, looking up at the artist with an affectionate smile. She had caught his expression exactly; his Joker chin and mouth, the almost patronizing droop of his eyelids.

"That one was painted in Durand-Ruel's gallery after one of the Impressionist shows—about eighteen-eighty-nine, I think," said Pierrot. "I remember the evening well, if not the exact date. Everyone was there that night, Pissarro, Tissot, Redon, and Degas. And what a jolly group they were! Except Degas, that is. He was a little drunk and gloomy. Probably had lost at the races again. Poor Mary and her father were forever lending the fellow money, for rent and clothing and materials and so forth. And he was forever taking it straight to the racetrack to bet on some complete loser on a 'hot tip.' Compulsive, I'm afraid. Sometimes I wonder how Edgar ever managed to do as much work as he did. He never did make much of a living from it, and if it weren't for Mary and her father, I'd hate to think what would have become of him. But there you are: that was dear Mary.

And later, when her father died and she moved out to the country to Mesnil-Beaufresne, all her artist friends followed her there, and all were welcome. She was as much a mother to everyone as she was a colleague and master in her own right. Why, she even hid me at her house once when Arlequin was out to kill me—and she told him off right properly, too, when he came knocking at the door. For all her years of living in France, she always remained every inch an American, and she wasn't the least bit intimidated by Arlequin's bluster. In fact, she found him rather comical, and used to infuriate him by laughing out loud at his posings and Don Juan airs."

Pierrot set the painting beside the other and sat down again. "Oh," he exclaimed reflectively, "why are there so few artists like Mary? But then, she was a woman; every inch a woman. Isn't it strange how the greatest of the women painters always managed to remain as women faithful to their men as well as faithful to their muse? Even Kahlo and O'Keeffe, fiercely dedicated artists both, stayed faithful to their crazy husbands until they could no longer bear the pain of being cheated on. And neither Rivera nor wily old Alfred Stieglitz was an angel, I can tell you that!"

The old man picked his teeth thoughtfully and stared lingeringly out the moody window. It was nearly noon, but the light remained wan and chilling. Suddenly he fixed me with a bright look. "Would you care for some champagne?" he asked.

"Pierrot, I just woke up," I protested.

"Very well, then," he said, with a disapproving cluck. "But you will of course forgive me if I have some. It is a special day for me, after all."

"Special?"

"Why, yes. It is special for everyone. Tomorrow we leave this baffling century behind for good: the Oistrakhs and the Presleys, the Einsteins and the Tellers, the Roosevelts and the Hitlers, the Picassos and the . . ." The old man's mouth turned down in distaste, ". . . the Warhols." With this, he got up and took a bottle out of the refrigerator. "And myself," he continued as he struggled with the foil and wire wrapped around the top, "I will be leaving America at long last. And it will be a welcome farewell."

"Where will you be going?"

"Oh, back to Paris first, I expect. I need to see my Colombina before I head on. It has been such a long time, my friend."

With a loud *pop,* the cork exploded against the ceiling, and the old clown poured himself a sparkling glassful and sat down. He closed his eyes in ecstasy and raised the glass first to me in toast, then to his lips. "Ah, that's the stuff, *mon ami.* That's the stuff."

I watched him a moment, then turned my attention back to the portraits. "Pierrot," I said, "do you have a portrait by Warhol?"

The clown sputtered in his drink, and put his hand to his throat. "Mr. Peters, please! Do let's be serious. You should have seen by now that I collect only good art. I have added very few new portraits to my collection in the last few years: a Hockney, a William Newman, a Bacon, a Joe Shannon, a John Alexander, and a lovely Gilliam. But I would rather be forced to spend a year in a cage with Arlequin than hang a Warhol on my wall."

"Why does Warhol displease you so?" I asked, a little startled at the vehemence of his response. "I agree he's not the greatest thing this country ever produced, but I can't think he was the worst."

He shot me a critical look, and deliberately swallowed the rest of his champagne before answering.

"My friend," he said then, "Andy Warhol was one of the single most destructive forces in American culture; possibly *the* worst influence on its art. He was the towering, rotting vegetable stock that symbolized everything wrong with the country's values, its loss of faith in magic. His art—if we can honestly call it that—was essentially nothing more than a highly visible symptom of the creeping decadence that began in the fifties, and has now fully flowered into the cultural stasis that threatens to poison every level of American society. In many respects, it was Warhol's popularity that ushered in—or made acceptable—the cult of stupidity. He was more than just a product of contemporary American culture; he was a champion of it. As a paradigm, I suppose his work has its educational value, but then in epidemiology so does anthrax, but one wouldn't want it in one's home."

Warming to his jeremiad, Pierrot poured himself another glass

▼

of champagne and adopted a professorial look, with his mouth drawn taut and his forehead creased. "It was largely due to the example set by Warhol that young artists opted for the money and the high life as opposed to the life of integrity and dedication. The man himself was practically characterless; banal in thought and deed. But he recognized a way to make a buck when he saw it, as they say, and also saw how easily one could manipulate a system that craved style and status; a system that had little patience with or use for substance.

"You see, my friend, culture is tricky enough a thing to sustain without letting blatant philistines assume a lead role in the business vox populi. The fact that during his lifetime Warhol attained such cultural authority was a measure of the insidiousness of the cult of stupidity. But then the CEOs of a greed-based system are *not* stupid. They may be devoid of true intelligence, but they are anything but stupid, and the ascension of Warhol and his ilk merely provided them with another means of manipulating society— perpetuating the stupidity, as it were. It was largely due to Warhol that extreme liberals got it into their heads that one could arbitrate what was or was not valuable to American culture by some sort of democratic consensus; a ridiculous idea, of course. Cultural authority has never been and never will be decided by consensus—not if the culture is to evolve in any discriminating fashion. A culture desperately needs its guardians and arbiters, and they will ultimately come down on several sides of every question, and will in their own time inevitably be pragmatic and, of course, unpopular. So it has been for centuries, and will, I suspect, continue to be so. Except here, that is, where I fear the process has been neutered beyond redemption. The overt capitalism of the system has forced many artists, critics, and other would-be arbiters of American culture to unwittingly become Marxists in their insistence on politicizing every aspect of the arts. Cultural anarchy cannot be far off."

The old man shook his head, then flashed a quick smile. "But there I go again," he laughed. "Warhol always affects me like that."

"I'll never mention him again," I said—and meant it.

"Good," Pierrot said, and got to his feet. "Well then, if that is over with, may I suggest a more enlightening way to spend our last day together?"

"Certainly," I replied, and was suddenly saddened by the prospect of his departure. "What did you have in mind?"

"You said once that you wanted to visit the Metropolitan for some reason. If you wouldn't mind my accompanying you, there is a certain very special painting I would like to visit again before I have to go, and I would like you to see it with me. Is that agreeable?"

"Of course." I wondered what picture that could be, but figured it was best to wait and see. Pity he was going, just as I was learning his mysterious nature. "When do you want to leave?"

"As soon as possible, *mon ami*. That way we can take our time, and still leave the evening free for a proper ringing in of the new millennium. I would like to wander about a bit, to fix the city in my mind." He looked suddenly pensive. "It may not be here very much longer—at least not as it has been all these years."

▼
▲

Outside it was sharply cold, and a few stray lints of snow floated on the stiff wind, like the random bits of ash from a burning building somewhere. Pierrot stopped on the sidewalk for a moment and held out his hand, then took a deep breath. "Ah," he said heartily, "New Year's!" And we started up the street at a brisk pace.

But despite my companion's smile and renewed satisfaction with the day, I found it hard to summon a properly festive spirit. Rather than heading up the East Side, the old clown turned west on Fourteenth Street, and as we made our way leisurely around Union Square, any nascent excitement I might have harbored at the prospect of being present at the birth of a new millennium gave way to a vague anxiety; a creeping melancholy of the kind I'd felt on my fortieth birthday, in spite of how hard I'd tried to ignore the event entirely. And later, walking uptown along Sixth Avenue—quickly now, continually glancing over our shoulders for an empty taxi (what few there were on the road that strangely quiet afternoon seemed uniformly occupied)—I was aware that for the first time in my experience of the city, I could distinctly hear our footsteps, and those of the few other passersby echoing up the wide street, resounding hollowly off the towering concrete-and-glass facades. What with so little foot or vehicular traffic, the dirtiness of the avenue and sidewalks became distressingly obvious: crushed Styrofoam cups edged crablike along the gutters in the sooty wake of passing buses; scraps of fabric and paper litter skittered softly along walls or eddied about the steam issuing from pavement vents. The rank, cloying odor of jam-packed humanity that I had formerly associated with the subways now pervaded the upper airs, seeming to settle in and cling to our clothes and hair.

Decay. In the final hours of the century that had seen the city's rise to prominence as the cultural capital of the Western world after the decline of Paris, New York was dying. And to judge by the expressions on the faces of the scant pedestrians we passed, everyone believed it at last. As we walked past the Empire State Building, the titanic grey structure seemed almost to shudder with stillness. No crowds surged in or out of the massive lobby mall through the Deco doors under the wide awning; no one hawked T-shirts or magazines or hot dogs at the curb front. And as we hurried through the building's looming shadow along the littered perimeter of Herald Square, I glanced up at it uneasily, for the first time not so much in awe as in fear. The thought crossed my mind that a modest-sized earthquake here might easily topple the megalith, smashing ten or twelve entire city blocks into rubble. A slight shudder crawled up my spine. I'd never seen New York in such a mood, nor had I ever before entertained such morbid thoughts about it.

Seeing my expression and evidently guessing my thoughts, Pierrot seemed amused. "What a long face!" he said with a grin. "But everything dies eventually: races, cultures, fashions . . . cities."

"And you?"

The question caused him to look pensive. He glanced up at the bright sky peeping down on the shadowed street between the ranks of skyscrapers. "Eventually," he said quietly. "But I have a long

▲

time to go yet; and that is good news for you, if not so good for me."

I let the answer dangle there, and turned my attention to the avenue again. So he was to die one day like the rest of us, and leave artists to their own devices once more—as they had been for who could say how many millennia. As hard as it had been to accept the old man as authentic, it was now hard for me to conceive of Western culture without him, or at least without his crazy spirit. I recalled how out of place he had seemed in Japan; dressed in his fine kimono and sitting in Hokusai's studio. And yet something about his personality, something of his magical quality, had also been evident in the Ukiyo-e master's cryptic talk of the purpose behind his efforts to capture the truth of what was before him—and always doomed to fail. The clown's wistful recollections of past times and acquaintances bore something of the quality of Hokusai's ruminations on the inevitability of utter artistic failure, and at the same time the conviction of the validity of the process. I suddenly remembered an article I'd read some years back in a scientific journal concerning the archaeological study of ancient ceramic kilns in Moravia. The Czechoslovak kilns, dating to some twenty-six thousand years old, had been full of bits of blasted ceramic figurines and other objects that proved to have been fashioned to explode in the heat. The Paleolithic artifacts had been deliberately mixed with just the right amount of water or mammoth fat so that the glassy clay could not fuse properly during the firing process—tens of thousands of them. A particular line from the report stood out in my mind: "The high fracture rate encountered . . . strongly suggests that what was important was not the final durable product but rather the process of making and firing the objects."* Was this in fact the same esoteric impulse that Hokusai tried to explain, and Pierrot's life seemed to exemplify, at work so very long ago? Could early man already have had so refined a concept of the entropic nature of existence? And if that were so, did it imply that

---

*Vandiver, "The Origins of Ceramic Technology at Dolni Věstonice, Czechoslovakia," *Science* 246 (November 24, 1989): 1002.

the making of art in all its forms was essentially an expression of futility? Was Pierrot's lifetime effort to attain the love of his Colombina also ultimately futile?

But the questions were too many and too large to contemplate just then, so I walked beside my companion in silence for another couple of blocks until a cab finally responded to our whistles and waves.

There was a particular liquor store Pierrot wished to visit at Eighty-fifth and Amsterdam, so we skirted the park and headed up Broadway. The cabbie proved to be one of those stony-faced, barely grunting sorts whose presence tends to discourage open conversation, so we spent the ride in silence, staring out the windows on either side, watching the city pass. I was relieved to see that there were more people about on the Upper West Side, though still fewer than I would normally have expected. Snug in gaily colored coats and scarves, they tramped up and down the wide sidewalks, gathering at storefronts to check out the post-Christmas bargains garishly displayed in the big windows. Liquor stores, naturally enough, were particularly busy—the clown's favorite being no exception, and he stood in line for quite a while before emerging with an enormous bottle of champagne under his arm. At his suggestion we set out walking again, to cross the park to the museum. We ambled up the street past the rows of tall, elegant town houses closely hedging the manicured sidewalks, each with its carefully tended little garden and slender sycamore in its circular iron grille. Yet even here we saw signs that not all was well. On a few buildings, ugly graffiti marred the once beautiful brownstone walls, and here and there stacks of garbage and discarded furniture gathered about stoops and curbs showed where the occupants had either moved out or were in the process of doing so. For so many years one of the most affluent parts of town, it didn't look it now. Crossing Columbus, then Central Park West, we set off up a winding footpath into the bare trees, swishing through ragged rows of drifted dead leaves.

Within minutes of entering the park, the bleakness of downtown was all but forgotten. Though the city's towering buildings were still visible through the skeleton trees, they seemed insubstantial; as if merely painted on the backdrop to a giant stage that might at any moment be lowered out of sight. Bundled-up children scampered gleefully in the playground, scrambling over the monkey bars and whizzing down the bright red slides, plumed breaths hanging in the air behind them. And on the baseball diamond, adults engaged in an unruly impromptu game, while all around us coveys of lovely, leggy Columbia University students chattered to each other as they strolled or bicycled along the path, now and then tilting fresh, rosy faces to the sky, as if to take in what little sunlight groped down through the chilly clouds.

"Do you think it will snow today?" I asked the old man, who seemed quite preoccupied with all the young ladies.

"Perhaps," he replied, "but not till we least expect it." He grinned at me happily. "There is a great deal to be said for the winter. I know some complain that in winter the women wear too many clothes. But I think they look tantalizing in their wraps, with their cheeks flushed and their eyes shining. *N'est-ce pas?*"

"You don't hear me complaining."

Exiting the park on the east side, we turned right on Fifth Avenue and walked briskly down to the museum. Cold as it was, there were still plenty of people perched on the broad steps, reading or chatting with friends, and I began to feel positively seasonal as we wound our way up through the crowd and into the big building. Once inside the high, domed foyer, Pierrot practically danced up the stairs and headed straight for the Modernist wing. Now he was hurrying right along, hardly pausing to glance at the glass-cased rows of ancient Greek pottery teeming with elegant black figures on red ground, graceful as women themselves. There was almost no one inside. A few young students promenaded solemnly about in pairs, whispering to each other and pointing to various works. And the usual little bands of elderly folk clutched each other's frail arms unsteadily as they loitered to gaze at paintings through thick glasses, smiling and nodding to themselves like owls listening for mice in a quiet evening wood. But Pierrot wended his way among them skillfully, striding determinedly past the room full of Degas's beautiful pastels of bathers and dancers, past David's *Death of Socrates;* the Turners, Manets, and Goyas. He made a beeline for the big partitioned room that harbored the Gauguins, van Goghs, Matisses, and Redons. But he barely glanced at these. I cantered to keep up with him, as it was obvious we were nearing the particular picture he had in mind, and I was curious to see any image that could make him hurry so. Around a corner and past the Rodin display, into a small chamber . . . and he suddenly stopped dead in his tracks, almost causing me to run into him.

"There," he said, giving me a sharp look. "This is what I brought you to see. To give you faith."

Following his pointed finger, I saw that we faced one of Amedeo Modigliani's beautiful nudes. And though I'd seen the image many times, I found that in the clown's presence it assumed a clarity and brightness I'd not been aware of before—as if it had only just been completed. As if the paint weren't yet dry on the canvas. She lay languorously back against an indistinct arrangement of pillows and draperies. Her brown eyes looked brightly out at us; coquettishly, almost. The corners of her mouth were turned up in a wistful, satisfied smile. Looking at her as if for the first time, I realized that Modigliani had not simply painted an anonymous nude here. He had painted the portrait of a woman he had just made love to; a real, flesh-and-blood personality, not a faceless model. She seemed so real, in fact—despite his stylized, elongated rendering—that I felt uncomfortably voyeuristic staring at her. Because the artist had made love to her again with the paint, fondling every inch of her delicious body as he molded her under his brush.

Who was she? Like so many of his lovers, probably a harlot or poor barmaid he'd picked up at some cafe on Montmartre. He had seduced her with those big dark eyes of his, the curly black hair that framed the face of the handsomest man in Paris. And she had taken him back to a shabby little room somewhere, this derelict aristocrat with a box of paints and cheap canvas under his arm, absinthe on his breath—and she had let him make love to her. Perhaps he'd told her he was a personal friend of the famous Picasso's—a half-truth—or perhaps he had recited Baudelaire to her with his dark, mellifluous voice, or offered her a bowl of hash, which, no matter how poor he was, he was almost never without. And after they had slept together, after they had both recovered from the poignant, fleeting rapture of illicit sex, and the haunting, hollow feeling after climax, she had posed for him. And she had watched him work, eager for him again, stroking him with her eyes. And was he again eager for her? Perhaps. But now he was a painter, totally, all eyes; fascinated to the point of obsession with the sensuous curves of her lithe body, the graceful Y of her pubis and the heavy volumes of her full breasts. Now he was moved nearly to tears by the deep orange blush that welled under her skin, the impossible blackness of her hair. Quickly now, with deft strokes sketching her outline first in sensitive dry-brush lines of sienna, he filled his canvas with her presence. Now and then he paused in his efforts and tilted his head to swig deeply from a bottle of cognac. When he did this, the woman leaned forward to lay a coaxing hand on his knee. His black eyes flashed at her momentarily, then softened, and with a playful tweak of a nipple, he pushed her gently back.

"Presque," he said. "Almost."

I watched Pierrot's thin face as he followed the lines of the master's brush across her glowing form, as his gaze lingered on her face, holding her eyes for a while. He looked as if he were about to try to speak to her. Then an expression of deep sorrow slowly drew his features long, and behind his heavy-lidded eyes I could tell he was remembering something. He no longer looked like the Joker, with that sharp, mischievous glint I had come to know. Now he looked more than anything like a prematurely aged little boy.

"It was raining, I remember," he said softly, withdrawing from the painting's spell to address me. "No wind, it came straight down, soaking everything. There was no way you could escape it. The damp got into your clothes, into your skin—even when inside by a fire, you felt as if you would never be dry again. And it was cold."

The old man's eyes strayed to the painting again, and he

shivered slightly and tightened his collar about his throat. "The streets of Montparnasse—the yellow bricks of the old buildings even—looked as though they might revert to mud and melt away. It had been raining like that for four days, off and on. The Seine was red with clay and swollen well above the footpaths on the banks, at times looking as if it might come right up the steep stone steps of the embankment and spill onto the streets. Through the gauzy curtain of rain, Notre Dame hunched hugely in the distance, its flying buttresses giving it the aspect of a ghostly grey spider stalking down to the Pont Louis Philippe. You could barely see across town to the hill of Sacre Coeur. No one was about in the city. It was too miserable. A few artists gathered in the Cafe du Dôme with the workmen and elderly tipplers, hugging themselves against the chill, sipping cheap Pernod and rereading old newspapers. Nobody was cheerful.

"It was nineteen-nineteen. The shadow of the war still hung over our lives. Normalcy seemed utterly remote. There were still Americans all over Paris—some, soldiers, who had elected to stay for a while or had girlfriends there; others who were aspiring writers or artists pursuing the mythically carefree life of *la bohème*. In five short brutal years our world had changed irrevocably. All of the old European empires—the Hapsburgs, the Ottomans, and the families and territories of venerable royalty—were gone or slowly dying away. National boundaries had been redrawn in ways that could never before have been imagined. Families now were often separated by nationality, and the knowledge that the old Europe as we had known it for so many centuries was gone left a hollow place in our hearts, even as the death of so many young men left us with the unfit, the lame, and the loverless women. The young artists and poets—most of whom had been born in the eighteen-eighties—had seemed so hopeful and vigorous before the war, in spite of their uniform poverty. Now, like everyone else, they felt disenfranchised, puzzled, and aimless. So many of their colleagues had either left the country for America or had been killed in action. At the call to arms, Braque had signed up early, and had been seriously wounded. Apollinaire was dead. Franz Marc was dead. Owens was dead, and the minds of other poets shattered. Cubism—the bright banner that had been beaten into manneristic cliché by Gris and Léger—was dead. Those who had survived the fighting, the Jew-baiting, and general havoc with their goals and disciplines intact were busy working, it's true. But they were too often loudly drunk or grimly quiet and sober, fearful, I think, of what was to come. Already it seemed as if another war might not be far off. The peace imposed by the Allied military machine was uneasy, and few people, in their heart of hearts, truly believed it could hold.

"Picasso, by now famous and well-heeled since Kahnweiler had moved him from boulevard Clichy in the slums of Montmartre to the comfort of boulevard Raspail in Montparnasse, held court at the Rotonde almost every night; drinking and debating with his sidekicks Max Jacob, Cocteau, Andre Salmon, Camus, and Malraux. His was the *haute* intellectual set. They had money of their own and plenty of rich American friends. But so many of the others fell through the cracks—artists who were either unwelcome at the trendy agora, or were simply too poor to go, and too proud to barge in.

"And then there was the rain.

"One miserable afternoon I went looking for Modi in Montmartre. Since he had taken up with Jeanne and she had had the baby, I'd hardly seen him. Nobody had, except Soutine now and then, and of course Modi's self-appointed mentor, Zborowski. But neither of them had heard from him in weeks, although Zborowski said that the artist had left some canvases at his doorstep one night, rang the bell, and crept away. Modi didn't have a place to live, as far as I knew, and I was worried about him because he had been so sick the last time I'd seen him at the Dôme. But of course he was always ill, and his incessant drinking and drug-taking only made his frail health worse. Truly he was a man born to die young. Modi was the closest I ever came to breaking the one rule I must abide by: never to interfere. With him, I almost tried to change the future; almost tried to save him from himself. Because he was so special. Of all the artists I have known in my long life, only a precious few had that special quality he possessed: an interlucence that seemed to radiate directly from his soul. Not mere charisma—although he had that, too. But a kind of

▼

compelling spiritual vitality you could feel the minute he walked into the room. Even dressed as a beggar, as he usually was because he was a genuine mendicant even by the standards of the dreadfully poor art community, Modi had the dignified air of a young prince; dashing, brilliant, vital, penetrating. He was fiercely independent. While every other painter in Paris was making Cubist pictures in nineteen-fourteen, even as war was marching across France, Modi chose to paint and carve caryatids, inspired by those he had seen as a youth among the Roman ruins back home in Italy. Sensuous kneeling women in pastel roses, greens, and blues, with swan necks and almond eyes.

"But then he was the most overtly sensuous man I have ever met. And in spite of his frayed and shabby corduroys, and greasy, stained hat—or the way he sometimes smelled after having slept in gutters for days on end—women seemed curiously unable to resist him. And he serviced them like a stallion at a stud farm night after night, in return for a warm place to sleep, a bath, perhaps—some food, some company. Mostly though, for cognac, hash, or ether. But the paintings he made of them! He re-created them so beautifully you were tempted to caress their painted flesh. And although his paintings did not sell for very much—twenty-seven francs, I think, was the most Zborowski had been able to get for one—people were beginning to realize how unique they were; works of unvarnished genius. His portraits were greatly admired, too—even by Picasso, though Pablo was too proud and stingy to either say so publicly or buy one. Had Pablo bought just one of Modi's canvases, it might have made all the difference in the world to his career. But on second thought, perhaps not. Modi was too undisciplined and antisocial to wear well with the fashionable dealers and collectors. But a few of them were beginning to hover about the area like vultures. It was common knowledge that Modi could not last much longer, not with his expressed determination to drink himself to death. They hovered, some of them, in hopes of running into him on Montmartre, desperate for a drink or food, so that they might treat him to lunch or dinner in exchange for a picture. After all, wasn't Modi famous for giving his work away? The joke was that most of them didn't know what had happened the last time a rich Englishman tried to do that. Modi knew what he and his pals were about, you see. He ate the fancy lunch, yes, and he drank the wine and liquor poured for him every time he emptied his glass. And then he set the tablecloth on fire and danced around it until the manager kicked them all out and made the schemers pay for the damages.

"It took me almost till dark to find him. And I did so only because I chanced to run into Jeanne's father, Monsieur Hebuterne. Under any other circumstances I'd have considered that a most disagreeable event. He was a stupid, conceited, and moralizing man; a two-bit grocer whose view of the world was limited to the distance of vegetable bins, over which he bargained the very last sou from his mostly impoverished customers. I had to put up with his brutish derision of Modi—"That fucking useless little Jew," as he referred to him—for nearly an hour before he would tell me where they were staying. Hebuterne was a Catholic, you see, and the worst sort of bigoted, conservative Frenchman. The fact that his child had fallen in love with, and bore a child to, a poor Italian Jew galled him to no end. It didn't matter to him that Modi was one of the most famous artists in Montmartre, for he was the type of person to whom art could never be of any benefit—the type on whom it should never be wasted.

"Modi and Jeanne, as it turned out, had been staying several weeks at the studio of one Pierre Dumars, a talentless hack who later became a dockworker in Dieppe, but who was nonetheless a good friend to Modi and his woman. He gave them shelter when he could, and sometimes gave Modi canvas—a good thing, because if he hadn't, most of it would have gone to waste under his palette knife, and we would be left with fewer of Modi's paintings. Dumars had gone out of town for a few weeks and had let Modi have use of the studio. It was kind of him to do so, but no great favor, as I soon discovered, because the 'studio' was little more than a run-down toolshed without heat, plumbing, or electricity. It was in an alley behind the Bateau-Lavoir, where Picasso and Braque had lived nearly twenty years before; easy enough to find. But Modi was not happy, I think, to have been so easily discovered.

"When I saw him I was dismayed at his appearance. His high

cheeks had sunk to dark hollows under his big eyes, which glowed with feverish brilliance. His hair was long, matted, and bedraggled, and there was a sickly smell about him. With all the rain, there was hardly a dry spot in the place. It was dimly lighted by a solitary kerosene lantern on a little table, by which light I could see the mildew creeping on the walls. Jeanne was out with the baby. '*A faire marché,*' Modi said. Shopping. But everyone in Montmartre knew she was the more effective beggar, because her small child made her an object of special pity. Modi had always been too proud and too abrasive for such work, and now, by the look of him, he was much too sick to go out. So he stayed inside, a coarse, filthy blanket wrapped about his shoulders over his eternally soiled, baggy corduroys, drawing on cheap wrapping paper by the dim light. Between fits of coughing, he drank from a bottle of ulcerous cognac.

" 'Did Zbo send you?' he asked when he opened the door. Not so much as a hello.

" 'No,' I said. 'But everyone is worried about you, you know.'

"He laughed harshly. 'Come in, come in, *mon maître*. Everyone is concerned about the Jew painter, yes? As always. That is very funny, Pierrot.' He motioned me to sit down in a rickety wooden chair while he perched himself on the tabletop next to the lantern. 'Tell me, my friend,' he said, his deep voice hoarse and raspy, 'if everyone is so worried about Modigliani, why don't they buy his paintings, *hein?*'

"His bright eye held a crazy glint as he fixed it on me around the lip of his upended bottle.

" 'Modi,' I said gently, 'you know why people are not buying your paintings right now.'

" 'Right now? Is art so much a matter of fashion then, my old friend? I thought it was your business to look after things like that, Pierrot. I do not paint to be in fashion. Would you have me making those stupid little Cubist constructions of Léger or Gris? Or would you have me hanging some of Duchamp's urinals about the city, *hein*? We have Mutts enough in the neighborhood without those. I paint only to make beautiful pictures, *mon maître,* and if people decide such things are not fashionable, then they can all go fuck themselves!'

"He tottered to his feet as he said this, trying to look threatening; trying to achieve a measure of his old bravado and swagger. But he was too weak, and he had to clutch desperately for the side of the paint-covered table as his legs gave out beneath him. I half rose to help him, but he waved me back with a glare and struggled to sit down once more. Then, realizing how foolish he must have looked in his attempt to browbeat me, he burst into laughter. But, God! I hope never to hear such laughter again. It began as a deep rumbling in his chest, swelling and gurgling until it burst forth from his lips in gouts, literally. Great gobs of dark blood and phlegm clung to his stubbled chin. And still he laughed until he started to choke and gasp and clutch at his throat.

"I felt like crying. But I did not move from the chair. He said, *Je suis désolé, mon ami,'* when he had got control of the fit, and had wiped the blood from his mouth on a corner of the blanket. 'I'm so sorry, but it's all such a huge joke, don't you see? I mean you—or anyone else—coming here; tracking me down to inquire as to the state of my health!'

" 'I fail to see the humor in it,' I said. 'You should leave the jokes to me and take care of yourself so you can paint more. The biggest reason that people are not buying your paintings, Modi, is that there are none to buy. And you know that, my friend. Zborowski and Guillaume have most of the older ones—and how many of the newer works have you simply burned? Anyway,' I lied, as I noticed the smile creeping back to his gaunt face, 'I didn't come here only to see how you have been mistreating yourself, but to beg you once again to paint the portrait of me I requested five years ago. Do you not remember?'

" 'Yes, *mon maître,* I remember,' he replied testily. 'And do you not remember my answer?'

" 'You said no.'

" 'Yes. And the answer is still no.'

"With a gesture of dismissal, he reached for the bottle again.

▼

" 'But why, Modi? You have painted almost everyone else who ever asked you. And I would pay you handsomely for it, don't you see? Why, I could even advance you some money now—that way you could buy some food and a warm place to sleep. It would take you only an hour, Modi. That's all. And if you don't care about yourself, at least consider Jeanne and the baby. How long can they last, living in this . . . this hovel?'

" 'I never asked her to, *mon ami,* ' he said bitterly, and directed his stubborn stare to the floor.

"The long, uncomfortable silence that followed was accentuated by the heavy drone of the rain on the thin roof of the shed. I watched my tragic friend as he sat and rocked back and forth slowly, one hand around the bottle, the other whitely clutching his knee. His eyes became fixed in the middle distance somewhere over my shoulder. His head lolled slightly and I shivered involuntarily, because I sensed that his once magnificent fire was about to go out. The gurgling of his breath could be heard above the din of the downpour, and his pinched features and bright eyes left me in no doubt as to the seriousness of his condition.

"Then, in a quiet, deliberate voice he began to speak, his gaze still fixed on some imaginary point—beyond death, perhaps: 'Do you recall, my friend, when Berthe Weill gave me the one-man show at her gallery? When the cops closed it down because they said the work was "indecent"? That night I swore I would never again care what people thought of my work. If paintings of beautiful women, uncovered in all their God-given glory, could be called indecent, then society was indecent. Nobody says a word about Kisling's women, or Pascin's—and his are not only pornographic, they're poorly drawn. But,' he said, suddenly bringing his eyes to focus on mine and smiling impishly, 'everything I do is indecent. Why, I guess I'm just the indecent sort: a gamin of the lowest order, *hein?* Look at the life I lead. The cops have beaten me before, Pierrot, not simply satisfied with taking their stupidity out on my work. The filthy bastards have beaten me because I was in their estimation in the wrong place at the wrong time, wearing the wrong clothes; with no money, let's say, or,' he smiled grimly, 'no clothes at all. And did I sometimes do things intentionally to annoy them? Of course. Because they are so stupid; so easily tempted to use their fists instead of their brains. But decency never got me anywhere, my friend. All it ever brought me was ridicule.

" 'I remember the day at the Rotonde when his highness Picasso first deigned to sit and speak with me; to drink a beer with the troublemaking Jew. And afterwards, everyone wanted to talk to me. Not to ask about my work, or my opinion of this or that. No. They wanted only to know what the great Picasso had said. But I wouldn't tell them that. I never told anyone. But, for you . . . Do you know what he told me, Pierrot? What that charlatan had the nerve to say to me? He said that if I kept on drawing every day, I might one day be as good as he was! The ass!

" 'And do you know, my friend,' he continued, now glaring at me fiercely, 'I did the decent thing. I sat there and I listened. I didn't raise hell, or talk to him like the dog he is—or the dog *I* am. I didn't even spit in his face, because, as much as I dislike the man, I am in awe of the artist. Do you understand what I am trying to say to you, *mon maître?*'

"I held my tongue for the rest.

" 'I am trying to tell you that the man is not the artist, Pierrot. He is only a man, with the frailties and biases common to all men— perhaps more so. The artist is another man, over whom he has no control. I have no control. And the artist, Pierrot, is indecent. He sees far too much to be a decent man. He knows that nothing in life is decent; that the entire concept is a ridiculous abstraction. A comfortable crutch for mindless fools. Life is filthy, my darling clown, and it smells bad. The artist knows this. Every artist—every true artist— knows this because his eyes see too much. This artist cannot paint you, Pierrot, because he cannot see you. You are not wretched. You are not frail. There is nothing hurting or hurtful in you to feel in my gut. You cannot know that huge hollow feeling that gnaws you when you realize that, being flesh and blood, you cannot ever be the things you paint. So you make love to them, and the feeling only gets larger.

Or you paint them, and it is diminished somewhat, for a little while. But you, *mon maître*—I can neither make love to you nor kill you, so how in God's name can I possibly paint you? I am not Picasso. I am not Velázquez. I have never wished to spend my time reinventing the visible world, playing brilliant games with forms. That is for others. I can only paint things with souls—frail, fragile, warm things that will soon be cold and imperturbable. Things that smell fragrant now, but that will one day soon stink of decomposition. As a man, as your friend, I feel inclined to say, "Certainly, *mon ami,* I will make your portrait." But the artist says, *"Non."* The artist wants only to paint what is tragic, Pierrot; what is beautiful and doomed—not what will last forever.'

"And then with a laugh—at my downcast expression, no doubt—Modi got down from the table unsteadily and, wheezing like a bellows, he began rummaging through some pictures stacked with their faces against the wall of the studio. In the dull, unsteady light of the lantern, he looked like one of the room's tall, swaying shadows; insubstantial as a ghost. I listened to the rain and shuddered as he fumbled with the canvases. Finally he turned to me and said, 'Here, my friend. Take this. It is quite indecent.'

"And do you know what he handed me?"

I tried to force myself back to the present by focusing on the beautiful woman's face. "This painting?"

"Yes, *mon ami*. This painting. It is the portrait of a woman named Clara, a young British whore he met just before he took up with Jeanne, and after his long and painful affair with Beatrice Hastings—another English woman. But Modi refused any money for the picture, and I couldn't coax him into letting me buy him something to eat. 'Then you would be just like the others,' he said, 'and you can never be like the others.'

"I cannot tell you how hurt and lonely that last remark made me feel. It wasn't intended as cruelty on his part; Modi was wild but he was never cruel. It was simply the truth. And Modi always spoke the truth, whatever else you may say of him.

"But I took the painting and left him with his bottle, spitting blood and grinning fanatically. It wasn't until I walked out the door that I detected the faint smell of ether. He must have stashed it behind the stack of pictures. It took every ounce of self-control I possessed to keep myself from going back inside and attempting to physically drag him to a doctor. But he would have struggled to the death if I had. When I got back to Montparnasse that night, I searched out Zborowski at the Dôme and told him about Modi's condition. He and his wife said they would see to it that he got some medical care. I don't know how Zbo managed it—he made very little money himself as a poet and art dealer—but several weeks later he sent Modi down to Nice for the remainder of the winter, to rest where it was dry and fairly warm in the hopes that something could be done to save his lungs. But of course it was all too late: they had hemorrhaged. Zbo managed to sell a number of his paintings in Marseilles for some five hundred francs, and sent the money to him. The vultures were ready to buy now, you see.

"But Modi shortly grew homesick for Paris, and used the money to come home. He had spent his time in Nice at a whorehouse, painting the prostitutes who looked after him. And those are some of his loveliest works. They look like angels, those prostitutes. Like angels. By January he was dead; only thirty-six years old, but looking fifty. The morning after he died, Jeanne threw herself from a fifth-floor window at her parents' home. It killed her instantly, as well as the second of Modi's children in her womb. Modi's brother in Leghorn sent the money for a grand funeral, and it seemed that every artist in Paris turned out for it—even Picasso. And now, of course, it is a very rich man indeed who can afford to buy a Modigliani, and millions of reproductions of his paintings decorate millions of homes throughout the world, because now everyone knows how great was the artist, no matter how indecent the man."

Having finished his tale, and visibly weary from the intensity of his reminiscence, the old man turned and shuffled over to a bench in the middle of the gallery to sit down. I lingered before the painting a moment longer—Good-bye, Clara—then joined him.

For a long while the old clown sat head bowed, staring at his slender hands, their long fingers resting spiderlike on his pointed knees. "Now," he intoned softly when I'd settled beside him, "you understand why he is the only great painter by whom I do not have a portrait. He was far too single-minded, too committed to his own special vision of the world to be persuaded or bribed into painting anything he didn't feel empathy for. But that, of course, is precisely what made him so brilliant an artist. Such stubborn independence of character is necessary if one is to make truly great art of any kind. I never had the privilege to know Michelangelo Buonarroti, but I understand from my father that he was similarly impossible to coax into doing things he did not believe in. It is first a matter of feeling in the gut. For the artist, emotion is the very font of reason and intellect—and what can be seen with one's own eyes. The basis for true knowledge has no name or description as precise and cozy as 'intelligence' or 'IQ.' The mind that is truly at one with the world and capable of understanding it and, to some extent, communicating certain things about it, only has an identity of its own; the ability to recognize and respect something for what it *is,* before and after it has been categorized with a name for convenience.

"The greatest artists reveal with a brushstroke, a word, or a note something beyond what you or I see as a tree, call a cat, or sway to as music. If there were no such thing as language, a great painter would still be capable of provoking vast nuance in the mind of the viewer. It is no accident that only with Giacometti did I encounter a similar resistance to doing my portrait. Alberto did eventually oblige me, but the sittings were long and grueling, and my likeness disappeared under his brush no less than eight times before being resurrected to his satisfaction. And the result, as you might guess, is not so much a picture of me, as of what he felt I *ought* to look like. And the image today looks as if he x-rayed the back of my skull to bring my face fighting all the way through it."

Pierrot grinned tiredly. "I mean," he said, "I hope I don't look quite the skull and crossbones yet!"

I couldn't meet his eyes because, truth be told, he looked at that moment very old indeed—as though he'd aged twenty years in the few days I'd known him, and the jovial personality that had accompanied me to the museum earlier might well have been an illusion.

How strange for him it must be, I thought, to be alive in the world of today—he who had been present at so many cataclysmic events in ages past. After having witnessed the Reformation, the Napoleonic Wars, the French and American revolutions, the industrial and technological revolutions, two world wars, and all the cultural, scientific, and artistic developments of some five centuries—after all that, had the events of the last few decades that constituted my lifetime been particularly surprising to him? Was it all just part of a repetitive litany of events?—an endless play in which over time the characters and sets changed, but the plot remained essentially the same? Or had the twentieth century been some sort of watershed? From my own perspective I could no longer tell. After listening to Pierrot's stories for several days, history no longer seemed as telescoped as it once had. Just a vast circle going round and round, lives and events leaving no more substantial a mark on it than the chalk lines on a timing gear. But there was one distinction marking my age that his conversation had forced me to consider in some detail: when he spoke of Paris early in the century, the intense passion of Modigliani, the heartfelt gloom of ravaged postwar Europe, he was speaking of people with a sense of oneness with events and cultural traditions that seemed practically alien today—at least in America. I glanced at him to find that his eyes had closed and his old head had fallen to one side in a comfortable doze. His crepe-frail, blue-veined eyelids fluttered with a dream, and there was the faintest trace of a smile on his lips. Where might he be wandering to in his sleep, I wondered? The rainy streets of Montmartre, searching for Modigliani—or for Colombina? Rather than move and risk waking him, I turned my thoughts to some of the encounters I'd had with the artists of my own generation; among them some of the young tyros of the Postmodern movement back in the early eighties. Of the ones that came to mind, precious few communicated either in work or in person anything like the kind of fanatical aesthetic commitment that had charged the art of Modigliani, Giacometti, van Gogh, or Gauguin. Most of them, in fact, reflected on an artistic level (of sorts) the kind of inanity that invested so much of the society of the period. But of the artists who had not bought into the art-star fashion scene, there were a few whose singleness of purpose and talent shone through as a ray of hope in the general junk. I remembered, for one, a Virginia-based painter named Allen "Big Al" Carter, a black artist of phenomenal ability and of such energy that he managed to paint himself out of lodgings on almost a biyearly basis. Al made art out of anything. He was quite poor for much of his life, and was forced because of his immense output to paint with everything from Dayglo and house paint to Rust-Oleum and kids' poster temperas. He'd scrounge for discarded sheets of plywood, cardboard, and even wallpaper, and would make sculptures of almost any material that came to hand. And if anyone entertained any misapprehensions as to his purpose in life, he did his best in every respect to dispel any doubts, by signing his name "Artist" Al Carter. He was the kind of guy who traded paintings for engine work on his car. He painted and drew ceaselessly, regardless of the exigencies of tending to a wife and two daughters. And the most striking aspect of his work was that, in spite of his early childhood in the projects, his paintings only rarely reflected the awesome misery of his own people in the inner-city ghettoes of Washington, D.C., where the murder rate steadily climbed year upon year until it resembled the casualty list of a major military encounter. He somehow always managed to paint through that; through all the dope-peddling and killing and filth—or perhaps beyond it is a better way of expressing it. He made countless pictures on idyllic subjects such as fishing on the green banks of a lazy river, or making music. He drew stylized farm workers, cotton pickers, imagined African market scenes, mothers with children, classical nudes, and delightful cartoon characters of his own invention. His art though, while superficially full of fun and joie de vivre, was, like Modigliani's, essentially a huge, poignant wish. Not life's sordid details as he saw them about him, but life the way he felt in his big heart it ought to be. And his pictures could make you smile at their joyful idiocy, or keep you rapt with their sensitivity of line and expressive detail.

▲

But the times were not ready for Al. He was one of those who slipped through the cracks. The insidious golem of television had so altered the minds of the general public that they had difficulty absorbing any art form that didn't in some fashion pay homage to its all-embracing lock on popular culture. Al's approach was just too big and gestural and honest to be comfortable for most. Only the artists who were willing to play the game—like a game-show game—all the way to the bitter end got the attention of the media and the collectors. One of the most prominent of these in the early eighties was Robert Longo.

In 1984, I had done a tape-recorded interview with Longo for a magazine, and I recalled the afternoon of our confrontational tête-à-tête well. I'd met the artist a year before at the opening of one of his celebrated exhibits at Metro Pictures Galleries in SoHo. He was, I think, thirty-two or so at the time, and very much up-and-coming. He'd garnered gushing reviews in *The New York Times* and the popular art rags, a host of younger, politically active critics having placed him squarely in the vanguard of the burgeoning Postmodern realist movement. A year later his polished style and huge assistant-built wall constructions would launch him into fame and fortune, shows at major museums across the country, and an almost mythic persona.

Like so many others of his coevals, Longo appropriated for his art the most ubiquitous possible aspects of American pop culture. His pictures teemed with monkey-suited yuppies and black-clad shapely women posed as if slam-dancing or being shot and falling; nude bodybuilders with huge penises, faceless and flexing their muscles vainly; and giant, plastic-looking roses and bronze bas reliefs à la Ghiberti—all larger than life-size, and finished in metals, glass, and plastics of various sorts with machinelike precision. From a pecuniary standpoint, his was a highly successful style; he replicated contemporary culture and society bought it back from him—at greatly enhanced prices, of course.

As a youth, Longo, like so many other Americans, had discovered the passive lure of television, and the boob tube had made an indelible impression on his art. Even in college he'd begun to develop images and sculptures based on the characters and events he experienced on the screen. He also had a fascination for pop music and just about every conceivable kind of entertainment technology. These influences he synthesized into an art form that made its first big splash with a multimedia work titled *Corporate Wars,* which I'd seen performed at the Corcoran Gallery of Art in Washington in 1980. It was a display of almost cinematic technical prowess, and this, combined with his facility for incorporating virtually any manifestation of video culture even into his static assemblages, soon landed him on the mainstream art-world maps. He was a dyed-in-the-wool New Yorker who once described himself to me as being "like this guy who runs a pizza joint over in Brooklyn."

The afternoon of our interview, Longo seemed suspicious of my journalistic intentions. When I appeared at the door of his Fulton Street studio, which fronted on the quaint, touristy waterfront marketplace of South Street Seaport, he waved his live-in girlfriend (and later art star in her own right) Gretchen Bender into another room, placed a half-gallon bottle of whiskey on a wood slab table, and said challengingly, "Okay. Let's go for it."

At that time the artist was stocky; a rooster-headed fireplug of a cockalorum with lively dark eyes that darted here and there restlessly—to match the constant gestures of his small hands. Naturally, he was attired in the approved art-star fashion: black from head to toe. His confrontational attitude, despite his small size, recalled the intimidating nature of his work, most of which was designed to reflect the sheer massiveness of New York's architecture. (It was no accident that in his own portrait of Pierrot, a piece titled *Pressure,* he had depicted the young, white-faced clown psychologically crushed under the imposing facade of a modern office building.) When we sat down to talk, it immediately became clear to me that Longo took himself and his work very seriously. There was no question that he believed strongly in what he was doing. He was no sloganeer like Barbara Kruger, Jenny Holzer, Larry Johnson, or other art stars of the time. And his work wasn't designed to conform with some overweening popular rhetoric, such as simulacrum theory or the popular "anti-aesthetic." No, he simply responded with fidelity to the artificiality he saw about him, in the media or on the streets of his city. There was a kind of guilelessness to his conversation that was at once charming and chilling. And he was not at all above launching into energetic soliloquies in praise of his own work.

He poured us both a slug of whiskey (not the sort of thing I looked forward to in the middle of the day), I turned on the tape recorder, and we "went for it."

After describing in some detail how he had suffered for his art, Longo settled into a sort of half-formulated dissertation. "To be an artist now," he asserted, "is not simply to be an isolated being in your studio. It's to have a real serious awareness of all the activities in the world. I mean, instead of being the heart, I want to be the circulatory system. I know where the heart is. I've gone through a lot of changes: from having contempt for the collector to having a certain degree of respect for the collector. Understanding the collector, and bypassing the idiots that could buy my art and destroy me . . . ."

"What do you mean?" I interjected. "Shouldn't everyone be encouraged to buy art—or to look at it and appreciate it? To support artists? I mean, isn't that the point of interaction in the first place?"

"No!" he practically yelled. "The climate that exists right now is . . . There's a lot of excess money in young collectors. So you find these people who are buying what they fear, or what they aspire to. And what they fear is riding the subways. They'd rather own a piece of the subway than ride on the subway! Or eat out in French restaurants. My situation is . . . people like Cindy [Sherman] and I are like fucking satellites."

After only a few minutes of conversation I was confused, but I did my best to keep the conversation going; to keep it from getting too far from the work itself. "Then who is the audience for your work?" I asked at length.

"That's real clear to me," Longo said, getting louder and more demonstrative as he warmed to the subject. "My audience is a board of directors. Like my friends. I mean there are people who've got eyes that you make work for. Then, after that group of people, there's the art world. Then, after the art world, there's the faceless audience. We don't care about the art world. What I care about is, I care about the faceless audience."

"But how do you get by the art world?—I mean, they're the ones who exhibit and write about your work. They're the ones who make your money."

"You do it by conquering the art world!" he replied, tossing back his drink and gesticulating with his empty glass. "In America there's a peculiar thing: like conformism doesn't exist in a way. If I could get through the art world—like if I could get on the subway and ride through Harlem and back, when you come out on the other end you become an individual. Then you dictate the terms. Like, in relationship to the art world, I knew I was good. I just had to wait for them to tell me I was good. Then, instead of allowing the audience to put me in a situation where I had to worry about the next thing I made, or will they like it, I turned it around to where I have the audience worrying will they understand the next thing I make."

He smiled broadly, spread his arms, and proclaimed, "Now my work is an active participant in its own direction. Do you know what I mean? It's like I have to consult it about its next stage, rather than me personally invent a next stage. The difference is being able to work now. *I can work now.* I can do any fucking thing I want!"

He poured himself another glass of bourbon and sipped it. I considered what he had just said—or what I understood of it. It sounded more like the game plan for an advertising campaign than a discussion about art. Glancing around the big studio—which was not, however, the one where his assistants assembled his finished works—I saw that, aside from a few small preparatory drawings and Polaroids pinned to the walls, the place was almost empty. A solitary electric guitar was propped against an imposing stack of amplifiers and speakers in the middle of the floor of the high-ceilinged main room. Indeed, the musical equipment was more prominent than any of the visual arts accoutrements. Then it struck me: rock 'n' roll. That's what it was all about. He talked about the "faceless audience," not "the viewer." In fact, the more I thought about it, the more the connection became clear—the entire art-star phenomenon resembled nothing so much as the pop-star model. And when I considered Longo's imagery—and that of his cohorts—the role seemed to fit. It was an art of loudness and size rather than of tonality and intimacy; neon rather than transparent glazes; synthesizers rather than real drummers and musicians. Longo lived in and saw only a world of plastic, concrete, steel, and glass. That was the only world that was real to him, and therefore the only one he could depict. And he sold his images of that world to the "faceless audience" by packaging it as nearly as he could in the same way pop music was packaged. It was, after all, the same audience he wished to reach and be important to.

I looked back to the feisty little artist, who sat regarding me with a slight smile tugging at one corner of his mouth. "So," I asked, "what exactly is your work all about?"

"Look," he said, "success is about reinvesting your success to become more successful. And still more successful, and so on. And then you die. To get to the top, you critics want to make sure we've suffered. But right now I can walk out there and make a fucking major work of art. There's nothing between me and that. I wasn't born yesterday in relation to the game that's going on here. I'm a generation of artists that was prematurely rushed to the front—by culture. That's because culture's gone from an industrial organization to a service organization, and people aren't making objects. People are making millions of dollars writing "how to do it" books because the act of making an object is as intrinsic as walking. So people love to fix their faucets or their cars. What more perfect time to call back the artist, because he makes the highest level of object that doesn't do anything. The closest thing to being able to make an object is to buy an object. When culture doesn't need the artist, we die on the streets of starvation or drugs, or cut off our ears. And when they need the artist, they take us out to dinner. I'm aware of this shit."

It was clear that Longo knew exactly what he was about, and that he understood the system in which he worked as few entrepreneurs did. And to give credit where it was due, when it came to making objects, few artists could compete with him in terms of sheer glossiness, size, or presence. The guy knew who he had to impress in order to make himself successful, and he had certainly done just that. But was he right that it was society or culture that "called" the artist when it needed it? Wasn't Picasso living high off the hog, rich and famous, while Modigliani was dying in filth, neglected and miserable? Had Picasso also been the calculating entrepreneur that Longo was, able to sense what his "audience" wanted and provide it? Surely there had to be more to the creator of *Les Saltimbanques* than that. When I asked Longo about the emotional inspiration for his work, he spoke of the "numbness" he felt in contemporary society; the numbness he felt at images of bloodshed and horror he encountered nightly on the television screen.

"The thing is," he said, "to take that numbness and shove it up your ass." But the bottom line was always the same: to make objects that faithfully echoed the cultural and societal values that had produced a character like himself. "This culture made me," he was fond of repeating. "Now you have to deal with me."

The last question I asked the artist before leaving him to his television was, I thought, calculated to get to the heart of the matter. It did.

"What," I asked, "do you see in your heart when you're really trying to get at who you are?"

His brows knit for a moment, then he smiled archly and replied, "When I look into my heart, I see a Burger King commercial."

▼
▲

Pierrot stirred beside me and rubbed his eyes. "Do forgive me, *mon ami,*" he said, and stretched. "Some days I feel very old and very weary. I trust I didn't keep you waiting too long?"

"No. I've just been admiring the picture."

"Ah, the picture," he said, and shot me a quizzical look. Then: "Well. I think it's time we went home and prepared to celebrate the last night of the second millennium, Anno Domini—unless you had other plans?"

"None other than a bottle of champagne and a date with the television set."

"*Bon.* I have no television, but I do have a fine magnum of

Dom Perignon here, and although I have a generous capacity for champagne, not even I could drink it all by myself."

He grinned and rose stiffly to his feet. For a moment he stood before the Modigliani and stared at it intently. Then, with a slight bow to the beautiful woman, he turned and walked out of the room. She seemed to watch him go, and her colors faded just a little.

Outside in the brisk air again, I was surprised to find it nearly dark. All the people had gone from their perches on the stairs. I hadn't thought we'd been inside for so long. But then I suppose it can take just as long to remember a thing as it took to do it in the first place.

We stood at the top of the stairs for a moment, the old man surveying the scene with a look of satisfaction on his writhen features. The lights began to twinkle on in every direction, and Fifth Avenue became a river of flashing red and white. Presently, Pierrot turned to me with a sad smile and said, "It has sometimes occurred to me that New York is a city of night. It comes alive at sunset, and it is then that its wonders are most evident; its opulence, terrors, and material triumphs. But even at night you can sense its decay. It is a city that has reinvested its success to become more and more successful, and now it is about to die."

At that remark I eyed him suspiciously, but he didn't look at me. He said absently, "I'm sure you would feel better for a change of clothes and a shower, and so would I. So I shall go back home now. Shall we say eleven o'clock?"

"Sounds fine to me."

"Good. À tout à l'heure, then." And with that his weariness seemed to leave him, and he bounded down the stairs and soon disappeared in the thronged street. I lighted a cigarette and made my way down slowly. There was a cab conveniently at the curb, and soon I'd joined the river of lights, bobbing like driftwood back down to the Plaza. I watched as the streets gradually swelled with foot and vehicular traffic. Merrymakers were venturing out now in earnest, armed against the night in their fanciest finery as if to spit in the eye of the day's inevitable revelations. Yet still I felt rather moody and apprehensive, and as I watched the crowds of people all decked out in their fashionable apparel, with smiles on their chilly faces, it seemed to me they were merely turning their taffrails to show their coffins.

Back at the hotel there was a message from Eileen, so before getting into the shower I called the paper, braced to lie through my teeth.

"Corry!" she said in mock delight. "How's the piece coming?"

"Swimmingly."

"Well, I'm certainly looking forward to seeing it. Have you got an idea of what sort of art you want—I'd like to start laying the page out with Carl."

The answer, surprisingly, sprang through my teeth of its own accord. "Just two pictures—and they'll both be in the morgue: a Robert Longo work—any Longo. And a Modigliani. Any Modigliani."

There was a long silence at the other end. Then, "Okay, Corry. Whatever you'd like. But seems like an odd combination to me."

"It won't, not when you see the piece."

"Okay, dear. See you tomorrow?"

"Late."

"All right. See you then."

Standing in the shower with hot water streaming wonderfully through my hair and down my back, I tried to come up with a first line. The lead would have to be perfect; set the tone for the entire essay. Art may look dead, but it's only playing possum. Not gone, just hiding. Something like that. I realized that, since my few days with the old clown, though I felt depressed about the situation in New York, I'd actually begun to feel optimistic about art again. I wanted to look some more. I wanted to talk to Hokusai for weeks. I wanted to meet Goya and Watteau and Picasso and Modigliani. I wanted to go and argue with Longo over whiskey. I wanted to paint, myself. But of course I couldn't. I didn't have the magic. But somebody, somewhere, had to have it. Where?

After my shower, still lacking a lead, but getting closer, I dressed in my best suit and sat by the window to smoke and watch the city get into full gear for New Year's. Even the usually empty nighttime park was alive with lights, and fireworks had begun to zing into the sky from every quarter of the city.

I must have sat there for a long time, just watching and thinking. But it seemed only a matter of minutes before it was time to leave for Pierrot's. The cab ride back down to the East Village more than made up for the lost time: it took forever. Traffic was so heavy on Fifth Avenue I feared I'd miss things altogether. But at last, and only a few minutes past the hour, we pulled up at the now familiar iron gate, and the old clown was there to meet me. Tompkins Square Park was virtually empty as usual, but there were people about on the sidewalks, and for once the area didn't seem quite so forbidding. Upstairs in the apartment, Pierrot had placed lighted candles on every available shelf and table. All the electric lights were off, and the place looked, with its heavy tapestries and throngs of paintings, eerily medieval. The many faces of Pierrot flickered dimly from the walls like memories, and in that light the clown himself seemed almost spectral.

We sat down across from each other on the two period couches, between us a coffee table laden with cheeses, caviar, and various nuts and candies. The old guy had really gone all out for the occasion. With a theatrical flourish, he produced the huge, heavy bottle of champagne and popped the cork.

As he topped up two large glasses with the spitting and crackling liquid, he said with a grin, "I trust you will suspend your usual abstemious inclinations just for this evening. It will be our last together."

I eyed the size of the glass he handed me, and thought, Oh dear. It had, after all, been some time since I'd had a hangover. "I'll do my best to keep up," I laughed, and raised my glass.

"*A vôtre santé,*" he replied, and we drank.

Well, it was delicious. I regarded my companion and host fondly. I would miss him, I thought. "Are you never going to come back to this country, then?" I asked.

The clown took another considered mouthful of champagne

▼

before answering. "Perhaps," he said, after he had rolled it around in his mouth a bit, and swallowed with eyes half closed in ecstasy. "If the country is still here in a hundred years or so. But we shall see what develops. But for now there is not much point in my staying here any longer. The world has changed again. Priorities have shifted, and I must follow where my muse leads me. And for now she beckons me back to Europe. Remember: art necessarily follows both the concentration of available money *and* dynamic culture. This isn't to say that it's not made everywhere, and at all times. It is. But advances and stylistic refinements depend very much on stimulating and responsive environments. And the environment here is no longer stimulating or responsive. And, after many years of repression, war, and uncertainty, Europe has elected to reclaim her cultural dynamism. Who may say what will happen there in the next few decades? I certainly cannot. The revolutions that began in Eastern Europe a decade ago are not yet played out. But this country is stagnating, and I suspect that nothing short of a revolution here will arrest the process. This country has played out its role in the arts; done its appointed part. The role it played was that of asylum, a refuge for the crafters of the dynamic European culture that perished during the last great war. And for a time—a short time—this country served their purposes handily. It injected their vision with fresh blood, and they gave back a measure of their own values and aesthetic impetus. And for a time American art blossomed in response, and brought its own unique dynamics to the noble process. But great art is as selfish and single-minded about its esoteric goals as America is about its pecuniary ones, and when the two become mutually exclusive, art—always—must move on. You see, *mon ami,* money is only a potential byproduct of the creative process, not its raison d'être. Once the acquisition of wealth becomes an end to itself, creativity can only be stifled, because it becomes contingent on satisfying a demand; and demand is largely generated by the mindless many. As this country has become more conservative and censorial, as its corporate and governmental establishments have attempted to appropriate and control what the artist produces—and all, mind you, under the guise of 'sponsorship' or

200

edification—it has driven the true, independent artist into bohemian status once again. Those who are unwilling to accommodate the publicly sanctioned art world with its aid of grants and other public monies—which amounts to making art by consensus and is therefore antithetical to the process—those who would maintain their independence of the system, as they indeed must, can no longer function here. Because to survive economically they have had to abandon concepts of personal spiritual attainment, beauty, integrity, or humanistic philosophy. Because they have become the makers of trendy new objects to satisfy the public's hunger for instant gratification. They have become like Hollywood scriptwriters: working by consensus and according to formula, rather than by impulse and aesthetic inspiration. Such things cannot be tolerated if the muse is to survive. So she has fled, and I follow."

I considered the clown's unflattering assessment, and realized that an entire age was about to slip quietly under time's bridge, while the merrymakers were busy forgetting what they didn't want to know in the first place—celebrating an event that would be their last of any real consequence for some time to come. And while New York was crumbling, Madrid and Berlin, London, Paris, Belgrade, Frankfurt, and even Moscow were busily rebuilding, poised to assume once again the rich mantle of the guardians of Western culture.

And the irony was that America had provided the cash and the incentive, while forgetting herself.

"It's a rather gloomy sort of thought for a New Year's Eve," I said, and drank down my champagne.

The old man didn't reply, but filled my glass once more. Then, with a faraway look on his wizened face, he leaned back and stared out the big sitting-room window. We watched in gravid silence as the Manhattan skyline grew rosy with thousands of fireworks. The whistle and thump of them was clearly audible through the thick brick walls, and served to heighten the pensive quiet in the room. Pierrot produced a cigar and lit it in a candle flame, and soon the fine stench of tobacco filled the atmosphere. Turning my head to watch him, my eyes fell on the little gilt box, sitting on the end of the coffee table.

▼

The clown intercepted my glance and said, "Tomorrow it will be yours."

I laughed uneasily. "Does this mean Arlequin will be tracking me down to murder me?"

"Don't trouble yourself over that idiot," Pierrot said. "He'll follow me, not you. And besides, what is in the box would be of no possible use to him. He only thinks it would. But that is because he is greedy and stupid, and he wants everything in the world that might satisfy his avaricious urgings. He is a fool. Don't worry about him at all, that is my job. When you return, take the box to the *Saltimbanques*. There you will find the key."

And on that cryptic note the subject was dismissed. Knowing better than to pursue it further, I made a mental note to pick up the box when I left, and turned my attention to the food. And the more I ate the thirstier I became, and the more I drank. I started when the clock struck twelve, and the entire city burst with the din of car horns and the rattle of gunfire.

Pierrot smiled and raised his glass again. "Happy New Year," he said.

"Happy New Year," and we drained them.

How many glasses are in a magnum? I'll make a point of finding out one day, because I'm quite sure I drank half of them and I don't remember falling asleep. But I must have slipped away very comfortably on the cozy sofa. And when I awoke next morning the sun had obviously been up for some time, judging by how bright it was in the room. I sat up slowly, expecting the worst. But though I was pretty groggy, I wasn't in pain as I'd feared. For a while I just sat there in a bit of a fog, gazing out over the park. It looked less depressing now, bathed in bright sunshine, though it was still dirty and vacant. The old man must still be asleep, I thought, for there wasn't a sound in the apartment. So as quietly as I could I stood up and stretched stiffly.

The empty glasses on the littered table tinkled at the movement, and a voice called from the other room, "You are awake finally?"

The voice sounded vaguely familiar, but it wasn't Pierrot's.

"Who's that?" I called, and hastily started to tuck in my shirt and smooth my rumpled clothes.

There was the sudden rattle and clink of crockery in the kitchen, and a moment later a tall, dark-haired young man entered the room carrying a tray of coffee and cups. "You see," he announced with a bright smile, setting the tray down on the table, "I timed things just right. You woke just as I was about to make the coffee."

Feeling slightly self-conscious and out of place, I sat back down on the couch as the young stranger poured me a steaming cup and stirred in one heaping spoonful of sugar—just the way I liked it. He handed it to me, and began busily cleaning up the mess Pierrot and I had made the night before. He seemed perfectly at home, and acted as if he'd known me for years. But although he looked familiar, I'd swear I'd never set eyes on him before. So I sipped the coffee and tried to think of how best to introduce myself. Perhaps he was a relation of the old clown's, or a student of some sort.

Finally I asked, "Is Pierrot up and about yet?"

The question caused the young man to giggle loudly. He straightened up and covered his mouth—just the way the old man would have done—and his heavy-lidded eyes danced merrily.

"Oh, *mon ami,*" he exclaimed when he'd recovered from his giggling fit, "haven't you understood a thing I've said these last few days? *I* am Pierrot. Did you not recognize me? I thought you understood that I begin each new century young and vigorous again. Living so long would hardly be worth all the trouble if I didn't, *n'est-ce pas?*"

Of course I could only stare at him. And so doing I realized that the young man was indeed Pierrot; his wrinkles smoothed away, now looking the spitting image of the clown in Picasso's painting. His eyes were dark and lustrous, his forehead high and shining white, and his widow's-peaked hair now glossy black, full and thick. And when he grinned at me, tickled by the surprise he'd caused, there was the Joker again.

"Come, my friend," he said at length, "I will make us some breakfast, and we can chat for a little while longer. But then I must get started packing, for I have a plane to catch and my Colombina waits."

12

▼
▲

I WAS HALFWAY DOWN THE CORRIDOR TO THE ELEVA-
tor before I realized I'd left the gilt box sitting on the coffee table.
Flustered—as much at the prospect of having to return after such a
fond and final farewell as at having been stupid enough to have walked
off without it—I turned back and pounded gently on the center of
the silver star. With my face composed in what I hoped was an
appropriately sheepish expression, I stuck my hands in my pockets
and waited.

And waited and waited. Perhaps he was in the shower. Finally
I knocked again, more loudly this time, and put my ear to the door.
But no one answered, and there wasn't a sound from within. That's
odd, I thought. The way he'd been bustling about before I left, you'd
think I would have heard something. I decided to be forward and try
the door. I turned the knob, and it swung open. And I stood back
in disbelief.

The room was utterly empty; no partition with a Cézanne on
it; no old furniture, no rugs, tapestries, or Old Master paintings.
Even the big chandelier was gone. I stepped inside tentatively. "Pierrot?" I called quietly. But my voice echoed hollowly in the other
rooms, and looking down at the floor, I saw that my shoes had
scuffed footprints in the dust. There were cobwebs thickening in the
corners and piles of dead flies drifting in the grooves of the window-
sills. No question about it: this apartment had not been occupied in
a very long time.

My head reeled. Could I possibly have had the wrong flat? But no; looking back, I saw that the star was still on the door. Holding my breath with mingled feelings of sadness and trepidation, I walked toward the kitchen. Well, at least it was still the same grease-stained yellow. I surveyed the room with rising wonder until, with a skip of my heart, my eyes alighted on something on the dirty linoleum countertop. Under the circumstances I was prepared to mistrust my eyes entirely, but when I walked over to it there was no doubt: the little gilt box sat there, dull and dusty, next to an ancient empty cognac bottle.

I picked it up, blew the dust off of it, and hefted it carefully. Yes, it was the same box, and the little hasp was still locked tight.

"Thanks, my friend," I said to the emptiness, and turned my back to the melancholy winter light nudging through the filthy window panes.

Needless to say, I was now more anxious than ever to get back to Washington, to be able to open the box and, perhaps, understand at last all the old man had tried to tell me. I hurried back to the hotel, packed as if Aunt Christa were threatening to do it for me, and raced to Penn Station.

I just missed the departing Metroliner, and the forty-five minutes I had to spend waiting in the noisy, echoing station were just plain maddening. But the next train was right on time and practically empty, so, making myself as comfortable as I could, I settled back to fidget away the next three hours. When the conductor had taken the tickets, and the other passengers had relaxed into various modes of preoccupation and conversation, I withdrew the little box and inspected it closely. What could it possibly contain that Arlequin would fight for it so? A huge diamond? A magical scroll? That was more likely. It certainly looked a fitting container for something of the sort; the top was slightly arched, like the lid of an old seaman's chest, and decorated with a veritable tapestry of scenes containing tiny figures. Indeed, they were so tiny that it was virtually impossible to decipher what they were doing without the aid of a magnifying glass. More legible were the numerous decorations and inscriptions around the sides. These were consistent with the old Romanesque chests I'd noticed in Pierrot's apartment on my first visit there: fantastic animals chasing each other around the corners, and weird heads and laughing faces, like the gargoyles on European cathedrals. Where had the box come from? I inspected the bottom to see if there might be some sort of a maker's mark; a stamp, or a date. But what there was instead— and this was enough to convince me that it had indeed belonged to the old clown—was a moon-face, pressed into the bare bronze as if struck there with a punch.

Try as I might, I could learn nothing more of the secret of the gilt box. So eventually I put it back in my pocket, unfolded and switched on my laptop computer—and promptly turned my attention to the swiftly passing scenery. And as it rolled by the windows of the train, faces began to roll through my mind: the hollow, sunken cheeks and fever-bright eyes of Modigliani; the soft, sweet, round visage of Hokusai; the burly, pouting face of Goya. And then came the stern but understanding face of Fran, looking up from a sink full of dishes somewhere in Ohio. Each face in turn seemed clearer than the next, although I hadn't laid eyes on most of them: Watteau was there, Picasso, and the shaggy face of a Cro-Magnon, too. And presently I became aware that they were all speaking to me at once— urgently, in a dozen different tongues. And I couldn't make out the words. Then, above them all, materialized the face of Pierrot—or Pagliacci or Pedrolino or Pantaloon or Gilles or whoever he was— young and shining with youth, his broad, good-natured mouth half ·mooned in a merry smile.

"So what are you waiting for, *mon ami?*" he asked. "Don't you have work to do?"

I looked down at my computer screen and contemplated the keys. The screen announced READY in easy-on-the-eyes green, but I evidently wasn't. On impulse I typed, "Now is the time for all good men to come to . . . ," and fell asleep.

I awoke with a start, having realized that the train had stopped moving. I rubbed my eyes and looked out the window, elated to see that we were back in Union Station, and that the afternoon sun still shone brightly all about. Rudely shoving past the other passengers

▲

gathering their effects in the aisle, I leapt down the metal steps and dashed for the escalators.

Bolting out of the cavernous station, I hopped into one of the waiting cabs and headed straight for the National Gallery. I unloaded myself and my bags at the cobbled square and fountain by the East Wing and, having paid the hacker, I stood for a moment undecided. "Go to *Les Saltimbanques,*" he'd said, and there I'd find the key. But the old clown hadn't indicated whether it would be in the picture, hidden somewhere about the gallery, or delivered by some other agency. A very highbrow looking couple walked past me, up the steps through the shadow of Henry Moore's giant sculpture and through the revolving doors. To be honest, I felt a little silly standing there surrounded by luggage which I'd have to haul inside and up the stairs—all in the hopes of finding the key to a mysterious little gilt box left me by a character who might very well have been nothing more than a figment of my overactive imagination. I felt my pocket. The weight of the box nuzzled reassuringly against my hand. Well, *that* was real.

At last I hoisted my bags and shuffled through the doors; labored up the broad marble steps and into the room where the troupe presided.

Actually, I half expected to see old Pierrot upon entering, and I was a tad disappointed when he wasn't there. I set my bags on the bench in the middle of the room and, with my hand wrapped about the box in my pocket, I approached the Picasso. In no time it had me riveted, as usual. The mysteriously indistinct landscape, the moody-looking family of acrobats, and, off to the side, Colombina, so sad and distant and fair. I could almost see the night surface of the river Main behind her, weaving in and out of the complex greys and warm ochres of the background. I looked at the young man dressed in Arlequin's diamond-spangled costume. It was the young man who'd made me coffee in Pierrot's apartment, all right. Lustrous and virile he stood, hand on hip, brows knit, looking toward the love of his life. I studied each figure in turn for a long time, inspecting every detail of their costumes; checking their fingers and hands for concealed objects. I searched the perimeters of the composition for chance markings—but there was nothing remotely resembling a key of any sort; no incantation or hint of a clue. I looked around at the other pictures in the room, the Matisses and other Picassos, confident that something would suggest itself; a riddle perhaps, revealed in some subtlety of the combined paintings, or some peculiar pattern of color.

But there was nothing. Nothing at all. And I began to feel more the fool as I wheeled around the room searching corners of paintings, feeling under picture frames and, with difficulty, restraining myself from turning them over to check the backs of the canvases. Finally I went back to contemplating *Les Saltimbanques,* feeling like cursing it for its beauty, and beginning to grow anxious about the fact that I had to write a long essay by four o'clock the next afternoon. The light began to grow dim as the wintry sun sank away, and the glare of the artificial lights began to rob the painting of its pastel hues. Well, I thought at last, perhaps it was all just a crazy dream after all.

I turned away from the picture sad and frustrated. Nothing for it but to try again tomorrow. Just as well; I needed to get my things back to the house, take a shower, and have a bite to eat. As I bent to collect my bags, it dawned on me that I was very, very tired. In fact, I was actually looking forward to sleeping in my own bed again— screaming rug-rats or no.

"Hey, Mr. Peters!" a loud, jovial voice interrupted my ruminations. Carter.

"Hello, Carter," I said tiredly. "Don't worry. I'm on my way out now."

"Oh, it ain't that late yet, Mr. Peters," he said with a grin. "I was just surprised to see you here. Like I told the man, I figured you'd be in New York for another week or two like usual."

"Told what man?"

"The guy who gave me these to give to you," he said, and reaching into his breast pocket withdrew two envelopes; one small one like the ones the bank gives you cash in, and one letter-size. "Said you'd be needin' them for something, so I told him I'd hold on to 'em till I saw you next."

▲

I took the envelopes in my shaking hand, scarcely able to conceal the broad smile I felt bursting out behind my eyes. On pinching the smaller envelope I felt, sure enough, the shape of a tiny key. The larger envelope was addressed in a tall, loopy hand: "Mr. Corry Peters, Esq."

"Thank you very much, Carter," I said. "It was good of you to hold them for me—I was kind of expecting them."

"No problem, Mr. Peters."

The old guard smiled and turned to go, but I asked on impulse: "Wait, Carter? What did the man look like?"

Carter stroked his chin thoughtfully for a second. "You know, Mr. Peters, he looked kinda familiar, actually. But I couldn't as rightly say where I'd know him from. Kind of a tall, thinnish fellow; real pale-like. Nice smile, though."

"Thanks again, Carter. I owe you one."

"Any time, Mr. Peters," he said, and turned again to go. "But try not to hog the paintings, now!"

The moment the old fellow was out of sight I sat heavily down on the bench, glanced about to see that there was no one else coming, and tore the top from the little envelope. I tipped the tiny, elaborately intricate key out into my palm, followed by a thread-fine snake of gold chain. I pulled the little box from my pocket, inserted the key into the slot in the center of the gold hasp, and turned it. The lid sprang noiselessly open.

Like I say, it can be damned hard to account for things sometimes. And sometimes you're better off not trying. Suffice it to say that nothing I'd experienced in the last few days since meeting the crazy old man compared with what lay in the velvet-lined box on my lap. Nestled snugly in the deep blue folds of cloth was a single, flattish oval stone of dark green, red, and black. My hand shook as I took it from its secret couch and turned it over. Sure enough, there on the underside was the row of bone-white marks stretching from one end to the other. Its surface was duller now that it was dry, but I still marveled at its perfect shape, and I could still recall the giddy, silly sense of triumph as it left my hand and sped into the green-glass water, skipped a full seven times, and sank beneath an incoming wave.

▼

I don't have any idea how long I sat staring speechless at the stone. But eventually I put it back into the little gilt box, locked it up carefully, and put it back in my pocket. Then I opened the letter.

My Dear Mr. Peters,

By the time you receive this, I shall be long gone. Do not attempt to find me again: I have others to look to, and I never know where I will be next anyway. But before I close, a word about the stone.

It is, but for the fact that you held it in your hand once before, quite an ordinary stone in every respect. There is nothing particularly magical about it; or perhaps I should say, no more magical than anything else in nature; anything else your eyes or anyone else's may behold. It was once part of a deposit of Eocene marl; full of the remains of the various animals that died on the bottom of the sea over sixty million years ago (well before my time!). The white pattern is all that remains of an extinct shell—the turatella. The red is caused by bits of jasper; the black by phosphorus; the green is marl. It has been shaped and polished by many years of rolling in the surf. That is all.

But keep it, Mr. Peters. It will, I hope, always remind you that there is such a thing as beauty, and such a thing as reality. It only takes imagination to make of these things enduring art. And while it may be true that beauty is in the eye of the beholder, it is equally true that there are some lovelinesses we may all agree on. And reality is at the hand of those who have faith in magic.

Adieu,
Pierrot